"Where is Teresa?" Ms. James asked.

"I told you, she will come back as soon as I have the money."

"They will only pay when she is back. Tell me where you took her and everything will be over soon."

"I didn't take her nowhere. I told you, she went on a trip, she calls me every day, when I have the money I'll tell her to come back."

"What did you say to the officers?"

"That Teresa is an adult. She can go where she wants to. They thought so, too."

"Let me speak to her when she calls."

"You have talked to her way too much already. You ruined our life!"

"I'll call the police again. I don't trust you, Frank."

The guy raised his hand. I was at the outer limits of the parking lot. Neither of them had seen me so far.

"Put that away," Midori James said in an unnaturally high-pitched, panic-stricken voice. Then she threw herself against the car door and pushed it toward the assailant. The man struggled for a second to stay on his feet but quickly regained his balance. Ms. James tried to get into her car and pull the door shut behind her. The man tore it open. A shining metal object protruded from his fingers.

I ran toward them, disregarding the most basic principle of my training, jumped the guy from behind and caught him off guard. He stumbled backward, and with his whole weight on top of me, I knew I would fall. Then the force was gone; the man propelled himself forward, against the metal frame of the door. A scream came from the car, a stab of pure pain. I found myself sitting on the ground. Somebody ran past me. I started from my position on the ground, got to my feet, tried to pick up speed, but the guy had already jumped over the low concrete border of the lot and was dashing down the street. I knew I could not catch him.

Visit

Bella Books

at

BellaBooks.com

or call our toll-free number

1-800-729-4992

The Next World

URSULA STECK

Bella
BOOKS
2005

Bella Books, Inc.
P.O. Box 10543
Tallahassee, FL 32302

Printed in the United States of America on acid-free paper
First Edition

Editor: Anna Chinappi
Cover designer: Sandy Knowles

ISBN 1-59493-024-4

Acknowledgments

This book is dedicated to the memory of my mother, who taught me biology and so much more.

Once again my family and friends have given me invaluable support while I was writing this book. A huge thank you goes as always to my father, who continues to be there for me wherever I go. My sister, Eva Steck, and her partner, Kerstin Breitfeld, have read the manuscript at an early stage and have encouraged me to not despair. My "writing buddy," Natascha Würzberg, has also read the manuscript and given me great advice. Anne VanDerslice and Kimberly Tom, thank you for doing such a thorough yet fast last check of the final version. Your advice and green light have taken a big burden off my soul. Maren Metzdorf had an open ear to my problems finding the "gene expert" and then hooked me up with Andrea Sabiwalsky. Andrea, thank you for so patiently providing me with that insider information of a DNA lab I was searching for.

Finally, this book would never have been written without the support and trust of the women of Bella Books and particularly Linda Hill. Linda also hooked me up with editor extraordinaire, Anna Chinappi, who was not only wonderfully thorough and sensitive in detecting and eliminating my "Germanisms" from the book, but also has been incredibly encouraging, supportive and creative in all matters of her name-sister Anna.

Last but of course never least, I want to thank my partner, Yvette Fang, who has gone with me every step of the way, listening to crazy plot ideas and extended oral narrations of the story never ceasing to provide this incredible combination of honest yet gentle feedback that is her trademark and that I need to keep me going.

Biography

Raised in Europe and the U.S., Ursula Steck spent most of her adult life in Cologne, Germany, until she met her partner, a resident of San Francisco, in 2001. Since then she has been traveling between the continents. She has published three mystery novels in German including *Alles im Fluss* (In a State of Flux), 1999; *Feuerzeichen* (Fire Signals), 2000; and *Fass!* (Attack!), 2004; all with Grafit, Dortmund. She has also published various short stories in German and English. She is already well known in Germany as a lesbian mystery writer. *The Next World* is her first American novel.

It is an odd thing, but everyone who disappears is said to be seen in San Francisco. It must be a delightful city, and possess all the attractions of the next world.

—*Oscar Wilde*

(As quoted on the paling around Pier 3 in San Francisco)

Chapter 1

It was a subdued sound. A terrible, low thud, instantly swallowed by the aggressive squealing of tires when a car sped away. I had never before heard this particular cadence of noise, but I instantly knew what it meant.

I started to run toward the noise. I dashed down the dock, toward the street, through an opening between the warehouses, onto the wide sidewalk. The massive silhouettes of the financial district's high-rises shot up before me like supersized medieval towers, their tips sucked up by the city's fog.

My schedule as a security guard for Pier 3 hacked the night into neat little time-slices, dictating where I had to be at exactly which minute of my shift. It was Friday morning between 2:15 and 2:30. The Embarcadero, the four-lane street which runs along San Francisco's bay front, was empty. Something was lying on the brightly lit streetcar tracks that divide the north and southbound lanes. A human body. Thrown there by the car that I had only heard, not seen. But I had recognized the low sound of impact, when a fast, heavy vehicle had hit a human being with a cruelly understated tone of tissue tearing, organs exploding and bones shattering.

There was no indication that somebody had tried to brake the car, I recalled now while running across the Embarcadero. Only acceleration, an engine revving, then the thud, and a fraction of a second later, the screaming tires.

I knelt beside the limp body. It was a man, dressed in a gray business suit. His bright blue tie was wrapped around his neck. He lay on his side, his long, slender arms and legs in odd positions, like a rag doll tossed aside by an angry child. I touched his face—the short, brown hair, thin lines of blood running from the corners of his mouth, nose, even his ears. His skin was still warm, but I knew he was dead.

I am no medical doctor, but I have studied biology. I learned about the physical principles of life and death from only a theoretical, molecular viewpoint, not from experience and practice. But I knew this man. I had felt his spirit, his vivacity, his absolute love for life. I did not need to check any vital signs to feel that all this had passed away. My friend Jeff was gone.

Jeff and I had met four months before his death on a ferry traveling between Sausalito and San Francisco. I had moved to the U.S. only five weeks before. I was born in America. That made it comparably easy to immigrate even though I had lived in Germany since I was four.

I had found an ugly, overpriced apartment in the Tenderloin and was looking for a job. I was willing to do almost anything in order to make a living—except work at a genetic research lab ever again, the field I had been trained in. But the economy was bad. Nobody seemed to have waited for this one-eyed German-American of Asian descent who was prepared to do anything but the one job her résumé qualified her for. But I was not desperate.

My savings would last another three or four months, and I was thrilled by the adventure of being in an entirely new place, of having left my family behind, of finally being on my own.

Somewhere in the abyss of my conscience lurked the knowledge that I had done something unforgivable. After all I had basically abandoned Sarah, my twin sister, at a time when she needed help. But I had convinced myself that it would help her the most if I stepped out of our all too close relationship, forcing her secrets to surface without me eternally covering for her. But possibly I was just protecting myself from Sarah and the catastrophe she was steering toward.

I had not arrived at the point yet where I would allow this realization to surface and haunt me. And so I rode around the city in happy, carefree oblivion every day by bus and streetcar, taking long walks up and down the crazily steep hills, and often boarding a ferry to cruise the bay. My life had finally opened up before me, wide as the Pacific Ocean.

Jeff had given me a big smile when I had walked onto the outer deck of the ferry. We were the only two passengers who did not stay inside. It was late afternoon and the fog was rolling down the mountains of the Marin Headlands like a slow waterfall. The Golden Gate Bridge was already completely veiled. Only the sturdy feet of its rusty red pillars were still visible above the white-capped turquoise water. The air smelled of winter—salty, cool, crystalline, even though it was late June. I stayed at the far end of the deck, not in the mood to make small talk with a stranger, and held my face into the piercing wind.

Back on land I walked to a coffee shop in the ferry building. Sipping a hot mocha I stared out of the window. I could never get enough of this view across the shimmering, glassy water. Then somebody asked me if he could take a seat at my table. It was the man from the boat. He was balancing a gigantic cup of coffee. I looked around, hoping to spot a vacant table, perfectly prepared to let the impolite curmudgeon in me take over and send the guy away. But every chair was occupied. So I resigned myself, nodded with hardly concealed frustration and immediately returned to my concentrated staring into outer space. But it was no use. The man could stand it only for a few seconds. Then he smiled and said, "Your eyes are quite something."

"Which eye do you mean?" I answered. "The real or the fake one?"

I was wearing an acrylic eye the color of a green mamba in my right orbit. My left eye is dark brown. I am used to people staring at me. They also stare when I wear an eye patch or an artificial eye that is an exact match with my natural one. It's the fascination of asymmetry. As a child it comforted me that they also stared at Sarah, who has two perfectly proportioned eyes. That was before I figured out that this had to do with our asymmetrical ethnicity. Our mother is Caucasian, and our father's family had emigrated to the U.S. from China when he was a baby.

"Are you from the Philippines?" the man continued without a sign of embarrassment.

"No, from Germany," I said without further explanation.

"I have a friend in Hamburg."

"I don't know Hamburg."

"Which city are you from?"

"Cologne."

"What a great place!"

"Not really," was my imbecile answer. I was wishing I could just ignore this man like one of the seagulls outside begging for food. However, he had managed to slip a foot into the crack of my emotional steel door. When I asked Jeff later why he was so insistent on talking to me at our first meeting—by then I had found out that he was usually much more reserved—he answered, "It was somehow like falling in love. I thought you were beautiful and fascinating in a strange, wild way, and I wanted to know you. But I could tell that you are not particularly interested in men. At least not on a romantic level. You were just so totally oblivious to me that it felt like a fun challenge to try and talk to you."

It was an odd sensation, one of those feelings that are too complex to ever completely understand. But while Jeff was talking uninteresting nonsense and I was trying to be as aloof and gruff as possible, I began to like him. Maybe it was the weeks of solitude that started to get to me, against my own firm belief that this was what I desired most. Maybe it was his touching, clumsy insistence on keeping up a conversation.

He told me that his name was Jeff Rockwell and that he worked as a photographer and art director for an advertising company at Pier 3. He lived in the Sunset because it was close to the ocean, and one of his great passions was surfing.

Jeff did not much resemble the stereotypical California beach boy. He was thin and elegant, with fine, rather longish features, a wide mouth and so many wrinkles around his eyes that if you had only looked at those, you would have thought he was already in his sixties. But the rest of his face told otherwise. Later I learned that he was in fact only thirty-eight.

As much as our genes determine so many aspects of our physical destiny—the bone structure of our nose, the way we age, the weight of our heart—they do not carry the secret to our death. Sometimes they have something to do with it, as when a hereditary disease turns out to be fatal. But in the case of Jeff's death, his fate was determined solely by the acts and decisions of other human beings. And one of them was me.

When I remember my friend today, I cannot help but feel utterly grateful that I had known him, had been loved by him, had laughed with him. But along with every memory of Jeff comes the agonizing realization that he would still be alive if he had not talked to me that day on the bay.

Chapter 2

After I had met Jeff, my life changed. He told me about the job opening for a security guard for AdUp, the company where he worked, and a week later I circled the beige sandstone buildings of Pier 3 from nine in the evening to five in the morning, five days a week. The old warehouses had been renovated during the last years and turned into modern office space. Jeff often worked late, and many times when I passed the big window on the ground floor of the building behind which his desk was, he spotted me, met me outside with a cup of coffee, some chocolate or other treat, and joined me for a walk around the building. On the weekends he often invited me to his house where we cooked together, watched movies with some of his friends and talked for hours.

Through Jeff I met Mido, at least indirectly. And again none of us had a clue that this was another one of the many unconnected events that would eventually form a mosaic of disaster.

Like my friend, Mido often left the office after ten in the

evening. I saw her for the first time on my third day of work. I was passing the street side of the building when she exited the front door of AdUp. Pier 3 also housed the offices of a number of other, smaller firms, but the whole ground floor was leased to this huge advertising company. They had their own glitzy lobby behind the giant glass doors through which a rather small woman now tried to squeeze. She was not much taller than the two fat cardboard tubes she was carrying, and her limbs were forced into all kinds of knots while she was trying to fit through the door.

Of course I helped her. I had never worn a uniform of any kind before, but now my new blue clothes, the shiny brass badge of the security firm on my chest, and the walkie-talkie on my belt made me feel important in a silly way. *Serve and protect*, I almost called when the woman thanked me with a quick nod for the very unspectacular good deed of holding the door open for her. "You seem to be in a great mood," she said. "Enjoy your evening."

"I will," I answered, having a hard time concealing a stupid grin.

The woman looked over her shoulder while she waited at the curb of the Embarcadero for the traffic light to turn green. Her hair was dark blond, not as short as my own but also not long. It looked at the same time casual and stylish, as did her black pantsuit. But contradicting these props of the successful business-woman, she had the features of an up-to-no-good tomboy who was searching for the next tree to climb, with dimples and freckles and arched lips that gave her a perpetual ironic smile. Only her eyes were very serious.

When I approached her a second time to ask if she wanted me to help her carry the awkward tubes to the car, I detected the dark shadows of utter exhaustion or sorrow beneath her eyes.

"No need, I am used to these things," she only answered and crossed the street without looking back, entered a dark sedan in the company's lot and drove off.

"Midori James," Jeff said when I described her to him later that night. "She used to be a copywriter, but a while ago she got promoted to acquiring director. She makes the contacts with our most important clients. She is cute, huh?"

"Do you like her?" I asked instead of giving an answer.

"She is about as easy to crack as a hazelnut with a granite shell. Maybe I would like her if I ever got the chance to see more of her than the efficient exterior."

I have always been a daydreamer. As a little girl this was my way to find solitude and self-chosen company at the same time. I grew up with a maternal twin. Nobody around me, not even my twin sister herself, seemed to understand that the fact that because our DNA is identical does not make us one and the same person. Thirty-four years ago, when Sarah and I were born, it was still perfectly normal to dress twins in identical clothes and assume that we had the same needs and interests, tastes and likings, wanted the same friends and basically longed to be together all the time. For Sarah this was true. For me it was a purgatory of forced companionship and denial of individuality. In order to escape it, I made up my own inner world where I was a child without siblings, parents, teachers and relatives.

My tendency to daydream had stayed with me into adulthood, and while Jeff was still describing his unapproachable co-worker, Midori James had already entered my fantasy world where she became an attractive, uncomplicated, fictitious companion who during the next months would walk around with me on my lonely early morning security rounds. She was someone to talk to, someone who uttered interesting thoughts and with whom I could flirt, without demands or danger.

When I met the real Ms. James—every other week we would run into each other when she left the office—I gave her a reassuring *I am here for your protection* nod and was rewarded with one of her dimpled, broad smiles. Sometimes, when I got a closer look, though, I saw that her face had become even more tense and exhausted looking. But her occasional remarks were witty and sometimes unexpectedly personal.

"Beautiful moon tonight," she said once and pointed at the sky.

"Yes," I agreed, looking up at the bright, perfect white disc.

"Don't you sometimes feel like howling at it in despair?" the enigmatic Ms. James remarked and disappeared in her shiny black car.

The incomprehensible workings of chance have triggered such powerful human fantasies as religion and superstition. I perfectly understand the need to make up a greater pattern for the unexplainable. The minute details of destiny have such an enormous impact on yourself and the people you love, that it is often too painful to accept that everything was just a senseless matter of coincidence, the laws and forces of nature and human longings. I find myself asking what would have happened if my shifts had not run from Monday to Friday but from Tuesday to Saturday? Would Mido then have remained just a character of my inner movies? Or was everything that occurred meant to be and would have set in a day later without any of us being able to change destiny's course?

On Monday, October 13, my shift had started as usual. I walked over to the piers from Geary and Leavenworth where I live. It was an unusually warm and clear evening. No trace of the city's trademark wind and fog. The view across the bay was gorgeous. The light chains of the Bay Bridge led into a sparkling universe of little orange and white glows where Oakland and Berkeley lay on the other side of the wide water.

I checked in with Carlos, the heavyset manager of the night shift, who sat in his office inside the Pier 3 building. He handed me my walkie-talkie and told me to look out for two people he had spotted earlier on a bench at the far end of the dock. "If they fall asleep, wake them up. If they lie down on the bench or the ground, tell them to leave."

The worst part of my job was bothering the homeless people who take to the docks at night, hoping for a few hours of sleep in a dark corner before daytime security and the first morning commuters arrive. Fortunately Carlos hardly ever left his windowless chamber, so I generally ignored this part of my job description.

Carlos's main task was to watch the monitors that transmitted images from the dozens of surveillance cameras that hung all over the inside and outside areas. By now I had found out where the dead angles of the cameras were, and I just sent every tired sleeper to a corner where their image would not be caught on tape. I secretly suspected that Carlos also often kept his eyes closed when he recognized one of the regular night residents of the docks on one of his screens. He usually radiated the sincere wish to be left alone by anybody—burglars, panhandlers, demanding staff—but living beings who were quiet and harmless did not get in trouble with this grim-looking giant with the glossy dark hair.

At ten past eleven Jeff found me checking the back entrance of the building. He was wearing a black coat over his suit—AdUp had quite a strict dress code—and carrying a huge portfolio under his arm. With his other hand he was balancing a cup of mocha and a chocolate muffin. He handed me both, leaned the portfolio against a wall and lit up a cigarette for himself.

"Some diabetes for you and lung cancer for me," he joked.

"You forgot the obesity, stroke, cardiac arrest and amputated leg part," I replied, biting joyfully into the pastry.

"At least we'll go under all sweet and bouncy."

We leaned in one of the camera-blind corners for a while and studied the water that was black as charcoal dancing with tips of light. Jeff talked a little about his new project. He had taken pictures of forests after a fire for the visitors' center of Sequoia National Park and was now working with a copywriter on informational brochures and posters. Soon my friend yawned and said, "So much for the bounciness," stubbed out his cigarette and gave me a hug. "See you tomorrow."

"Sleep well."

For the next several hours I made my rounds without encountering anybody. I saw a light in one of the back offices of AdUp, but there was no movement inside. Probably somebody had just forgotten to switch off a desk lamp. At three fifteen, I passed the street entrance. I checked the door as usual. It was locked from the outside, as it was supposed to be. Originally, I had thought that I would have to chase vandals or even the occasional burglar off the premises. But I had been instructed not to ever go after an intruder myself, to stay in the background, inform Carlos by walkie-talkie and wait. By now I had not witnessed any potentially dangerous situation. I had come to the conclusion that my main task was to make my menacing presence felt in order to discourage any would-be criminal.

I had rounded the north corner of the building and was again heading away from the street. Then I heard steps. Midori James had left the office and was slowly walking across the Embarcadero. Even her shoulders looked tired today. She had never before stayed this late. She did not see me. I waited and watched her, feeling a little bit like a stalker. But after all I just wanted to make sure she would safely reach her car.

She crossed the streetcar tracks, entered the parking lot and opened the door of her sedan. Suddenly another person appeared by the car. A man. He stood very close to her and towered over her. Only the open door separated them. I had not seen him come across the parking lot. I still thought they would get into the car together. Maybe he was her partner picking her up from work. But something was wrong with the picture.

They talked. It was so quiet at this time of night that even at this distance I could make out a low murmur, which grew louder. I still could not make out what they were saying, but the tone alarmed me. It was time to get closer to the scene. Before I had reached the middle divide of the Embarcadero, Midori James pushed the car door against the guy. He shoved it back aggressively.

"Never ever call the cops on me again, do you hear me!" Raw rage carried his words.

"Where is Teresa?" Ms. James asked.

"I told you, she will come back as soon as I have the money."

"They will only pay when she is back. Tell me where you took her and everything will be over soon."

"I didn't take her nowhere. I told you, she went on a trip, she calls me every day, when I have the money I'll tell her to come back."

"What did you say to the officers?"

"That Teresa is an adult. She can go where she wants to. They thought so, too."

"Let me speak to her when she calls."

"You have talked to her way too much already. You ruined our life!"

"I'll call the police again. I don't trust you, Frank."

The guy raised his hand. I was at the outer limits of the parking lot. Neither of them had seen me so far.

"Put that away," Midori James said in an unnaturally high-pitched, panic-stricken voice. Then she threw herself against the car door and pushed it toward the assailant. The man struggled for a second to stay on his feet but quickly regained his balance. Ms. James tried to get into her car and pull the door shut behind her. The man tore it open. A shining metal object protruded from his fingers.

I ran toward them, disregarding the most basic principle of my training, jumped the guy from behind and caught him off guard. He stumbled backward, and with his whole weight on top of me, I knew I would fall. Then the force was gone; the man propelled himself forward, against the metal frame of the door. A scream came from the car, a stab of pure pain. I found myself sitting on the ground. Somebody ran past me. I started from my position on the ground, got to my feet, tried to pick up speed, but the guy had already jumped over the low concrete border of the lot and was dashing down the street. I knew I could not catch him. He remained a distorted image of dark curls, muscular shoulders and thighs and the smell of a leather jacket.

I ran back to Midori James's sedan. She was in the driver's seat but with her feet out of the car. Crouched over, she was covering her left hand with her right one, holding it against her stomach almost like a baby.

Her piercing scream still echoed in my ears. "Did he hurt you?" The words came out of my mouth like groans.

She looked up. Her car was parked under a bright light, and I could now make out the details of her face. She was so pale she looked almost green. Nevertheless, she smiled at me. For the first time I noticed that her teeth were quite irregular. Now I realized that was one reason why I found her face so intriguing. There was something imperfect and vulnerable in that image of cool determination.

"Can I see your hand?" I asked.

She slowly let go of her left arm and stretched it toward me. Already the fingers were swollen like a balloon. Blood ran down the middle finger. A dark blue bruise had begun to take over most of the hand.

"You need a doctor," I said, not daring to even touch her injury. "Did it get caught between the door and the frame of the car?"

She nodded.

My attempt at getting the man away from her had resulted in her hand being crushed.

"Don't even go there," she said, reading my mind. She pulled her legs into the car. "I got myself into this mess."

"He had a knife." I now recalled the scene completely.

She started to shake and pulled the car door shut. With her right hand on the steering wheel, the sedan rolled away but stopped when she had to make a sharp turn to exit the parking lot. I rushed toward the car and could see that her forehead was leaning on the steering wheel. I opened the door, fearing for a moment that she had lost consciousness, but Midori James looked up at me, white as a ghost.

"Do you drive?" she asked.

"Yes."

"Can you do me a favor and park my car again? I'll call for a cab."

13

"I can drive you."

"Never miss a chance to get off work early," she said with an unexpected grin, and I wondered for a second where in hell she still took her humor from. Then her eyes teared up.

I called Carlos. "I have to drive somebody to the hospital. I'll explain everything tomorrow, but can you take over the last round? I'll make it up to you."

"Why? but—" was all I gave him a chance to say, then I disconnected the walkie-talkie, opened the passenger door for Midori James and we drove off.

"Just stay on Embarcadero until it hits 101," she said when we stopped at the first red light.

"Is that the closest way to the clinic?" Her directions would take us toward a rather residential area.

"I do not want to go to any clinic. Just take me home. My hand will be okay."

"No way." From what I could see, every bone in her hand might have been broken.

She sighed and gave me a long look. I focused on the road, then turned right onto Market Street. I had no idea why, only that it took us off the route she wanted me to go. After some blocks I discovered a billboard advertising the emergency room of a small clinic. It promised you would not have to wait more than forty-five minutes. It was about ten blocks away. I knew the cross streets and made a right onto Geary.

Midori James stayed silent for a long time. Finally she said, "You are a good driver. Can I ask you something? I am sure you will think it is a stupid question, though."

"Don't worry."

"How do you compensate for the lack of three-dimensional vision?"

It was no stupid question. Of course a passenger in a car wants to know about the visual capacity of her one-eyed chauffeur. But most people were not so tactful.

"I lost my eye as a small child. The human brain has great

14

resources to make up for missing information. I cannot really imagine how it is to see with two eyes, but when they tested me for my driver's license I passed without problems. I do have to turn my head a little bit to the right. But then my field of vision is big enough."

"Your other eye must be very sharp."

"If you say so," I teased her.

"Well, I am hardly an expert on you," she joked back. "I don't even know your name."

"Anna. Anna Spring. And yours?" I would certainly not admit that I knew it already.

"Just call me Mido."

The receptionist at the clinic was a tired-looking woman with gray dreadlocks. She jotted down Mido's insurance information and asked us to wait in the next room. The smell of disinfectants and cleaning detergents barely covered the much more intense stench of sickness and human excrement. We sat down on orange plastic chairs that were bolted onto a linoleum floor the color of pus. Mido held her hand up. I tried to find somebody who could give us an ice pack but ended up buying two cans of Coke from a vending machine. I opened one can, gave it to her to drink and held the other as gently as possible against her injured hand.

"You have to report the man to the police," I said. Then I remembered snippets of their argument. "Or did you do that already? Has he bothered you before?"

"Frank is upset right now. And I understand him. Not that I like him, but making him even angrier will not help Teresa." Mido sounded contemplative, as if she was talking to herself.

"May I ask who Teresa is?"

"I can't drag you into this, too." She set down her soda, took the makeshift ice pack from me and held it against her skin herself. She seemed to press it quite hard onto the swollen hand. I turned my gaze away.

After a long time of mutual brooding, a tall middle-aged Asian woman in green scrubs walked up to us. "Ms. James?"

I stayed behind while the medical staff and Mido walked away.

"Good luck," I called after them. Mido looked back. "Can you wait for me?" she asked with unexpected shyness.

"I have no other plans tonight," I answered.

She gave me one of her crooked, charming smiles and was gone.

Chapter 3

When Mido returned, she looked as if she was sleepwalking, her eyes unfocused, her steps slow. Her hand was wrapped in a thick white bandage. The green-clad woman showed up behind her. "Nothing's broken. Here's ointment you have to rub in three times a day. And here are some painkillers." She handed me a tube and a plastic bottle. "Make sure she does not drive or operate a machine under the influence of the medication. Her hand will take a while to heal, but there's nothing to worry about."

"Did you hear her? No caterpillar operating today, okay?" I said as we slowly walked back to the car.

"Where do you live?" Mido suddenly mumbled.

"On Geary."

"I know it's a lot to ask, you have already been very good to me. But can I stay at your place for a few hours? Until I feel awake enough to drive home."

"No problem. But as I said, if you'd rather go home, I can take you."

"I'd rather not right now."

An undertone of fear rippled in her voice, and the alarm bell in my mind rang very loud and shrill.

I found a parking spot around the corner from my apartment. The building was typical for this area of the city. A ten-story eighty-year-old dirty-white structure with high, narrow windows and a stucco facade. It had once seen good times, but that was very long ago.

Fortunately the building had an elevator, a rattling thing, stinking of rotting carpet and urine. I would not use it under different circumstances, but today it took my dazed visitor and me safely to the second floor. The moment Mido saw the huge couch in my living room, she sank down on it, took her shoes off, stretched out and fell asleep. She was still wearing her wool jacket. I got a blanket from my bedroom and covered her.

I was not tired at all. I would usually stay up after my shift anyway, prepare something to eat, watch some TV or read a book, do grocery shopping in one of the corner shops and go to bed at around eleven in the morning. The best part of my day had only just begun.

My apartment consisted of two rooms and a rather spacious kitchen. The furniture, which came with my lease, looked as if it had been left over from a brothel of the twenties. It was all dark wood, strange curves and velvety upholstery. The burgundy armrest of the couch carried a bandage of olive-colored military camouflage material, and the headboard of the bed was a patchwork of green threadbare brocade and pink terrycloth.

The walls were the most inconspicuous element of the place. A former tenant had painted all of them the same grass-green and I had no intention of changing this. It felt like I was living in a forest, where somebody had dumped some old pieces of furniture and kitchen appliances in a clearing and I had made them my own.

Somebody must have once removed the doors between the rooms of the apartment and lost them for good. So now I tried to move about quietly. I took a shower, happy to finally get out of my stiff uniform, put on a pair of bright blue jersey shorts and an over-sized T-shirt. Something was wrong with the heating in the apartment and it went on and off randomly. Today it was going full blast, and the temperature contributed to the somewhat tropical feel of the place. I had taken out my green acrylic eyeball, cleaned it and stored it in its box and replaced it with a brown one that matched my real eye.

Clean and alert, I went to the kitchen, stir-fried some catfish with red peppers and corn, boiled enough rice for two and set a portion of the meal aside. Then I poured myself a glass of orange juice, ate and drank and tried to make some kind of sense of what had happened during the last several hours. I was not very successful. Finally I reached for the book I was reading, *Animal Dreams* by Barbara Kingsolver, and entered the fictional world, which I so often preferred over the real one, anyway.

A moving shadow behind me brought me back. Mido had entered the kitchen on bare feet. She had taken off her jacket, rolled up her wool pants and looked much more alive again, with tousled hair and a rosy shimmer on her cheeks.

"It's hot in here," she said.

"It's the heating."

"I would never have guessed."

The kitchen window could only be opened a tiny crack. I felt no further need to explain the conditions of my apartment to her. It was self-explanatory, I figured.

"Would you like something to eat?"

"I'd love to. It smells great."

I quickly heated up the portion I had saved for her. Mido stood next to me at the stove while I was stirring the food in the pan. I could almost see the crown of her head, so much smaller was she than I. She smelled of sweat and sandalwood. Our arms were so close to each other that I could feel her warmth, which was even hotter than the air around us.

A moment later the meal was ready. She ate ravenously and washed everything down with juice.

"How does your hand feel?"

She looked at me as if she had already forgotten all about it. She was right-handed, and her bandaged left hand lay in her lap like an inanimate object.

"It hurts. But not too badly. That shot the nurse gave me really knocked me out. It's wearing off, though, fortunately. I'd rather hurt than feel like a zombie."

She had emptied her plate.

"Would you like anything else? Chocolate, a sandwich?" I asked.

"Chocolate would be great."

"Cake or bar or cookie?"

My guest let out a loud laugh. "Cookie!"

I produced a bag of double chocolate chip cookies and we finished most of it in the next twenty minutes. The part of Mido that had reminded me of an impish, androgynous girl at first sight became more pronounced while she devoured the sweets. It made me happy to see her like this.

I hope she comes back, I suddenly thought. Something felt right about this woman in my kitchen, sitting at the table, her legs stretched out, her hair spiking off her head in many directions, her lips ready to laugh. I detected a little amber speck in her right eye. Otherwise her irises were dark blue, almost violet.

"Where did you come from?" she asked, looking around the room. "This place doesn't look as if you've lived here long."

"I'm from Germany."

"Oh, and you came to this country to work as a security guard?"

Suddenly I had enough of our small talk. "No, I came here because I had to put some distance between me and my family. I used to work as a geneticist, like my mother and sister. But I needed a new start. To see things more clearly."

"Like your whole life?" Mido asked, sounding perfectly serious and full of empathy now.

"Yes."

She only nodded slowly in reply, stood up. "Now I have to get back to my own life. It was wonderful here. Thank you for the refuge."

"Come back whenever you want."

"I'd love to," she replied without a smile.

Again Mido wanted to call a cab; again I persuaded her to let me drive her. If Carlos fired me because I was AWOL, I would apply as a limousine driver. It was fun to steer the luxurious black sedan, an Infiniti, up and down the hills. Mido directed me through the city, the outer Mission district and finally through the Excelsior. It turned out she was a fourth-generation San Franciscan and knew the history of the town like nobody I had met so far. "Over there is Sam's Barbecue." She pointed at a wooden shack at the side of the road. "It does not look too impressive, but Sam makes the best broiled oysters in the city."

Many of her stories centered around food and I realized we shared a strong passion.

"Make a right turn over there and just stay on the street until it ends, that's where I live," she finally said.

Music came from the back of the car. I recognized a wimpy electronic version of "Ode to Joy."

"My cell phone!" Mido tried to reach her bag on the backseat but could not grab it with her right hand. Her rush to answer the phone bordered on panic. I pulled to the curb, stopped the car and found the cell phone for her. She held the little box to her ear, her hand trembling.

I continued to steer the Infiniti down the road, staring ahead, trying to give the impression I was not listening in on the conversation. The street grew narrow and small trees appeared on the sides. The wooden houses we were passing looked not exactly grand, but many of them were well kept, painted in pastels; the minute front lawns were bright green, encircled by flower beds: a neat little fairy-tale neighborhood. Some buildings, though, were raggedy, beaten-up siblings of the nicer ones, with sunken-in porches, yellow, dusty yards and broken bicycles and car parts strewn around.

"I told you I'm working on it . . . But if she doesn't want to . . . In the end it's her decision . . . You cannot force her." Somebody at the other end continued to interrupt Mido. She had sounded anxious from the beginning of the call but became severely frustrated in the end. "Leave me alone . . . That's not true . . . !" She threw the phone on the backseat, and looked even paler than before.

"Bad news?" I asked.

Mido just pointed at a driveway. She retrieved a little remote control device out of her jacket pocket and pressed a button. The door of the garage in front of us opened.

"I hate this car, but the company wants me to use it. So I'm hiding it."

Her home was a small one-story clapboard building. Not much different from the other houses on the street. But it was painted a beautiful dark red and partly covered in light green vines speckled with white flowers. I admired it while the automatic garage door closed behind us.

"Thank you so much for everything," Mido said, sounding as distant as I had known her before the parking lot incident. She unlocked her front door. "Shall I call you a cab? Of course I'll pay for it."

"No need," I answered. "I saw a bus stop on the way here."

"I'm sorry that I'm not more hospitable. The call I just got . . . I have to take care of things. But I'd like to take you out in the next few days. Dinner, lunch, you choose . . ."

"We'll figure it out," I answered. "When you feel a bit better."

"I'll be back in the office tomorrow. I'll look for you."

"My shift starts at nine p.m."

"I know." She stepped into her house.

It was as simple as that. There was one last glance, a little smile, the promise of a next meeting. And then Mido closed the door, locked it behind herself and disappeared.

Chapter 4

The bus ride from Mido's place back to the Tenderloin took more than an hour. Finally I trudged up the hill to my house with heavy legs, looking forward to my bed. When Martha Bega's voice reached me, I tried to pretend I was too tired to hear her. But that would have meant being too tired to hear the siren of a fire truck.

"Hey, chicky. Come in for a moment." As usual, my noisy, annoying neighbor lurked in the doughnut shop on the ground floor of our building. Often I was lucky and she had found some police officers who frequented the place to chat with. But today she was the only customer. She pushed her wheelchair with rocket speed, came after me and then managed to block my way.

"Chicky! What's up? You don't talk to me anymore?"

"It was a long shift," I lied. "Have a good day. See you later."

But between me and the door sat a two-hundred-and-fifty-pound former detective sergeant of the SFPD who was bound and determined to present me as a fool, one of her favorite pastimes.

"You never heard of California employment law? They can't do that to you. Overtime has to be paid time and a half. And since when do you have to drive pretty women around on your job?"

Martha's apartment was at the front of the building. When she did not spy from her position in the doughnut shop, she was on the lookout at her living room window. She did not sleep very much. She had told me that lying down caused too much pain in her back from when she'd been hit by three bullets from an assault rifle.

Martha was always groomed fantastically. Her long salt-and-pepper hair streamed over her shoulders like a nocturnal river, and her almond-shaped black eyes were made up in an intricate Cleopatra fashion. She radiated relentless authority, and I usually just patiently answered her questions, looking for a polite excuse to quickly get away. Today my brain was too dead for politeness and I just said, "Let me through. I'm tired."

Amazingly, Martha let me pass, even patted my arm. "Get some rest, chicky."

That *chicky* crap had started right after I had moved in. When Martha had seen me in the hall the first time she had called, "Look, what a spring chick we have here." I had no idea what her reference age for spring chicken was, but I obviously still fell into that category.

With a weak little sigh of relief I closed the apartment door behind me, slipped out of the denim jacket and jeans which I was wearing over my jersey shorts and T-shirt and sank into bed. Sleep was gracious enough to come fast and dreamless.

I shot out of a deep black hole just ten seconds before the clock radio began to play that night. My heart pounded with alarm. I could not exactly say what had come over me until the memories of the last night and morning set in. I went to the kitchen, toasted bread, opened the peanut butter jar, sank in a knife. Visions of an enormous sharp blade appeared before my inner eye. The image of Mido's injured hand came back. Suddenly it looked as if it had been cut up. Streams of blood ran down from it, gushed onto the pavement.

A vivid imagination is a force you can't do much against. I usually embraced it and tried to use it for my pleasure and mental balance. Only when my mind's eye veered toward my sister, Sarah, did I doubt the usefulness of an active imagination.

Thinking about Sarah, I began to search for my phone. I never had a landline installed in the apartment but used the throw-away cell phone I had purchased during my first few days in New York before I had boarded the plane to the West Coast. My twin wanted to know where I was, and keeping a phone number with an East Coast area code was an obstacle against her finding out. I did not want to be cruel. I had thought of disappearing without leaving a trace for my family. The phone was a compromise. They could leave me messages. I also left the occasional voice mail on my sister's box. If she picked up, though, I ended the call.

Once a day I turned on the phone mainly to hear if anything had changed with my shift—sometimes co-workers wanted to switch hours—and to have the occasional chat with my best friend. Heidrun and I had met on our first day at the university. After graduation she had found a job at a hospital in Frankfurt where she worked as a genetic counselor. She was the only person in Germany who knew where I was.

Today, though, there was no message from Heidrun on my voice mail as I had hoped, but after I had entered the password, I heard Sarah's voice. "Talk to me, Anna. Come on. I know what you think. I have great news." Her voice was clear and bright. It sounded more familiar than any other voice in the world. I pressed the delete button and switched off the phone.

Carlos did not fire me when I came back to work that night. I bribed him with a cake, from one sugar addict to another. He gave me a questioning look, opening the box I had set in front of him, and an expression as close to bliss as I had ever seen appeared on his face. My present for him was a marzipan crème gateau and I knew the whole yellow and pink flower-decorated affair would be gone by the end of the night.

The chances of seeing Mido today were slim, but the worry that was gnawing at the inside of my chest became more vicious when Jeff confirmed that she had not shown up for work that day.

"Did she call in sick?"

"I don't know. I didn't ask. But she's management. She doesn't have to stick to the regular schedule. With all the overtime she puts in she can just stay home a day, anyway. But I'm sure she'll be back tomorrow. We have a presentation for one of our biggest clients in the afternoon. I didn't know you followed her work hours so closely," he said.

We sat on a bench by the water. It was three hours into my shift, and I was allowed to take a fifteen-minute break now. I told Jeff about the events of the previous night. He did not indulge in office gossip. And he was my friend. I wanted to know if he had any idea what the scene in the parking lot could have meant.

Jeff had worked almost until midnight. "The presentation is driving us all crazy." He sighed and looked even more exhausted than the day before. Still he listened to my story with full concentration. "I don't really know the woman," he finally said. "But she seems to be tough and I'd say she can take care of herself." He fell silent for a moment, searching for the right thing to say next. "But I know you like her and that it's hard not to worry. And it *is* strange, what happened last night. I'll get her phone numbers for you. Then you can check on her, if you feel you should."

I did not call Mido that night. But when I returned to work on Wednesday evening, Jeff was already on the lookout for me. "Mido didn't show up today. Big Susan is not amused. I asked Peter. He told me she left a message saying that she would be back on Monday. He tried to call her, but she didn't answer the phone."

Susan Bradley, nicknamed Big Susan by her employees—in another time they would have been called her subjects—was the owner of the agency. Peter, as Jeff now explained, was her assistant. I had seen Big Susan only three or four times. She would usually get picked up in a bright red Ferrari by her chauffeur, who drove up to the sidewalk and stopped so close to the front door that his boss could enter the car practically unseen. However, their ritual involved him leaving the driver's seat when she arrived at the door; he'd get in on the passenger's side and she would drive the car off herself. Jeff had told me that although AdUp was making good money, most of Big Susan's riches were inherited. She lived with her mother, one of San Francisco's eleven billionaires, in a mansion in Pacific Heights.

Big Susan was a petite woman with a feline face and spiky, light orange hair. She wore Armani style suits the few times I got a glimpse of her before she darted off in her four-wheeled rocket.

When Jeff had broken the news of Mido's no-show, my nervousness instantly turned into a bitching monster. "Did they send somebody to look for her?" I inquired.

"She is an adult. She left a message. Susan called her. That's about as much as the company can and will do."

She is an adult! Where had I heard that before?

I had programmed Mido's home and mobile numbers into my cell and tried to call her every hour during the course of the night. She never picked up. The voice mail on her cell phone was turned off, but I left a message on her machine at home each time. "Please just let me know that you're okay," was the same message I left.

I cannot say today why I did not rush to her house immediately. It probably had to do with the way we are conditioned to be unintrusive and keep a well-mannered distance with new acquaintances. Work ethics may also have played a role as well as a severe shyness in personal matters that I don't like to admit, even to myself. As soon as I had handed my walkie-talkie over to Carlos at five a.m., I dashed to the Hyatt Hotel on the corner of Market and California, entered one of the cabs waiting there and asked the Rastafarian driver to take me to Mido's address.

Chapter 5

The neighborhood was quiet this early in the morning. Behind very few windows I detected light. I had asked the cabdriver to drop me off at the last intersection before Sunnyvale Avenue, Mido's street. I wouldn't have been able to say why, but it felt better to approach her home on foot.

The small house lay in total darkness. Even its red color, which had been bright and lively in the daylight, now blended in with the predawn shadows. A faint, sweet scent of flowers hovered in the air. I rang the doorbell and listened hard. But there was only silence, sinking down on me like a heavy weight. And of course nobody opened the door.

The garage was locked. There was a small path around the back of the house. I remembered the penlight on my key chain. It cut a tiny white hole into the darkness. I peeked through windows into black rooms. My knee hit against something hard and a sharp pain predicted a big bruise. When the sting subsided, I could make out my attacker: a wooden bench.

I pulled the heavy thing toward the garage and cursed when it made squeaking noises that resounded like screams in the looming stillness. Finally it was in the right place. I climbed on top and stared through the narrow window of the garage door.

The weak beam of the light touched a cement floor. I moved it up and hit something shiny. The dark finish of the Infiniti? After I had probed some more, I was sure that the sedan was in the garage.

"Can I help you?"

The man's voice came from right behind my back. In a reflex reaction, I shot around and jumped from the bench.

A strong flashlight was directed at my face. The person holding it was invisible to me. I reached for the light, managing to push it away. Now the beam illuminated the space between us and I could make out its bearer.

He seemed to be a pilot. He looked so flawless in his uniform and cap, golden stripes on his shoulders, brass wings on his lapel, it felt as if a TV commercial had come to life. He was only slightly taller than I, with a broad chest and the set jaw line of a fifties movie star.

"I'm looking for Ms. James," I managed to say.

"If she did not open the door, I guess she is not at home," he stated with the arrogance of an educator patiently repeating the obvious to a less-than-sharp student.

"I work for her company," I replied quickly. "They asked me to pick her up for an early morning meeting. I was just wondering if there was a misunderstanding, and maybe she drove to the office already by herself."

"She usually does her own driving. I can't recall her being picked up before, particularly not by somebody on foot." The man's face would have been almost boringly good looking in its clean-cut perfection, if it hadn't been for the little moustache that kept moving when he talked, almost like a second upper lip.

"She injured her hand. I work for the security staff of her company. They asked me to take a cab here, help her with those cumbersome portfolios and drive her downtown in her own car." My

29

brain spit out lies with an ease that should have worried me had they not come in so handy. "Have you by any chance seen her leave already?"

The man shook his head in contemplation. I waited for him to volunteer some more information, but he just studied me as if I were a harmless but utterly strange species from another world.

"Okay, I should call AdUp and find out if she has arrived there already," I finally said.

"Yes, you'd better do that. I'll help you put the bench back."

"Don't worry. I'm sure you have a plane to catch."

Now the guy smiled a little. "Yeah, but there's always enough time to assist a lady."

We carried the bench back to its original spot. Then the pilot lifted his hand in a farewell greeting and started down the driveway. On the sidewalk he looked back and gave me another inquisitive stare. I pulled the cell phone out of my pocket, pretended to also walk away from the house, pressed some buttons, talked to the computer voice who told me I had dialed a number without a connection. Mr. Airline eventually entered an unexpectedly old and ratty white station wagon that was parked in the driveway directly opposite Mido's house and drove off.

I waited until his car was out of view. Then I turned around and walked up to the red house again.

I made another trip to the backyard. Gray dawn now invaded the house and revealed the silhouettes of furniture. I looked through every window once more and spotted beautiful plants in most rooms. From what I could see they were the only living beings currently present in this house.

When I had reached the front door again, I carefully checked the perimeter to see if the next shift of the neighborhood watch was walking up the driveway. But nobody was in sight. Then I bent over and looked through the mail slot. Newspapers were lying on the floor. I pressed my face closer to the slot, trying to make out the dates on the papers, and almost fell forward. The front door had swung open. I gathered my balance, stood up and slipped into the house.

I closed the door behind me and called Mido's name in reaction to the surprise over my own brazenness. "It's Anna. Are you here?" No answer.

One of the newspapers was from Wednesday, yesterday, another one from today. I wondered if this paper had been delivered just now, while I was sneaking around in the back. Next to them lay a letter, which upon a closer look turned out to be an electric bill. Then there was a postcard with the picture of a winking baby wearing a black leather cap and a dog collar studded with spiky silver rivets.

I stepped into the kitchen. Tuesday's paper was on the table, still folded. Countertops and sink were empty. The place had a somewhat sterile air as if it was used only on special occasions.

My first impression that the house was empty was confirmed when I looked into the other rooms. Mido was into white and cream-colored fabrics. Her furniture was at once simple and beautiful. The hardwood floors were polished. Bright pictures with jungle motifs added colors to the rooms.

Most of the many plants looked healthy and in good shape, even though their soil was dry. Only two hibiscuses, which were in full bloom, had limp leaves and flowers. I resisted the urge to water and save them. I did not want to change or touch anything in the house.

The closet in the bedroom was open. It looked as if a tornado had ripped through its shelves. Blouses were scattered on the floor, as well as sweaters, panties and bras. I experienced a moment of embarrassment, faced with such private items of a woman I had fantasized over since I had first seen her.

Wooden hangers were strewn around. A number of business suits, though, were hanging in an orderly fashion on a rack and thick winter sweaters were neatly stacked on the top shelves.

Adjacent to the bedroom was a small den. The moment I entered it, I sensed something missing. The room contained a desk with two drawers, both of which were closed. In a bookcase was a row of bright blue photo boxes. On the desk stood a rather old-fashioned fifteen-inch computer screen, mouse and keyboard, and a printer. Next to them was an empty file tray.

I retrieved a tissue from my jacket pocket, wrapped it around my fingers and opened the drawers. One was flat and contained an assortment of pens and pencils and some sheets of stamps. The other was more spacious and crammed with tape dispensers, scissors, tubes of hand cream, gift ribbons and a wild assortment of other useful home office items.

An empty shelf underneath the photo boxes caught my eye. Fine dusty lines drew the silhouettes of three rectangular objects, each about two inches wide and eight inches long. The pattern had the exact shape of the bottoms of office ring binders.

I gave the desk another long look, and suddenly I knew what was missing. There was no computer. At the back of the screen an aimless cord dangled to the floor. The wire tail of the mouse led across the tabletop and ended halfway down the desk unconnected, as did the keyboard and printer connections.

In the living room I couldn't find a clue to anything unusual. I checked if there was a door to a basement or attic anywhere but didn't detect one. Before I left, though, I wanted to find out what was wrong with the lock on the front door

It was a not particularly well-protected door. There was only a single old-fashioned lock. It looked as if the door had been merely unlocked and not pulled fully closed. When I had leaned against it, the short latch had just snapped back.

A phone rang in a corner of the hall, and the sound hit me like a blow, interrupting my thoughts about the front door. The answering machine clicked after the third ring. Mido's voice sounded. "Nobody here. But I'll call back later if you leave me the necessary details."

The caller hung up.

It was a rather old-fashioned combination telephone/answering machine. There was no caller ID display. I punched in *69. A phone rang. Nobody picked up. Then I pressed the redial button. A deep female recorded voice said, "Ruth's office. Leave a message after the beep."

"Anna Spring here. Could you please call me back." I left my number.

I played Mido's incoming messages. Many were my own, but equally as many were hang-ups. Two came from AdUp. A male voice asked to get in touch as soon as possible. Then there was a woman wondering if Mido was still up for dinner on Wednesday. She didn't leave a name or number.

All but one of the phone messages had been recorded on Wednesday. The tinny computer voice announced the call was left on Tuesday at four fourteen p.m., about six hours after I had dropped Mido off. The message came from a man with a low gravelly voice. "Somebody is coming by to pick up the documents. You have gained access to them illegally. All this must stop!"

The man's words felt like a punch to the stomach, though I wasn't even the addressee of his threat. I was frustrated that the caller had not left anything else I could work with. *Mido, what is this all about?*

Next to the phone was a notepad. The top page was almost completely covered with crazy doodlings drawn in a frame around some words. There were psychedelic ornaments and faces. Some of them looked like skulls, with huge, panicky eyes and wide open mouths. The drawings almost covered the letters in the center frame. But a few words were still legible: *duncker, 32 bleeker, ask anna.*

Ask Anna! *What in the world do you want to ask me? Or is there another Anna in your life? And what kind of trouble are you in?*

I still hadn't solved the puzzle of the open front door. The dominatrix-baby on the postcard grinned up at me sardonically. When I had stepped over the threshold of this house, I had also crossed a border of the mind. By now my worry for Mido had become stronger than all inhibitions. I turned the card over. It carried no stamp or postmark, so it must have been delivered personally. The handwritten words read: *Hey crazy. Why don't you call back? I left you so many messages. Don't forget I will always be your friend. You know that I don't hold you responsible for anything that happened. You just wanted to help. I would be devastated to lose you. Love Rita.*

Chapter 6

"Ruth, Rita, Bleeker, Duncker, Anna," Jeff repeated the names like a chant.

"Can you find out who these people are?" I wanted to know.

It was a chilly, foggy morning. The Sausalito ferry was about to leave; its horn sounded loud and longingly. Half an hour before, I had decided to pull the door to Mido's house shut. Even if somebody leaned against it like I did, at least it wouldn't swing open. Then I flagged a cab and came back to the pier. Jeff was already sitting in front of his computer, and I signaled him to meet me outside, where I told him the whole story of my break-in.

He shook his head after having mulled over the events for a while. "It doesn't make any more sense to me than to you. Let's see if Peter is already in, maybe he has an idea who these people are." Jeff disappeared around the building.

The ferry's white silhouette melted into the misty air over the water. I was deep in thought about my next move. Was it more harmful to act than to do nothing? I have always been a very private person, protected my own affairs with jealous discretion and tried to stay clear of other people's secrets as well. What would Mido say, when she found out I had practically broken into her house? Or was she in real danger, and only I could rescue her? I wanted to shake off the last question as a symptom of utter hubris. But then, what would be worse? To piss off Mido and have her never talk to me again, or to ignore the worrisome facts as well as my own nagging intuition and not help her when she was in desperate need?

Jeff returned. He had found Big Susan's assistant. "None of the names rang a bell with Peter."

"And Mido hasn't gotten in touch with them since yesterday?"

"Nope."

Worry is infectious. Jeff looked as contemplative and serious as I felt. "Duncker, 32 Bleeker, ask Anna?" he said again.

"Uh-huh."

"32 Bleeker could be an address. Let's check if there is a Bleeker Street in San Francisco."

This time I followed him back into the building. AdUp did not believe in cubicles. Their main office was so vast that the desks strategically dotted the giant room. The center of the space was taken up by a big conference table. With its turquoise carpet and the light green tabletops, the space seemed like an extension of the bay outside, mimicking its waters and islands.

Most of the desks were still empty at this time, shortly after nine. In a corner, far away from Jeff's desk, two women leaned over some posters spread out before them.

Jeff pulled an extra chair over to his computer. First we checked the street directory of San Francisco on the Internet and got results for a Bleeker Avenue in the Mission District. Apparently, though, it was so short it did not have a number 32. There was no Duncker Street, Avenue or Boulevard. When we Googled the names separately, thousands of entries popped up. Finally we tried the combination "Duncker+Bleeker."

Most entries referred to two biologists by the names of Bleeker and Duncker from the beginning of the twentieth century, who had both described a number of new fish species, particularly in the coastal regions of Australia.

"Did Mido show any special interest in marine biology lately?" I asked Jeff.

"Very unlikely."

"No campaign for a sushi joint or a deep sea aquarium?"

"Not that I know of."

Then we found a more promising link. It led to the Sacramento phone book and referred to a Sheryl Duncker, 246 Bleeker Street in California's capital.

"It's not the same address," Jeff said.

"Can't hurt to call," I replied.

I dialed the number on my cell phone.

"Hello," a female voice answered.

"Am I speaking to Ms. Duncker?"

"How can I help you?" The woman had the polite suspiciousness of somebody not sure if she was dealing with a telemarketer, missionar, or the Office of Homeland Security.

"I am searching for an old friend and was told that she is in touch with somebody named Duncker in Sacramento."

"Oh," the woman only replied.

I waited, hoping that curiosity would break the ice.

"That's interesting. What's your name again?"

"Johnson," I lied. "Anna Johnson."

"Hmm. And who are you looking for?"

"Midori James."

"I am sorry. I have never heard of her."

I feigned disappointment. "You were my last hope. Do you by any chance know anybody else called Duncker who lives on Bleeker Street?"

Her hesitation told me that she knew the person I was looking for.

"In number 32?" I probed.

"I am sorry. I can't help you." The woman's voice was brittle with mistrust.

"I am sure this is the Duncker address I'm looking for." I did not have to force a tone of excitement. "It would be so great if you could give me the phone number."

"No," the woman answered. She was seriously annoyed that I had tricked her into revealing something she would rather have kept to herself. She hung up without a good-bye.

I tried my luck with 411. As I expected, no other Dunckers were listed on Bleeker Street. Meanwhile, Jeff had continued to surf the Web, but he came up with as little news as I.

"I'll drive to Sacramento," I finally said.

"When?"

"Now. I'll rent a car over at the Hyatt."

"You're tired. Get some sleep. I'll go with you later. After work."

"Then I'll have to work."

"How about the afternoon?" Jeff tried to bargain with me.

"Rush hour. We won't make it back before nine."

"There's nothing to do here today that can't wait until later," Jeff finally said. "Let me drive you there now." A deep line had formed between his eyebrows. He worried about me as I worried about Mido.

This was the last moment when I could have said no, when I could have saved his life. If Jeff had not been such a loyal and stubborn friend, or if the human mind were not such a test tube of ignorance, naiveté, love, generosity—and violence.

I pointed at my dirty uniform: "Could we quickly stop by my house?"

"Sure."

We drove over steel bridges and through valleys. The grass was burned ocher and the water of the inlets and rivers shifted from gray to blue-green-white. There were thousands of clapboard houses along the route; an oil refinery squatted on a hillside; and outlet malls, highway crossings and billboards encroached upon the wild countryside. Their efforts were in vain, though they managed to give the hills the strange flair of a foreign planet being explored by ugly spacecraft.

Jeff's Chevy carried us to Sacramento like a huge ship. My friend looked small and fragile and, behind the wheel of his over-sized SUV, oddly lonesome. Jeff had been married when he was in his twenties. His wife, Lisa, a Hong Kong–born American, was a photographer, too. They had met at the art academy. Lisa had been killed in a traffic accident more than ten years ago. That was all Jeff ever told me about her. He said he had never since felt the urge or need to fall in love again.

With a printout of a map of West Sacramento, we found our destination without problems. Bleeker Street was a long suburban lane lined by houses that seemed to all stem from one litter of the same mother house—modern, luxurious and frighteningly unin-ventive two-story buildings. Most of them were painted the color of pale flesh. Some were white. Each had a front alcove, fake roman pillars, whitewashed garden walls, crew-cut front lawns.

House No. 32 had the color of a freeze-dried salmon. We parked across the desolate street. When we left the car, finally a sound brought the street to life. The barking of dogs emerged from the backyard of No. 32. Tiny dogs, excited dogs, I thought, considering the high pitch of their yelps. And before we had made it all the way to the garden wall, sleek little bodies appeared behind the iron fence gate.

Two chihuahuas and a smooth Yorkshire terrier greeted us with an aggressive stance and showed their vampire front teeth. Jeff and I both bent down outside the gate to greet the little monsters, but as soon as they met us eye to eye, the three heroic watchdogs took off and jumped up the front steps of the house, yipping in panic.

A man appeared on the front steps. In the same moment a woman slowly walked around the corner of the house. Both stared at us. I rose to my full height again.

"Sorry, we didn't want to scare your cute dogs," I said.

The man just nodded and closed the door behind him and the miniature predators. The woman looked at us with a shy smile. Like

38

the dogs she was petite. Her hair fell to her shoulders in a clean-cut bob. Her features looked Scandinavian, with the high cheekbones, straight, narrow nose and full mouth you would expect in a long-legged towering fashion model. But the woman was barely five feet tall. She wore a white jersey dress. A still small pregnant belly protruded from her tiny frame. She was around forty.

"Mrs. Duncker?" I asked.

She nodded.

"I am Anna Spring. This is my co-worker, Jeff Rockwell. We are looking for Midori James. She was supposed to meet you or your husband today."

My assumption that she was married wasn't contradicted. I continued, "And now urgent matters have come up at the agency. We can't reach her on her cell. So our boss asked us to drive up here and see if she is maybe still with you."

Jeff was wearing one of his elegant gray business suits. I had changed into the most formal pants I possessed, soft beige corduroy five-pockets, and a white blouse. For lack of any more official footwear I had put on red sneakers, the creative touch of an advertising agency's staff, I hoped.

Mrs. Duncker approached the gate but did not open it. Her head reached only to my shoulder. She had to tilt it to look into my face but then avoided my eyes. "Ms. James was—"

The door to the house opened interrupting her, and the woman quickly turned her head and looked in the direction of her husband, who now also walked over to us, no dogs in tow.

"What's up?" the man asked.

"Mr. Duncker," Jeff stated.

"The one and only." The guy's voice was quite high. He was tall with hanging shoulders and thin, black hair cut as short and neat as the grass underneath his feet. His gaze had the piercing force of a drill. He was dressed in a pinstripe suit and bright blue tie. Under the left arm he carried a leather briefcase; car keys were jingling in his right hand.

I repeated the question about Mido's whereabouts.

"I have no idea who and what you are talking about. You say you come from an agency?"

"As I said, we are just looking for our co-worker, Ms. James."

"I don't know a Ms. James." The man rubbed his chin, as if trying to come up with a clue. "Do you, Mindy?"

His wife rubbed her thumb over a little black speck on the garden wall. It was a dead mosquito baked onto the otherwise impeccable white stucco. When she had scratched it off, a red spot remained. Mrs. Duncker shook her head.

"I am sorry," the man said with a broad smile. "But we cannot help you here."

"That's strange," Jeff wondered. "I am sure Mido mentioned you as an important new contact for our firm. Aren't you the public relations director of your company?"

"Wrong again," Mr. Duncker said, still smiling. "I am the CEO."

"That could be the explanation," I bluffed. "Maybe Mido named you as the man in charge. But then the meeting was in fact set up with your PR manager. If you could give us the name, I am sure he or she can help us."

"I don't believe a word of what you're saying," was Mr. Duncker's answer. "And I suggest that you leave now."

"Isn't your company working in biotechnology?" Jeff probed.

"That's quite far-fetched." Mr. Duncker recovered his fake smile. "It's an industrial bakery. But we do work with yeast, as you can imagine."

"Can you think of anything that Ms. James would have wanted to discuss with you?" I inquired with growing despair.

"I ask you one more time to leave and not bother my wife and me anymore," Duncker said, his eyes as piercing as ever. He did not utter a more concrete threat and he did not have to.

The Dunckers stared at us while we walked back to the car. A real-life wedding cake couple behind an iron fence. Jeff and I had no choice but to get back in the Chevy and drive off.

Chapter 7

"Biotechnology?" I inquired.

"A crazy guess," Jeff admitted. "*Ask Anna!* Maybe Mido needed your genetic expertise."

"It's also possible she wanted my knowledge as a security guard."

Jeff chewed on his lower lip. "Mido had the Dunckers' private address written down. Maybe there is another connection than a professional one."

"Documents," I said. "Mido is or was in the possession of documents that somebody else wants. And her computer is gone. As well as a number of file folders."

"And she was threatened by a man named Frank who wanted money he could only get if someone named Teresa would come back. Now we only have to find Ruth and Rita and the confusion is complete."

"Damn." For a second I had to smile about our absurd potpourri of intelligence.

"Don't you think Mido would call you if she really needed your help?" Jeff said.

"And what if she can't?" I answered.

The skyline of San Francisco appeared in the distance. Once again the fog was rolling in and the city seemed to hover above the clouds.

"Maybe there's something in her office that could give us a clue," Jeff finally suggested.

"That's true."

"I'll do some snooping around."

"Can we go together?"

"It's less conspicuous if I do it alone."

Jeff dropped me off at my place at four thirty that afternoon. He made me promise I would lie down and get some sleep. l sank onto the bed fully dressed, slipped out of my shoes, curled up into a fetal position and closed my eyes. My head was spinning as thoughts chased one another and evaporated. Ideas turned into pictures—of Mido's house, the empty rooms, the Dunckers, and finally the image of a woman in shackles, chained to the wall of a medieval dungeon. Her chin had sunk to her chest, I could not make out if she was alive, dirty wet strands of hair covered her face, and she was wearing a bloodstained shirt. I tore my eyes open to escape this horrifying vision.

I got up, showered, put a TV dinner into the microwave oven—it was teriyaki chicken—changed into my second clean uniform, ate the meal without tasting a single ingredient and left the house. Today I did not wear an artificial eye. Exhaustion could make it uncomfortable to place the acrylic prosthesis in the orbit, so I covered the socket with a blue self-adhesive patch.

It was eight thirty, enough time to walk to the bay. I strolled down Geary Street, pulled out my cell and checked the voice mail. No message. Union Square was buzzing with life. I studied the face of every passerby, hoping in vain that I would detect Mido's crooked smile, her beautiful features, the serious eyes I was so desperately searching for.

Jeff came out of the building as soon as I had started my rounds. Walking beside me, he pulled something from his pocket. A postcard. It was of the kind where several small photos are pieced together. *Greetings from the Big Apple* was printed across. On the backside was another handwritten message. It was a different script than the one on the card in Mido's house. It read:

Dear Mido, I am fine. I had to leave Frank. The pressure was too big. I will get in touch soon. Don't worry about me.
Teresa.

"I found it on Mido's desk. I could not look around more yet. Too many people. But I'll try later," Jeff explained.

"Now we know at least a bit more about Teresa." I studied the postmark. "It was mailed on Monday from New York."

"Yeah, but take a closer look at the pictures," Jeff said.

Unsurprisingly they showed New York landmarks: Empire State Building, Statue of Liberty, Staten Island Ferry, World Trade Center. "Wait," I said. "This card must be quite old. Do you think they still sell them?"

"I have no idea. I guess not every little souvenir shop has taken cards with the Twin Towers off the shelves. And there are possibly people who even search for such cards as rarities. But would Teresa do that?"

"Who knows."

"And why was the card sent to Mido's office address and not her home?"

Again I could only shake my head in wonder as I slipped the card into my pocket. Maybe its aura would give me a revelation.

"Our conversation this afternoon keeps circling through my brain. As if there was something in it that should trigger a memory or a clue," Jeff said. "But I can't really put my finger on it."

"What kind of clue?"

"It's too vague. Let me try to track it down some more before I set your wild and beautiful mind onto the wrong track." And with a little wink he left.

The night closed around me like a dark tunnel. The fog over the water never lifted and the lights of the Bay Bridge seemed to come from a faraway galaxy. Jeff did not show up at midnight for my break. I knew he had not gone home yet. He would have looked for me to say good-bye. Several lamps were still lit in AdUp's space, but I could not make out what was going on inside.

By two in the morning, I still had not heard or seen Jeff. Then Carlos called me on the walkie-talkie: "Activity in section C, check."

My boss was in love with this kind of lingo. I liked to play the game, too, and answered, "Check C, understood."

Section C was the southeastern perimeter of the building. I walked there slowly, tried to make out from the distance what kind of activity Carlos had detected. There was some movement on the ground close to the fence by the water. A shadow wobbling among shadows. Somebody inside a sleeping bag was crawling forward.

"Wouldn't it be easier if you rolled up the bag and walked?" I asked when I stood next to the person.

"Sure," was the answer. A friendly, muffled voice.

For a second we were just two human beings exchanging conversation. The sleeping bag belonged to a woman. She had cropped brown hair, a skinny face and no front teeth. She could have been my age or a hundred years old.

"Can I help you?" I asked, knowing that nothing I had to offer would help her at all.

"It's cold here," the woman said. "Maybe it's warmer over there." She continued her crawl.

I had no idea what to do. My task was to make sure she would leave the premises. If she didn't comply, I would have to call the cops. Overkill in my opinion. *Great security guard you are*, I said to myself. My decision-making process was interrupted by a sudden sickening sound.

There was the thud, the squealing tires, the percussion of my own steps on the pavement. When I ran and ran, the engine revved up. It was so far to the next corner, light-years to the street, an eternity until I had made it across the lanes to the body lying on the tracks. The next seconds burned themselves into my mind and would haunt me forever. When I bent over Jeff's body, the realization and disbelief crushed me like a killer wave.

I touched my friend's face. It was warm, his eyes half closed, without focus, the wrinkles around them deeper than I knew them, as if dirt had settled there. I waited for Jeff's mouth to open and say something, anything, to crack a joke, make a remark about the expression on my face. I wanted to roll him on his back, arrange his limbs in a better position, make him more comfortable. And there was the blood. A thin, bright red line running from his ear. I wanted to wipe it away, but I did none of this. I was paralyzed by the knowledge that he was beyond help, that Jeff was dead.

Forcing myself, I searched for a pulse, frantically pressed my fingertips on his neck, then his wrists. I looked up, searching for someone, anyone. The headlights of a car shone in the distance. I stood up, raised my arms and waved.

The lights approached fast and I felt a kind of relief. But something was wrong with these lights. They came at me too quickly, and they were in the wrong place. I was standing in the section for the streetcars. The vehicle should have been to my left. But it raced up in the middle of the tracks, aimed at me. I shot to the side and stumbled up the embankment to where the palms stood. I used the nearest trunk as cover, and I was certain that the vehicle would run over Jeff's body. Then it braked and backed away, its motor singing a high-pitched tune. After a few yards it stopped, the lights still headed at me.

The car was nothing but a dark image behind blinding lights. I could not see its color or make. We waited—the machine and I.

I pressed the talk button on the walkie-talkie and whispered,

"Carlos, I need help. On the tracks. Across from the front entrance. Call the police."

No answer.

The car began to move. Slowly. In my direction. I couldn't take my eyes off the headlights. Everything was painfully bright. I waited, frozen. When the vehicle was only three yards away from Jeff, I darted from behind the palm, ran across the car lane onto the parking lot and headed for the darkness at its farthest edge.

Behind me the engine roared, again the singing tune of backward driving, the healthier sound of the first gear, then jumping to second, it came closer. I didn't turn my head, I only made a mad dash.

Shrubs blocked my way and I fought them with closed eyes. Behind the bushes there was another empty street, a small park and lawns leading to Embarcadero Center.

I heard nothing behind me. My instinct told me to stay on the lawn, make it across the open stretch and head for the narrow lane that led into the mall. The car couldn't get in here. But maybe somebody followed me on foot. I kept running. A sharp pain stabbed my flank. A familiar sensation. Harmless cramps. I welcomed them. They took over, subduing the unspeakable horror of the last minutes.

The entrance to the Hyatt Hotel appeared to my left. I ran inside. A doorman said something—I couldn't make out what as I looked for a crowd, witnesses, safety. The lobby was on the second floor and the escalator was much too slow. I jumped up the steps two and three at a time. A big hall opened before me. In front of the reception desk was a little cluster of people—late night check-in.

I stayed close to them. Pulled out my cell phone. Pressed a button. The display remained dark. Dead batteries.

"I have to make a call," I yelled. "There was an accident on Embarcadero."

The concierge shoved a phone across the desk. Hotel guests stared at me. I started to cry and only realized it when I tasted salty liquid in the corner of my mouth. I dialed 911.

46

After I had sent the police to Jeff, I wandered back to the escalator. I wanted to be with my dead friend but at the same time feared returning to the scene more than anything. I waited in front of the hotel until I heard the wail of sirens. They grew deafening, and an ambulance shot by. It turned onto the Embarcadero.

At first I stayed in the shadows of the high-rises on Market Street, then I ran down the big brightly lit boulevard and stayed on the streetcar tracks. Blue lights quivered in front of Pier 3. I stumbled toward them, sobbing uncontrollably.

Chapter 8

The ambulance left the scene soon after I arrived. The paramedics had confirmed what I already knew: they could not do anything for Jeff. Two police officers stood beside his body. Strong uniformed arms held me back when I wanted to come closer. I explained that I had called them, that I was a witness, and a security guard for the pier, that Jeff had been murdered.

A tall, female officer with pink hair asked me for my name and proof of identity. I produced my U.S. work permit.

She looked at it and gave me a smile that was warm and experienced at the same time.

"Tell me exactly what you saw."

I did, up to the point when the car was waiting for me to come out from behind the tree.

"So you did not actually see the accident, but only came to the scene later," she said when I had finished.

"Yes," I said. "But I am sure Jeff was killed on purpose. Why else would a car hit him on the tracks? And then chase me onto the embankment?" It seemed to cost me my last remaining strength to stay concise.

The officer thought about my answer. "We'll find out where he was hit. With high-speed impact a body could actually be thrown onto the tracks from the car lanes."

"And why then was I chased?"

"We'll process your statement," was all she said.

She gave me a long look and I knew she was thinking about my eye patch.

Another police car appeared and parked next to the first one on the sidewalk. Two male officers climbed out. They quickly conferred with the police who guarded Jeff's body. I saw them stare at the ground, shake their heads, then they walked to the Pier 3 building and entered. *Why is the door open?* I asked myself. I felt a moment of odd relief while this trivial security guard worry occupied my mind. *And where is Carlos?* That was my next, more troublesome thought.

"My boss should be somewhere around," I said. "Did you talk to him? Carlos Soto."

"I believe somebody reported a break-in at one of the offices," the colleague of the female officer informed me. He was a sturdy guy with a broad face, thick nose and Asian features. We still stood close to Jeff's body. No streetcars ran at this time of night. I did not look at my friend, but I did not want to leave him either.

"Maybe I should see what's going on," I said finally. "Maybe Carlos needs help."

"The officers are taking care of that, I'm sure," the squat officer said. He sounded somewhat uncertain, though. His gaze seemed to ask his partner, *What are the procedures in a case like this?*

"Did you see anything connected to a burglary?" the pink-headed officer asked me.

The woman with the sleeping bag came back to my mind. Did she break into the Pier 3 building after I had left her? I had no idea. I shook my head.

"Then you better stay here," the officer decided.

Space opened up around me and became a vast vacuum where thoughts could not be contained, feelings spread out eternally, a single heartbeat became so forceful it could knock the next one out and kill you in an instant. The officers just whispered to each other, the car lanes remained empty, all movement had ceased.

Suddenly there were headlights again. A dark blue sedan appeared on the northbound lane, pulled over and parked parallel to the police vehicles. A slight woman in jeans and a leather jacket walked up to us. She was African American like the officer next to me. But that was about the only similarity. She appeared to be half the weight of the uniformed officer, her hair was short and naturally dark brown. She had a narrow face, a slender nose, slanted eyes and thin lips. "Detective Sergeant Julia Wayne," she introduced herself.

Detective Wayne asked the uniformed officers about the events, they gave their report: a 911 call, a dead person on the tracks, white male, approximately forty years old. Witness appears on the scene. Security guard Anna Spring. She reports suspicious car.

Then the detective turned to me. She smelled of tobacco and stale smoke. A fragrance that reminded me of Jeff and our jokes about the perils of cigarettes. The plain irony of this thought made me numb, so I was able to report my story all over, calmer this time. Detective Wayne took notes and nodded after I had finished. "No license plate, no vehicle description?" she said and continued, "Crime Scene should be here soon. Let's see what they'll find." She knelt down next to Jeff, let her eyes wander over his body.

"Anna!" Carlos's voice suddenly sounded through the night. He stood on the sidewalk, waved at me. I walked over to him. One of the officers who had gone into the building earlier appeared next to my boss.

"Big burglary," Carlos said. Sweat ran down his forehead and shone on his upper lip.

"Jeff is dead," I weakly replied.

50

Carlos knew the staff of AdUp. They often passed by his door and waved a greeting. Carlos didn't talk much to anybody. But he was certainly aware that Jeff was my friend. Carlos's face twisted in pain.

"Mainly vandalism," the officer informed me. "We have to wait for the staff to come back and assess the damage. It's hard to say what is missing and what has just been smashed."

I was allowed to take a look at AdUp's space from the door. Computers were lying on the floor, screens were shattered, papers flying all over the place. I focused on Jeff's desk, and I could not see his computer anywhere next to it. Mido's office was in an extra room off the main space. I had no view of it from where I stood.

"I think Mr. Rockwell's PC is gone. And you should check if anything is missing from Ms. James's office," I said flatly.

Carlos looked at me questioningly. Julia Wayne had joined us inside the building.

"It's a complicated story," I said.

"Let's hear it," she answered.

She went to get a tape recorder from her car. Then she led me to a quiet corner of the lobby. We sat down on a bench and I told the detective about the events of the last several days, starting with Mido's encounter with Frank in the parking lot and ending with my escape to the hotel. I felt that I was mixing things up, that I forgot to mention certain details. And worse, I feared I was maybe getting Mido and other people I didn't even know into trouble. But I also felt that I owed it to Jeff to give the professionals who would investigate his death as much information as possible.

When I had finished, Julia Wayne nodded, her gaze contemplative. Finally she asked me why I thought all these events were connected.

Isn't it obvious? I wanted to say but instead answered, "Wouldn't it be a bit odd otherwise?"

"My job is a school for the art of oddities. But we'll keep your statement in mind. Let's see what Forensics will find."

Wayne asked me for my address and phone number. "We'll get

in touch, if we have more questions. You can go home now. And no more detective work for you. We'll do the job from now on."

There was concern in her voice, almost warmth. It was the kind the pink-haired officer had radiated: professional, humane, detached. Rage against the detective and her institution to which she referred with this strange usage of *we* surged up in me. I wanted to yell at Julia Wayne, shake her, force her to feel the same anguish I did. But I just stared at the woman while she gathered her recorder and microphone.

"Before I forget," she finally said. "Can you give me an address or phone number of a relative of Mr. Rockwell?"

Jeff's parents were dead. "He has a sister who lives in France. I don't know if her last name is Rockwell or if she has taken her husband's name," I told the detective.

Jeff's family were his friends. So I gave Wayne the name and address of his closest buddy and surf companion, Ethan. He and Jeff had gone to high school together. I knew I should inform Jeff's friend myself. I looked at my watch. It was twelve minutes past four. I would do it later.

The doorway between the lobby and AdUp was covered with yellow tape: *Crime scene, do not cross*, it read.

One black-and-white was still parked on the sidewalk. Detective Wayne walked over to the open back door of a white van. Two men in luminescent orange vests and blue coveralls heaved a longish gray shape into the van. For a second I thought it was the woman in the sleeping bag again. But then I knew it was Jeff.

I began to run, away from the pier and toward the Ferry Building. The Big Ben clock on its tower pointed out that it was not yet five in the morning. My shift was not over. But it didn't matter. I would never again work as a security guard for Pier 3.

Chapter 9

Sleep is a dangerous place when your mind is a hurricane, loaded with heavy debris. But I couldn't run anymore, couldn't stand, couldn't even sit. I sank onto the bed, naked, my clothes thrown into the farthest corner of the room. At one point everything became quiet. Later I rose from a chaotic place and opened my eyes to bright light. It was 9:09 a.m. I got up, aware of tasks at hand but not knowing what they were exactly. Jeff's face appeared before me, smiling. My heart began to pound, hard.

I washed and dressed myself, grabbed the corduroy pants I had worn to Sacramento the day before, and slipped into a black T-shirt. The night before replayed itself in my mind in every detail. I collected my security guard uniforms, carried them in a big heap down the stairs and dumped them on the next street corner.

Almost back at the house, I remembered my wallet. I found it in the pocket of one of the pants. And then Teresa's postcard from New York came back to my mind. I had forgotten to mention it to

Julia Wayne. And now the card was gone. I searched the pockets of both sets of uniforms but couldn't find it. Perhaps I had lost it during last night's desperate flight.

A man whose face was covered with sand-colored hair like a stretch of prairie was watching me. The moment I turned my back to the clothes, he walked over to them. When I stepped back into the house, he was already carefully inspecting one of the jackets.

Martha was waiting for me in the hall. "Hey chicky, I didn't know you liked male visitors at night," she exclaimed. Her expression was a mix of amusement and threat as usual, but there was also something different about it today.

"Me neither," I answered, trying to sound disinterested.

"The guy said he was your friend. Wanted to surprise you after your shift. I told him to piss off."

"Where did you see him?"

"Right here. In front of your door."

"And when?"

"Shortly after four a.m. Heard a noise in the hall. I swear it sounded like somebody wanted to break into your place. Wouldn't have bothered, otherwise. It's not as if I'm curious."

This was one of the boldest lies I had heard in a long time. Martha produced a wide grin. For a moment I actually liked her.

"What did the guy look like?"

"Baseball cap, six-foot-three, athletic, white, dark eyes, stubbles, a bit like that guy from the *Bachelor*, third season."

"Sorry, but I didn't watch it."

"I forget you're an alien. I can't draw suspects, but with a good sketch artist I could make a great picture for you."

"What did he wear? And could you see his hair color?"

"His hair was all covered by the cap. Green baseball cap, dark blue jeans and a black turtleneck."

Every mug shot I had ever seen on a crime show flashed up in my brain. "Did he leave right away, when you told him to?"

"My little Glock may have convinced him faster."

"You pointed a gun at him?"

"It was just lying in my lap. Harmless like a toy dog."

"I guess I have to warn my visitors to wear bulletproof vests in the future," I said.

"So you did know him? Sorry, if I scared off a beau. But I thought you were a ladies' kind of gal."

I had never talked with Martha about such personal matters. But I was also not astonished that she knew. And for the first time I was extremely grateful for her obnoxious curiosity and brazenness.

"I have no idea who it could have been," I admitted. "Thanks for chasing him away."

Martha's grin became wider. "Always there at your service, chicky." Her voice sounded as tender as it could ever get.

Back in the apartment, I looked for my personal documents, gathered some clothes, a little picture album with photos of my family, some books, the charger for my cell phone, an almost empty journal—I had never been good at documenting my daily life—a small first aid kit, toiletries, sunglasses, the cleaning solution for my acrylic eyes, the containers with the eyes themselves, and a box of patches. I threw everything into a duffle bag, locked the apartment, which now contained not much more than it had before I moved in, and left.

I walked down the street, entered the first big hotel, looked for the receptionist and asked if they offered rental cars. He gave me directions to an Avis station around the corner. The clerk, a blond woman with very high hair, heavy makeup and a friendly shy smile, filled out a form, asked me for my driver's license and finally for a credit card.

"Can't I pay cash?"

"I am sorry, but we require a credit card."

I had credit cards, but they can be easily traced. Then I remembered a MasterCard my twin, Sarah, had once forced upon me. It was a partner card under her name. I had told her I didn't need an extra credit card, particularly since she would receive the bills and I would have to repay her. It seemed like an entirely impractical arrangement to me at the time and another attempt of my sister's to gain control over me. But she had looked so disappointed when I refused the card that I had finally put it into my wallet.

Sarah and I did not have the same last name. Our parents had not been able to decide on a mutual family name after we were born. Their marriage had been difficult from the start. The compromise that my father suggested was to give Sarah his last name, Yan, and name me after my mother.

"I am using my sister's credit card," I said to the rental car agent. "I hope that's okay."

She looked at the card for a moment, checked my driver's license, asked for my passport, which I dug out of the duffle bag, finally nodded and said, "Sure."

She then filled in Sarah's credit card information, while I still wondered if my idea wasn't a bad one. I could easily transfer my sister the money via online banking from my German account—that was not the problem. But when she received the statement, she would know that I had been to San Francisco. But this would happen in a few weeks, and I decided that it was the least of my problems right now.

"It will take about an hour to get your car ready, Ms. Yan," the clerk informed me, after she had made a phone call. She looked at the forms again. "Ms. Spring," she corrected herself. "They have to drive it over from the airport."

I walked across the street to a Chinese restaurant that offered dim sum. I selected some chive dumplings and pork buns. Already the buns were more than I could eat. I paid and a little later wandered up the street and into the first hair salon I encountered. It took about twenty minutes, and I left the shop with only about an inch of hair left. In the next shop I bought a black wool cap and arrived back at the rental car agency strangely satisfied. A burgundy-colored Pontiac was waiting there for me.

Ethan Chin lived not far from Jeff's house out in the Sunset for the same reason our friend did—because it was close to the ocean and its waves. I had never tried surfing myself but shared my friend's love for the sea. I made a short detour to the Pacific and stood on the top of the cliffs for some time. The surf was low today, little gray waves crouched onto the sand. I inhaled the salty air. Its flavor blended with the taste of tears in my throat. A seagull screamed greedily high above me. There was a smell of tang and fish and decay, and the horizon was strangely close.

The Chins' yellow stucco house was located three blocks from the beach. At this time of day Nora, Ethan's wife, was at her dental office on Balboa Street; Linda, their three-year-old daughter, would be at preschool. But Ethan was a writer and worked from home.

It took a long time before he opened the door. His eyes were swollen as if he had been hit by a severe allergy attack. But then he embraced me. Held me so tight it almost hurt. Ethan was not very tall but strong, and I realized he was crying.

"They have reached you already," I mumbled after a few moments.

He let go of me, led me into their kitchen, pulled out a chair at the table and poured me coffee from a thermos.

"Half an hour ago," he said. "San Francisco police department. They wanted to know if I had his sister's address."

"I wanted to call you, too," I apologized weakly. "But then it didn't feel right, so I came—"

"It's okay," Ethan interrupted me and we both knew that nothing was okay anymore.

"Do you know his sister?"

"We all went to school together. Mary. She's two years older than Jeff and me. She went to Europe to study and I haven't seen her since. The detective, I think her name is Wayne, asked me to meet her at Jeff's place later. To go through his stuff. Address book, etc. I'm sure we'll find Mary's number."

"Did Wayne tell you about the investigation?"

"Well, it was an accident. I guess they are still searching for the driver. DUI probably." Ethan's fine-lined features looked heavier than usual.

I was struggling not to jump up and furiously throw the coffee cup against a wall. Instead I began to count the flowers in the kitchen. Everything was painted in reds and oranges: pictures of roses hung on the walls, big blue petals were airbrushed on cabinet doors, and vases full of dahlias stood on the table, the windowsills and the countertops. I made it up to twenty-two blossoms, before I could focus on the conversation again. "I don't think it was an accident."

"But what else . . . ?" asked Ethan. "Why would—?"

"I don't know," I answered quickly. "I . . . it's just a notion . . ." Now I cursed myself. It would be crazy to pull yet another friend into this maelstrom of suspicions and secrets.

"I thought Jeff had left all that behind," Ethan said.

"What?" I asked.

"Well, I thought you knew. But there were times when I feared he would die young and possibly from an unnatural cause."

Jeff and I had only briefly talked about our respective pasts. He had told me that there had been years after his wife's death when he had led a suicidal lifestyle. "Let's say there is hardly a drug that my body doesn't know by all its nicknames," he had explained to me one night on the beach. "But don't worry. That was a while ago. I've been clean and sober ever since my chat with the dragons."

The chat with the dragons had started one evening when he had broken down in a club and had remained in a coma for several days.

"I'm sure the police will find out what happened," I said, forcing conviction into my voice that I didn't feel.

I stayed with Ethan for another half hour and told him an abbreviated version of the story of the night before. I conveyed the police's theory that Jeff might have been thrown onto the streetcar tracks by the force of the impact of the vehicle that hit him. In my account, the anonymous car became possibly driven by somebody who was just afraid to get out and help because he or she was scared of a trap. I could almost feel my tongue split while I uttered these thoughts that in fact I felt were total nonsense. Then I asked

Ethan not to tell the police any of this so that they would investigate unprejudiced.

Ethan promised to contact Jeff's other friends. I left him my cell
phone number and asked him to call me anytime. He walked me to
the door and when I drove off, I saw him still standing on the front
steps, staring up at the sky.

Chapter 10

I followed Geary Street back into the city. The wide main drag was not congested at this time, and it felt as if I was being pulled back to the bay on a string. I found a parking space right in front of Pier 3 and walked inside. The doorman knew me and greeted me with a smile. I peered into Carlos's booth, but it was empty as expected.

The crime scene tape now dangled loose from AdUp's door. The vandalized office looked even sadder in the merciless daylight. AdUp staff crouched on the floor, sorting through sheets of paper, gathering computer parts, piecing together torn-up poster drafts.

I asked the first person who crossed my path, a friendly woman with an Annie Lennox haircut, where I could find Peter. She pointed at a man who was talking to a group of people.

"I told you, she will take care of everything in a while. Right now she has to inform clients." Peter sounded strained. His dark, straight hair was pulled together tightly in a long ponytail. His face was pale, his eyes huge and light blue. The gathering broke up and I approached Big Susan's assistant.

"Hi, can I talk to you for a moment?"

"Sure, let's collect all the crap that's lying around, start a little fire and have s'mores and a pipe." He sighed and then gave me a second look. "You're one of the security staff."

I couldn't recall ever having seen the man myself.

"Right." I nodded.

"I can't believe what happened to Jeff. You are his friend, he once pointed you out to me."

"Uh-huh." I decided to seize the opportunity. "And I wondered if I could take a look at his desk. There might be some personal stuff his family would like to have."

"Sorry, can't let you do that. Come back tomorrow—or better, the day after when we have sorted through this chaos. I promise to save all of Jeff's personal items."

I wondered how those weird eyes would look if Peter ever broke into laughter. "The police let you all come back in here already. Isn't that a bit early?"

"Took some convincing on Ms. Bradley's part. But we have burning deadlines, are missing them actually, as I speak." Peter turned away and rushed over to a desk, where a man was signaling for him.

How did Big Susan convince the police? I wondered. After all, it was a crime scene. And how did the vandals get into the office, to begin with? The windows consisted of safety glass and were extremely hard to break. I did not spot a shattered one.

Maybe they came in through the lobby door, I thought. The whole building was wired with an alarm system, but because AdUp's staff often worked so late into the night, it was not always easy for Carlos to figure out when to switch on which part of the alarm network. If Jeff had been the last one to leave the office last night, and I was quite sure he was, he should have informed Carlos.

I was standing in front of one of the inner doors. It was painted turquoise, matching the color pattern of the office. Big red Chinese letters were drawn across the upper half, spelling out something I could not read. But then there was much smaller English writing underneath: *Susan Bradley, CEO*, it said. I walked to the next door. And here the letters revealed *Midori James, Acquisition*.

I tried the knob. Miraculously the pattern of unlocked doors continued, and I slid into the room. There was no key to lock myself in, so I grabbed a chair, quickly carried it to the door, positioned the back under the knob and hoped for the best.

A faint musky scent hovered in the air. It reminded me vaguely of incense. The room had the same style as everything else in Big Susan's realm—office supply chaos on a background of ocean colors. The desk was toppled, paper clips and pens were strewn around, a giant potted palm was knocked over, and little brown stones covered the floor.

Something was different here, though, than in the big office. No paper lay on the floor. The file cabinets were empty, as were the transparent acrylic trays that had been thrown to the carpet. No computer equipment whatsoever was to be seen. I opened the desk drawers. They were as barren as oyster shells after a feast. I looked around a little longer. Then I was sure: Somebody had been very thorough in eliminating every snippet of paper that had ever existed in this room. I studied a picture frame that lay underneath the desk. The glass was broken, the photograph partly ripped out. It showed four women, two Asian, two white, two in their twenties, two in their fifties. They looked like mother-daughter pairs. One of the younger ones was Mido. All of them wore big smiles.

I fought against the urge to pick up the picture and save these happy images. But I had already been on forbidden territory too long. I opened the door a crack, peeked through the gap—it looked as if nobody was around—and left Mido's office.

"Ms. James is not in today," a voice came from my right, my blind side. I had not even made out an approaching shadow. I closed the door, pretended I had just wanted to enter from the outside.

Susan Bradley studied me intently. "I know you from some-where," she continued.

"Nighttime security," I helped her. "Not very successful though."

She looked around. Her expression hardened. "This is very troublesome. It will take us weeks to get back on track."

I had never seen her up close, and I found myself searching for signs that she had grown up so incredibly rich. Were there maybe less traces of sorrow in her face than those of us carry who have to struggle to pay for our very existence? But it was the same as with all royalty: What you inherit is just the myth. Susan Bradley's physical self was in no way different from a poor person's. I was in fact astonished to discover the many fine lines coursing over her features. She was at least ten years older than I had originally thought. Much closer to fifty than forty, which did not make her any less striking. There was something fanatic about her, though. A certain fixedness of her gaze.

"I am sorry to hear that," I said. "And also that you will have to find a new art director."

The rims of her eyes softened a bit, but her stare didn't crack. "It's a terrible loss. I figure you are the witness the police men-tioned."

I nodded.

"Can you come into my office for a moment."

I followed her.

Her space looked untouched. "I lock the door when I leave," she explained. "I have formerly had to deal with staff who could not resist the boss's property. I suppose the invaders did not want to bother with the lock," she said.

"Or ran out of time," I added.

She offered me a seat on a formal-looking couch. Her room was about double the size of Mido's with windows covering two walls. Susan Bradley sat down on a chair opposite mine.

"Jeff was a very creative person," she began. "A great photogra-pher. It's hard to accept all this talent can be destroyed in an instant."

And all this soul, I thought to myself.

"The detective I spoke to this morning said that you have seen the car that killed him?"

"I'm not sure."

She leaned forward in her seat, glued her stare onto my face once more. "I understand you must provide the police with all the information. But I have to ask you not to talk to the press. Suspicions multiply like rats and an advertising company that has been dragged through the media is not particularly attractive to clients, even though I recognize the hypocrisy." She smiled now, sarcastically, and quickly continued. "I am sure it was just an accident. Jeff could be absentminded sometimes. I have seen him run across the Embarcadero without paying much attention to the traffic."

Suddenly her gray eyes, which were cleverly highlighted by silver makeup, sparkled even more. It took me a moment to realize there were tears. She pulled a neat white cotton handkerchief from the pocket of her elegant suit, unfolded it and dabbed her eyes.

"I was wondering if you have heard from Ms. James." I pricked through the momentary crack in Big Susan's armor.

"She'll be back on Monday," she answered with freshly recovered inscrutability. Big Susan looked at me with curiosity but did not ask what I wanted from her staff, or how I knew Mido.

And had her reply come too quickly? Or just innocently? Not doubting what her faithful employee had promised in her last message? I contemplated these questions while I walked back to the car. The traffic was dense on the Embarcadero now. I looked at the street, desperately trying to imagine Jeff's last seconds. Had somebody called him from the opposite sidewalk? Had he been chased? Was there some kind of emergency he was running to? One thing I knew for sure: Jeff had never just run onto a street as his boss had wanted me to believe. He always waited religiously for the red light. His wife had been killed while she had dashed across Market Street, trying to catch a streetcar.

The landscape narrowed into a tunnel of fleeting colors. My foot accelerated the rental car faster and faster. I was headed for Sacramento, but in effect I was speeding away from myself, from the devastating thoughts and the feelings that were tearing at my inside like furious predators. Only the day before, I had passed this bridge with Jeff, only a little more than twenty-four hours earlier my friend had sat close to me in his car. We had chatted and I had contemplated his fundamental loneliness and how he had built himself a new life with his friends after his wife's death and his breakdown. A life that was now over.

Suddenly the back of a bright orange truck came closer. I braked, stepping onto the pedal with all my strength to avoid crashing into the standing vehicle, which turned out to be the tail end of a bad traffic jam. My frantic race had come to an end. The car closed around me like a cage. I began to shiver and finally couldn't hold back my own wild tears anymore.

Eventually I turned on the radio, found a station where one of those spiteful hatemongers was verbally bashing all kinds of minorities. He was a wonderful scapegoat. "I'd like to strangle you, too," I raved, "and stab you right in the heart and fry you alive with onions." Fortunately, the traffic cleared and I could speed again.

When I was only five miles away from the exit to Bleeker Street, I checked into a Motel Six. The decorator of the room had been in love with shades of dirty green. It smelled of insecticide. I dumped the duffle bag on the bed, plugged in my phone, which needed to be charged, and called Carlos's cell. He didn't pick up, I didn't leave a message. I would try him again later.

I had borrowed the Sacramento yellow pages from the reception desk. There were a number of bakeries listed, most of them small shops advertising their homemade breads and pastries. Two of the numbers, however, could belong to bigger manufacturers, wholesalers that targeted retailers and not private customers.

I pulled out the prepaid phone card, which I otherwise used to make low-cost calls to Heidrun in Germany. Using it now would block the display of my own number on the other end. I called the first bakery, hoping against all odds that somebody was still working there on a Friday at four fifteen in the afternoon. An automated message dashed my optimism: "Please call us again during our business hours . . ."

The second number belonged to Gold Corn Bakeries and here I was luckier. An energetic female voice answered my call. "Brenda speaking, how can I help you?"

"I am looking for Mr. Duncker. Is he still in?"

"Let me put you through to his office. I don't know if he has left already."

"Mr. Duncker's office." This time I was greeted by an another female, equally efficient but with a younger-sounding voice.

"Susan Bradley here, can I speak to Mr. Duncker, please."

"He is in a meeting. Do you want to leave a message?"

"Maybe I should call back later. Can you tell me when I can reach him?"

"I'm sorry. The meeting is in the city. He will probably drive straight home afterwards."

"Hmm, it is rather urgent. Can you please give me his home number? I have it somewhere, but I'm calling from out of my office."

"I can't do that, you must understand. But I can tell him to call you back as soon as possible if you leave your number."

I gave her a fake number.

"Good-bye, Ms. Bradley," was her final cheerful greeting.

I could not tell if the woman in Duncker's office had ever heard of a Susan Bradley. Or had recognized that my voice did not belong to her.

Chapter 11

Darkness slowly crept over the streets. I left the car a few blocks from the Dunckers' residence on a busier road lined by shops. It still did not feel particularly comfortable, but I had inserted my brown eye. When I wore an eye patch people tended to stare at me and could remember me more easily.

The neighborhood was as dead as on my first visit. Either the residents here did not believe in procreation or they kept their children behind closed doors. Only in one driveway was there a tiny bicycle lying around. Even the air was sterile.

The shadow of a little sycamore tree gave me some cover while I checked out the Dunckers' house. From what I could see, only one window on the ground floor was lit. White kitchen cabinets were visible. Mrs. Duncker moved around inside. I could only hope that she was alone—her husband out for a while with his important business contacts.

The driveway was empty, the garage door closed. After some

more minutes without a male shape showing up behind the kitchen window, I walked up to the gate, tried to open it, but it was locked, so I rang the bell. Lights flashed from everywhere. I waited for troops in camouflage gear to jump out of the rosebushes, but only Mrs. Duncker appeared on the front steps, dressed in white again. She saw me and instantly stepped back into the house. One of the dogs managed to slip through her feet, though—the terrier.

I pressed the doorbell once more. The little dog barked bravely behind the fence. Fear or excitement or just the frustration about his physical disadvantage colored his voice with hysteria. I thought about ruining my karma for good and snatching him as a hostage. For the moment it sufficed to say "Hey doggie, doggie!" The originality of my words overwhelmed even the beast, and his barking rose to new heights. Eventually the woman of the house re-emerged.

Mrs. Duncker did not tread over her doorstep. She merely said, "Conan," in a soft tone. Conan did not even blink in reaction to his owner's voice.

"Conan, come here," Mrs. Duncker tried again.

"Could you please let me talk to you," I called, certain now that her husband was not in. He would otherwise definitely have shown up by now.

I leaned over the gate, dangled my hand over the terrier's nose. He became even more excited, jumping up and down, making a wide variety of squeaking sounds he certainly believed were extremely frightening.

"My friend, whom I was here with yesterday, has been killed." I shot the biggest arrow first and thought I saw Mrs. Duncker stiffen a bit more when she heard the news. She was still standing at the top steps, too far away for me to be sure.

"I need to know about Ms. James's visit to you. You said she was here."

"She was . . . I can't tell you anything. It was a misunderstanding. You have to leave. My husband will be here any minute."

Sometimes a question not uttered is in itself a perfect answer.

Mrs. Duncker did not ask me anything at all. And I became even more convinced that she knew something. Something so important that I wanted to lift her up at the ankles and shake it out of her. And she appeared light enough for this stunt to be possible. On the background of the big, dark house, she looked as if somebody had shrunk her on purpose—a mad scientist who dreamed of being a giant.

"Please," I managed to say. "You have to tell me what's going on. Other people are in danger. I am being threatened myself."

The hum of a motor approached, a giant black Mercedes turned into the driveway.

"That's him! Go away," Mrs. Duncker exclaimed with panic.

I knew my one small chance had vanished and I quickly walked around the next street corner, where I hid in the shelter of the garden wall, hoping to eavesdrop in on the couple.

But there was only his "Good evening, darling. Sorry I'm late. What's up with Conan?"

The dog was still yelping at the gate in frustration.

"Oh, you know the little bastard," his wife replied. There was in fact something like a happy laugh in her voice, which had been terrified just seconds ago. "Always trying to show how important he is."

"Conan," Duncker now called. The dog became quiet. A door fell closed, and I bowed low in admiration of Mrs. Duncker's acting skills.

I heard the sound of footsteps behind me. I resisted the urge to jump up, shoot around and try my nonexistent karate moves on whoever was approaching. Instead I sank down a bit more, pretended to tie my shoelace, hid my face between my knees.

"Are you sick?" somebody asked. A young voice. I looked up and into the face of a boy. He was maybe thirteen, carried a baseball bat and glove. His freckled features under brown curls looked truly worried.

"No, it's just my sneaker. Look, now it's okay again." I rose to my full height, lifted a hand in farewell and started to walk away.

"I haven't seen you here before," the boy said. He was only a step away from manhood and already protective of his territory.

"I was just visiting friends," I answered.

"I'm sorry if I'm bothering you." The boy smiled. "My parents taught me to look out for strangers in the neighborhood."

"It's okay," I answered. "Have a good evening."

Now the free-ranging curiosity of the child took over. "Did you visit the Dunckers?" he asked.

"Yes." I nodded.

"How is Mrs. Duncker? She hasn't been well lately, you know. She used to let me walk their dogs. I like animals. But my mom is allergic. So I can't have my own. But now Mrs. Duncker only nods when she sees me, doesn't talk to me or invite me to come in. I hope she'll be better soon."

I was oddly touched by his sincerity. "Yeah, she hasn't been well," I said. We spoke from within entirely different universes, this kid and I—his honest and clear, mine full of deception and obscure.

"Maybe when she has the baby, she will feel better." The boy sounded full of hope.

"Hopefully," I agreed. "She likes children a lot."

"It must be hard that she lost two babies already."

"That's true." I had to control my breath, so close to important secrets. "I am an old friend. And she did not even tell me what happened."

"Nobody knows, really," the boy said, importance carrying his voice. "Mom thinks either they were premature and didn't make it, or they died in her. Because her belly was already quite big, and then from one day to the next she wasn't pregnant anymore, but there was no baby."

"That's very sad."

The kid's eyes shone with compassionate fascination.

We parted with a friendly good-bye. The boy asked me to say hi to Mrs. Duncker from him. "I'm Jason, from down the street."

Back in the car nausea welled up in me. *Food*, I thought. The socket around my artificial eye felt as if it was on fire. I made it back to the highway, drove for a while, and finally turned into the parking lot of one of the many strip malls. In the bathroom of a diner I exchanged my eye for a patch. In the restaurant I then ordered a double cheeseburger, fries and a huge Coke and devoured everything within five minutes. I stared out of the window, at the moving lights of the cars on the highway, the multicolored neon signs of the gas station and the shops. Nothing anchored this place in time and space. It could have been anywhere in America, any day of any year. Nobody I knew had an idea that I was here.

I went through everything that had happened that day. Organized what I had seen and heard and decided to drive back to the motel. The room looked even worse than in daylight. The cold light from the ceiling lamp did not help with its color pattern. But I was oddly glad to be here. I searched for the journal in my bag, made myself comfortable on the bed and wrote down everything in my head. Then I looked at the pages for a while, drew lines between names, waited for an epiphany to pop and finally had to realize that I was at a loss.

What did Mido have to do with Mrs. Duncker's life? Her lost babies? Was that even the connection between them? Was there a connection at all? Or had my nervousness created a crazy fantasy here?

And if so, was Jeff's death then totally unrelated to everything that had happened in the last days? Had he died the same way as his wife many years ago—as a victim of a mere twist of chance?

And how about Mido's disappearance, Frank's threats against her? Her empty desk at home, the break-in at AdUp? I had to admit that it was possible that all these incidents were in fact unrelated.

In science you have to be aware of two possible fallacies—of making connections where there are none, and of not seeing connections that are in fact there. Many connections cannot be fully explained but are widely accepted as valid. The placebo effect, the healing influences of acupuncture, even a lot of medications have proven effects but not fully explained mechanisms. Sometimes, we simply have to take things on faith.

71

I plugged in my phone again. The mysterious Ruth, the last person called from Mido's line, entered my mind. She had never called me back. And then there was Rita, the sender of the postcard. Where were they located in this maze of entangled connections or crazy coincidences?

My cell phone displayed a new message. It was Sarah again. Her last call seemed centuries ago. "Hey, sweetie. I have to tell you something. It's so exciting."

My sister's message sent a chill down my spine as had many of her remarks in the last years. Sarah was drifting into a world of her own. Connected to reality only by ever thinning threads. She was making up people and events that didn't exist, getting excited about news she had completely fabricated. Over and over I had tried to talk to her about it, alert our mother, but neither was receptive to my warnings. I was too close to my twin and felt she was spinning me into her fantasy web until I started to doubt my own perception—after all there was always enough truth in her stories to make it difficult for me to prove her entirely wrong. In the end I felt that all I could do was break away and run. But then I also had to admit that I missed my twin more than I had ever thought I could.

There was a second voice mail, from Carlos. "You tried to call me. Try again."

"Carlos here," he bellowed when he picked up.

"This is Anna."

"Where are you? Why are you not here?"

"My shift only begins in three minutes." I could not resist playing with him. Felt a sudden lust for a little cruelty.

"So you're on the way."

I imagined his big face with its eternal look of resigned worry.

"No. I'm . . . I'm not feeling so well. I'm afraid I have to call in sick."

"Very late." All hope had left my former boss's voice.

"Listen, Carlos. I also want to put in my notice. After what happened last night, I can't come back."

"We'll talk about that later. Not good to make decisions when you have a fever."

I almost had to giggle about this self-confident diagnosis from a distance. "Sorry to let you down. Maybe you can try Theo. He likes to put in extra shifts. And otherwise don't worry. There's not much more to steal at AdUp anyway."

"We'll lose the contract. Didn't do our job."

"What did you see last night?"

"Saw you at the back, talking to sleeping bag. Next thing you're gone."

"And then?"

"Not like you to just disappear, to not make sure the sleeping bag is gone. I went to look."

"Why didn't you call me on the walkie-talkie?"

"Tried, you didn't answer."

"And why didn't *you* answer when I called you?"

"I . . . I left it inside. Was sure I would be back right away. But the woman with the bag wanted to talk. Took a while. She asked me to come with her over to the next pier, to show me something important."

"And you went with her."

"Yeah." Carlos sounded inconsolable.

The woman and her urge for a moment of importance and human contact may have saved Carlos from being injured or even worse. The people who had raided AdUp had been efficient and merciless.

"When I came back, everything was broken."

"Where did they break in?"

"Lobby door."

My guess had been correct. They had probably slipped in through the front door when Carlos went out. Or when Jeff had left.

"What did you see before you entered the building again?"

"What do you mean?"

Carlos wasn't usually so slow. Guilt must have fogged his brain.

"Did you see somebody run away? Or a car take off? Anything like that?"

"Nothing."

73

"Didn't you see Jeff lying on the tracks?"

"No."

Jeff had been hidden behind the embankment. It made sense that Carlos had not detected him. I had heard the sounds of a car. That was why I had looked in that direction. When Carlos had come back, the car and I were already gone.

"What did the woman want to show you?"

"Huh?"

"The woman in the sleeping bag. You said she wanted to show you something."

"A dead bird. A big bloody thing. Right in front of the coffee shop. Not our territory. Took me a while to convince her that the cleaning crew would take care of it in the morning."

"Did the police tell you anything else about the break-in? Do they have an idea how many people came in, what is missing?"

"They didn't tell me much. Want to send somebody over in the next days. To point out better security measures." Now Carlos sounded clearly offended, although I had to secretly agree with the officers. There was a lot of room for improvement.

"You did what you could." I tried to comfort him.

"But it wasn't enough. I couldn't even keep them from ransacking my own office."

"What?"

"All the surveillance screens are pureed. Control panel smashed, too."

I had a hunch. "Did they take anything?"

"Not really. The printouts of the work schedules are gone and the Rolodex with the addresses of the staff. They also took the folders with the personnel files. Fortunately all of those are only for my use. There are copies in the company's main office."

"Be careful tonight, Carlos," I said. I thought of Theo, the other nighttime security guard. He was about double my weight and at least five inches taller—for his own good I could only hope that nobody would mistake him for me.

Chapter 12

The epiphany finally came, but it was a minor one, more like a good idea. I had fallen asleep not long after my talk with Carlos. I was in my clothes, stretched out on the green and olive motel quilt under a raw fluorescent light. When I woke up, it was still dark outside. There was no clock on the bedside table. A moment of confusion passed, then I remembered my watch. It was 2:34 a.m.

And then I thought, Rita! Rita's postcard had been delivered personally. Maybe she had driven by Mido's house, had dropped it off. But maybe she had not used the U.S. Postal Service only because she lived close by, within walking distance.

At four a.m. I gave up going back to sleep. I took a lukewarm shower, enjoyed a short moment of strange pleasure when I washed my now so short, furry hair, and dressed. Today I could fit in my brown eye without trouble. The few hours of sleep had done wonders. I put on black jeans, a white shirt and a burgundy velvet jacket. Usually I only care about my appearance when I am in a carefree spirit. Now it suddenly seemed important to be acceptable looking under any circumstances. Not only for strategic reasons, it also had something to do with an urge for basic dignity.

I had checked into the motel under Sarah's name and had given her credit card information. Now I only had to collect my belongings from the room and throw the key into the drop-off box.

The freeway was only yards from the parking lot. With its never-ending traffic it seemed like a giant living creature. A dangerous worm, roaring through the dark early morning, incredibly fast and eternally long. I started the Pontiac, exited the parking lot and soon became another bump in the worm.

The drive back to San Francisco took a little more than an hour. The toll plaza to the Bay Bridge was already busy. I paid my entrance to the city, crossed the tunnel under Treasure Island and finally spiraled off the bridge into downtown.

It was still much too early to pay anybody a visit, so I pondered stopping by my apartment but decided against it. For a while I drove aimlessly through the city. Finally, a rundown-looking café on Polk Street with a big sign in the window, boasting twenty-four-hour Internet access, lured me in.

I ordered a cup of coffee and was astonished to be asked the long list of options: espresso or cappuccino, single or double, decaf or regular, and so on.

"Just a regular coffee, please."

My emergence had obviously saved the heavyset motherly waitress from a slow and painful death by boredom. She brought me the coffee at my seat in front of the computer and came back every three minutes to check if I needed a refill.

"It's okay," I said after her third visit. "I'll be fine for a while."

She sighed, went back to the counter and stood there waiting for customers like a sailor's wife waiting for the ship to come back to shore.

My Internet search was not much more purposeful. I randomly Googled AdUp, Gold Corn, Duncker, Midori James, Jeff Rockwell, Susan Bradley. Of course AdUp had its own Web site and my requests for Jeff's, Big Susan's and Mido's names all led there. The site showed some samples from AdUp's recent campaigns. The Sequoia poster, Jeff's last assignment, popped up on the first page. The site also listed some of the advertising company's biggest clients. I copied their names into my journal, recognizing only two of them—the National Park Service and the Arthouse Movie Theater Group.

Jeff's name also appeared on many sites about photography. He had won a number of awards, and his photos had been shown at numerous exhibitions. Apparently even the San Francisco Museum of Modern Art had purchased two of his pictures. He had never told me about any of this.

Gold Corn bakery also had a Web page, a glamorous affair showcasing dozens of pictures of beautiful breads and other baked goods. And of course it named its CEO, Horatio Duncker.

Time had passed quickly and almost all tables were now occupied by breakfast guests. It was shortly after nine a.m., a good time for another trip to Mido's neighborhood.

Once again I left the car a safe number of blocks from my destination and walked from there. It was a sunny, mild morning. But the gentle air had not yet lured people outside. I reached Mido's house without running into a soul. When I glanced through the back windows, the rooms looked exactly as I had left them on Thursday morning. I was not surprised, but I was still disappointed.

Back on the street, I sensed that somebody was watching me. When I looked around I spotted a man standing on the front porch of the house opposite Mido's. He was dressed in faded blue jeans and a black Giants sweatshirt. I instantly recognized him as the pilot I had already bumped into the other day. The man lifted a hand in greeting. "Still on the lookout for Midori?" The red moustache performed its own little strange moves as it shot up under the man's nose.

I walked over to him. "Not today. Ms. James had to go on an unexpected business trip, you know. That was how the mixup on

Thursday occurred. Somebody had forgotten to tell my boss, and now she needs something from the office delivered to a friend who lives in this neighborhood. My boss wrote down the name and address for me. But I must have lost the note. Do you know anybody named Rita who lives around here?"

"Interesting line of services that your company offers."

"We are very service-oriented."

"And because you can't believe that Midori is really gone, you had to sneak around her house once more."

"She also asked us to check if she had closed all windows tightly."

"And if they hadn't been closed tightly?" The man smiled—friendly, flirtatiously.

"Then I would have closed them."

"From the outside?"

I pulled a key ring, which had the keys for the rental car on it, together with my house keys, from my jacket pocket, let them dangle in front of the pilot's face for a few seconds. "I guess I would have let myself in with Ms. James's keys and closed them."

Pretending to be hypnotized by the pendulum of keys, the man said, "Rita Takahashi lives over there."

He pointed at a house on Mido's side of the street. It was the third building to the right. In most respects it was a twin of the red house but for its color, which was dark blue with the paint chipped in many places and the wood shining through.

"Thank you," I said, turning to leave.

"You won't have much luck right now. I saw her walk away just when I came outside."

"Maybe somebody else is home."

"She lives alone. But she'll be back soon. She went for her morning exercise."

This guy certainly kept a close watch over his female neighbors.

"Would you like to join me for a tea on the porch?" the man asked. "From there we can spot her when she comes back."

"Sure," I answered, stepping up to the porch. His house was

bigger than Mido's. The first floor was raised, indicating there was a full-sized basement. It looked as if there was also quite a spacious second floor.

"Donald Mayer," my host introduced himself, after he had come back outside with a tray carrying a pot of green tea, cups and spoons, and a plate full of muffins.

"Anna Spring," I answered.

Mayer set down the tray on a small round table in a corner of the porch. He had offered me one of the two chairs placed there.

"So you don't have to fly today," I said.

"Nope. A day off before a Europe leg."

"Not a very family-friendly schedule." The pilot's private life did not particularly interest me. But there was something about the way he looked at me that provoked my comment.

"Very true. My girlfriends always complain about this, too."

He poured me tea, a little smug smile on his face, and I wondered if he was talking about consecutive or simultaneous girlfriends.

I changed the subject. "It's a nice neighborhood."

"Yes, and the neighbors almost feel like a big family."

"You must really take an interest in one another here," I replied. The man was wearing a strange cologne, very sweet, with a lot of vanilla. It physically weighed down the fresh morning air.

"You have to put some work into a good neighborhood. I only bought the house five years ago, but Midori has lived here all her life. And she has done so much for this street." The pilot was leaning back in his chair, legs stretched out, hands entwined behind his head. He pointed an elbow toward the muffins. "Help yourself."

My inside made growling, hungry sounds. I bit into a chocolate muffin, partly annoyed with myself. I did not want to owe this man anything, not even gratefulness for a piece of pastry, but then the rich bittersweet cocoa filled my mouth, and I didn't care.

"How did she do that?" I asked, then corrected myself. "I mean, what is it exactly she did for the neighborhood?"

"This used to be a blue-collar area with good, hardworking

79

people back in the fifties and sixties. But then many of the original owners died. Their kids moved away. Houses began to fall apart, the city didn't spend any money on fixing things. In many of the neighborhoods not far from here real lowlifes moved in, gangs took over the streets. But not here. When Midori's parents passed away, she kept the house, encouraged other people from her generation to stay, too. Founded a neighborhood initiative, got city funding for renovations, spread the word when a place was being sold. That's how I heard of this house."

"Through Ms. James?"

"Not directly. But a girlfriend of mine knew a friend of hers who wanted to sell. Got a really good deal, too."

Again he used an elbow to indicate I should help myself to another muffin.

Possibly it was just the lazy nonchalance of this gesture, a movement which to me conveyed a profound disrespect even though it was intended to be inviting, that sent my dislike for the man over the edge and made me want to get away from him as quickly as possible.

I stood up.

"You have to leave already?" Mayer asked. "I thought you were waiting for Rita."

"I have used up too much of your time already. And anyhow, I'd like to take a little walk around the neighborhood. Catch some fresh air."

"Even fresher than on my porch?"

Yes, I wanted to say, the air would be fresher almost anywhere than around you and your horrid perfume. But of course I kept quiet. All humor had suddenly vanished from the man's features and his eyes seemed to have petrified, so hard was his gaze.

"Is that Ms. Takahashi?" I said, desperately hoping that the woman in black jogging gear who was walking up to the blue house was the one I was looking for.

"Yes."

"Good-bye then. Work calls."

I had almost made it down the steps when the man said, "Maybe I could take you on a flight over the city soon. I have a little Cessna. You'll be impressed by the view. All my girlfriends couldn't get enough of it."

"No thanks. I'm scared of heights." Which was not true, but a handy excuse.

"What a pity. But you would certainly not say no to a dinner invitation? I know some great restaurants."

"I have a phobia of restaurants, too. Have a good day." Already on the sidewalk I added, "And thanks for the muffin."

The pilot followed me down the porch steps, picked up a garden hose and turned the water on. The last thing I saw of the man was a little twitch of his strange moustache. It could have been involuntary. It looked like a whisper, though, and his lips quite distinctly formed the word "bitch."

Chapter 13

Rita Takahashi opened the door only seconds after I had rung. I realized I knew her from somewhere and I tried to remember where I could possibly have seen her before.

"Good morning. Can I talk to you for a moment? I'm a co-worker of Mido's at the agency. My name is Anna."

"What's up?" Rita asked, a mix of suspicion and friendly interest on her face. She studied me quickly, assessing my features. I was used to that and I imagined her inner questions: *What happened to her eye? Which part of Asia contributed to this one?* There are people who claim to be able to determine at first sight if somebody has Chinese, Japanese or Korean roots, but I don't belong to them. Her last name was my clue to Rita Takahashi's heritage.

"We haven't heard from Mido in days. I was wondering if you have an idea where she could be."

"Come in."

The woman led me into a big room, the size of Mido's bedroom, office and living room combined. Half of the space was an artist's studio. A large paint-splattered easel stood in the center, and jars filled with bright pigments were lined up on a work-bench. Canvases leaned against a wall with the painted sides out of sight. The only visible painting was attached to the easel: A composition of black, red and purple, not quite finished. Flower petals were flying around in it—it was a psychedelic vision of explosives blowing up a bouquet of roses, an image of terrifying beauty.

In the other half of the room was a bed and a couch. The bed was unmade, the couch cluttered with shirts and pants. On the floor lay more clothes, books, CDs and a wide variety of other things, from magazines, dirty cups, open bags of chips to leather bracelets, a dog collar and other jewelry.

The lady of the house wiped some of the stuff from the couch, offered me a seat and asked, "Want some water?"

Before I could answer, she left the room. There was the sound of liquid splashing from a faucet, and she came back with two glasses and a plastic pitcher. She poured herself a glass, gulped it down and mumbled, "Help yourself," then sat cross-legged on the floor.

It smelled of sweat in the room, of unwashed cotton, turpentine and flowers. A big bunch of purple roses, half withered but still radiant, stood in a dirty glass vase opposite the easel on a chair.

"Okay, Anna. I haven't seen Mido in weeks. And anyway, why do you think I would know where she is?" Rita Takahashi had a dark, husky voice. She spoke fast while her eyes steadied themselves for a moment on my face, then returned to their erratic wandering over my body, the room, her own legs and back to my face.

She was wiry, almost scrawny, her hair short and bleached with dark roots. She frequently brushed through it with her fingers, urged it to stand off her head in ever new shapes. Her face was small with full lips and round eyes whose outer corners pointed upward. She looked like an entirely sad character from a Japanese cartoon. And suddenly I knew where I had seen her before, albeit much happier looking—in the photograph in Mido's office. There a younger version of Rita had smiled into the camera, next to a woman who looked as if she was her mother.

"Mido once mentioned you as her friend and neighbor. So I asked around," I said.

A moment of hope seemed to cross Rita's face, as if something she had waited for would unexpectedly come true.

And out of a similar impulse I began to tell her my own story of the last week. Almost the whole story. I didn't confess my attraction to Mido, but I admitted that I had walked into Mido's house, had found the postcard there and read it. The only option I had at this point was to trust this woman.

It seemed to take forever to recall what had happened. All the while my host looked at me, full of concentration, suddenly calm, collected. It seemed I had never before in my life spoken for so long without being interrupted. When I told her about Jeff's death, Rita sank her eyes even deeper into my own, encouraging me to continue, to keep talking.

I ended with the events of the last evening and told her about the Dunckers' lost babies.

Rita looked out of the window for a few seconds. Eternal seconds. I was shaking a bit, and wrapped my arms around myself.

"I was afraid Mido was in trouble," Rita finally said.

"Why is that?"

And then she told her own story. I listened with absolute fascination. It was a horrifying tale, extraordinary, but in many aspects also terribly commonplace.

Rita and Mido had grown up together. Their mothers had been neighbors and friends, such close friends that they decided to let each other name their respective daughters. The girls were born only two months apart, and during childhood they were best friends. Then they attended different high schools and had quite different adolescent experiences. Mido was an honor student— ambitious, goal-oriented, possibly with some teenage arrogance.

Rita was more of a rebel. She was into punk and pot and at that time the two girls seemed to live on different planets. Mido later earned a bachelor's degree in journalism at San Francisco State; Rita went to an art school. Both had moved away from the neighborhood when they were eighteen. Eventually, fate brought them back to the houses of their childhood.

Mido's father died when she was in her early twenties. Her mother was sickly, and Mido moved in with her. In 1995, when Rita and Mido were twenty-two, Mido's mother passed away.

"The same year that Ryoko, my sister, left," Rita explained. Her voice became strangely flat when she said this.

"Where did she go?" I asked.

"We never learned. She would write to us—in the beginning. Said that she had met somebody, that they were happy with each other, that she wanted to start her own life. She was only nineteen, you know, and had never been a difficult teenager like I was. Maybe she felt she hadn't got enough attention. My parents informed the police, even traveled to some of the places where her mail had been posted—Pennsylvania, New Jersey, later Canada. But they never found her."

After some months the Takahashis didn't receive any more mail from their second daughter. "It broke my parents' hearts, you can imagine. Finally, they moved back to Japan. They had been first-generation immigrants and had never really overcome their homesickness. My father could retire early. They were thinking of selling the house, but then I was looking for a new place to stay. In fact, it was Mido who convinced me to move back here. She had decided to keep the place after her mom's death. She had this dream of good friends all living together in this neighborhood."

"Do a lot of your friends live around here?" I wanted to know.

"Not really. Somehow it didn't happen. I actually don't care very much for many of the people who moved here in the last years. However, I manage to be left alone. And Mido doesn't have a lot of time for friends, she works so much. Also, until lately, we've had each other."

I would have liked to ask if they were lovers, but didn't dare. Rita answered the question anyhow, smiling a little when she said, "We were almost like a married couple at times. After I had come back here, we became best friends again. I had a full-time job then, too. As a Web designer. At night we would hang out together, cook dinner, tell each other everything that happened. And on the weekends we went on trips. Every now and then one of us dated somebody, but it would never really work out for either of us, and afterward we would laugh or complain about it, and regret that our sexual orientations weren't as compatible as the rest of our personalities. I'm thoroughly hetero, you know."

Everything had obviously gone smoothly for the two women for a long time. And then Rita lost her job, two years ago. At the same time, Mido's career grew more and more demanding. AdUp expanded despite the economic crisis, but the competition threatened to devour its employees.

Rita and Mido remained friends, but they didn't see each other so often anymore. Rita took on various minimum-wage jobs— cashier, waitress, parking lot attendant. She had less money than before and struggled to keep the house, to afford material for her painting. She also had less time.

Mido had not been blind to her friend's difficulties. She looked for job openings for her and tried to get her into AdUp.

"But somehow the whole situation paralyzed me," Rita said. "I did not present myself well enough and didn't get the position. I was very depressed. It was almost as if I only then fully realized the consequences of Ryoko's disappearance. Before, I had been sad, sometimes furious how she could do that to us. Now I suddenly felt I would never see her again. My little sister . . ."

She stopped talking, fixated on the picture on the easel as if she could set it in flames simply by thinking it. "Hopelessness is a color, you know," she finally said. "It's all colors at once, a scorching bright white. There are no contrasts anymore, nothing is special, nothing matters, it burned out my very existence . . . and then Mido made a suggestion."

Rita got up, walked around the room, left it, and came back with a refilled pitcher of water. She looked less haggard now, as if the chance at this confession had suddenly pumped new life into her veins.

Mido had broken the news to her carefully. She seemed to expect a rejection. But she said that she would feel bad if she didn't at least tell Rita about the possibility. After all there was enough money in it for her friend to live independently for quite a while. And she would also help somebody—immensely.

Rita never learned exactly how Mido had heard about the offer. She believed it was a connection through one of AdUp's clients. Mido just said there was this couple who desperately wanted a baby. Only the woman had lost her uterus and could not carry a child. So they were looking for a surrogate mother, somebody to have their embryo transferred, go through pregnancy for them, give birth, hand over the baby, get paid generously.

"It's strange, but I didn't even think the request was so odd. I agreed very quickly," Rita explained. "Of course the money was a great incentive. But originally I also thought it would be quite a creative task, in the true sense of the word. That is, until all the medical procedures started. I had kind of blanked out how helpless you feel, when you are lying in such a chair with your feet in stirrups and a doctor's instruments inside your vagina."

"Did the woman still have her ovaries?" I wanted to know.

"I . . . I don't know," Rita said, surprised about my reaction to her revelation. "Why is that important?"

"I'm originally a geneticist," I said apologetically. "Somehow I can't keep my brain from thinking in DNA structures. If she could still produce egg cells, choosing in vitro fertilization and transfer of an embryo is understandable. Otherwise, the couple could have just asked you, if you would be willing to get inseminated with her husband's semen. That's much easier than in vitro."

"I can't believe I never asked about any of that," Rita mumbled. "How could I have been so stupid!"

"Most likely, it was really the only way the couple wanted it," I comforted her. "Possibly, the woman's ovaries were still intact—or they had frozen embryos or egg cells from before she had them removed or the prospective parents wanted to use a particular egg donor."

"Maybe if I had known more, things would have turned out differently." Rita tousled her hair in a nervous, almost wild gesture.

She had become pregnant after the first attempt at transferring three embryos. One had settled into her uterus and everything had looked fine during the first months.

"They asked me to come in for ultrasounds every couple of weeks and never said that anything was wrong," Rita continued. "I was so sure the baby was okay. I was already in the twenty-first week when they called me and said there would be another test necessary. A detailed ultrasound. It didn't seem bad, just like the ultrasounds before."

Rita's face suddenly seemed to relive a state of shock. "But then they called me days later and said there was something wrong with the baby. That I had to come back and have an abortion. It sounded so easy. As if somebody had put the wrong part into your car and now it had to be exchanged. I told myself it wouldn't be a big deal. I would still be paid some of the money. And after all, it wasn't my baby. But then it was so awful."

A second trimester abortion. It could be a true trip to hell for everybody involved.

"I could not keep myself from imagining the baby," Rita continued. "How it must have looked, if it had felt any pain. Before the abortion, it had already moved inside of me, and I could feel that it was alive. After it was gone, I became even more depressed."

"On top of it all, your hormones were bungee-jumping," I mused.

Sometimes, things can go so wrong that doctors would recommend second- or third-trimester abortions. Sometimes, the mother's life was also endangered. It was an ethical question of the deepest proportions. Many parents thought it was more than they could take to raise a child with a disability. Others wanted the baby, no matter what, and sometimes even had to listen to insults from the medical community who believed they were irresponsible, bringing a disabled human into the world.

"What was the problem with the baby?" I asked Rita.

"I don't know exactly," Rita said. "They just told me it was disabled and it had to be aborted."

"Do you by any chance have any of the medical records regarding the procedure?"

"No."

"Where did all this happen? Who were the doctors?"

"It was a clinic in Reno. I had to go there for the embryo transfer and later for the abortion."

"Can you give me an address, a phone number, the name of the physicians who performed the procedures?" A new excitedness rose in me, much like floating on a life raft on the ocean for weeks and now seeing land, realizing it may still be just a mirage.

Rita rubbed her forehead, "Kelly," she finally said. "The doctor who transferred the embryos was called Kelly by the nurse."

"And the nurse's name?"

"Everybody just called each other by first name: There was Kelly. And then the nurse was called Jane. During the abortion there was another doctor. His name was John."

"But you must have been at the facility for a while for the abortion. There must have been other staff around."

"No, it was always just the three. Jane took care of me before and after the operation. Then they drove me home. I was still bleeding, but they said I would be okay."

"They drove you home?"

"Yeah. I got picked up here each time and driven back. In quite a big car. The driver's name was Bob," Rita said, happy she could still come up with this information.

"And the clinic's name?"

"I have no idea. After Mido had made the connection, they always just called me to let me know when the pickup would be. I didn't pay very much attention where we went. Somewhere in Reno. On the outskirts. It was dark each time we arrived there.

Also, when they took me home. I think we actually drove through a strip of desert to get there."

"Who performed the ultrasound?"

"The early ones, only Kelly. Then for the last one John was there, too."

"How did they look?"

"I'm not sure. They wore masks and caps. Like surgeons, you know. And plastic goggles."

"They always wore this outfit? Even during the ultrasounds?" I asked incredulously.

"I never questioned it," Rita said, exhaling quickly. "It was a strange arrangement altogether, wasn't it? I mean, playing cash cow for a rich couple is not exactly an everyday dream job. Once I realized that I was merely an object for these people, I wanted to get it over with and insulate myself from the circumstances."

"Did you ever meet the prospective parents?"

"No."

"But you know who they are?"

Rita shook her head. "It was part of the deal. I wasn't allowed to know anything more than what they told me at the clinic." Again she looked as if she could not believe how another earlier self could have been so gullible. She continued, "But look, I took the money, so I shouldn't complain. It was my own decision."

"How much did they give you?"

"Five thousand."

"That's not a lot for such an ordeal."

"They paid me fifteen hundred a month for living expenses up to the abortion. And I would have received two hundred thousand if the pregnancy had not been terminated. I knew what I had gotten myself into."

The price for the baby being so high, the doctors must have been reimbursed quite nicely as well. I was sure they would have wanted Rita and the fetus in their own care and control under any circumstances. *Reno, town of incredible gambles*, I thought. "In case of an emergency—after the abortion or even before, during the first pregnancy months—what did they tell you to do?"

"They gave me a number. Said I could call there day and night."

"Do you still have it?"

She jumped up, left the room and came back a little later, carrying an organizer bursting with scraps of paper and business cards in many shapes and colors. Rita searched for a while, then she produced a pink card with a handwritten phone number.

I copied the number into my cell phone's speed dialer. My head was spinning as it tried to process everything I had heard in the last hours. Rita's story raised more questions than answers. "How much does Mido know about any of this?" I wanted to know. "Apart from the first contact she made, of course."

"They said to me that I must not tell anybody anything, not even her," Rita whispered, then gulping down another glass of water.

"But she must certainly have known of the abortion."

"Yes. I mean, I didn't tell her in detail. She was still working like crazy. I didn't see much of her. However, I couldn't believe it when she asked me if I could do it again."

As sad as it was, I was not so astonished that the people from the clinic may have wanted her to try it again. A pregnancy after the first transfer was a good result.

"Kelly called me first and asked. But I refused. And then Mido showed up. I can't say that she was very pushy, but she asked me to at least think about trying it another time. That it would mean so much to the couple. That I had proved to be such a good physical match for their embryo. They even offered more money than the first time."

"But you declined, and that led to your falling-out with Mido," I made a guess.

"We didn't have a falling-out. I just said I didn't want to do it. Mido apologized and said she would never ask me again. That was it."

"Do you know why she never returned your calls?" I inquired, remembering the text of Rita's card.

"That's what I wanted to find out. Mido has never been a

person who sulked. She tells you directly when she is angry or has something on her mind. I figured she must be feeling guilty or ashamed. There was no reason for that, I wanted to tell her. Also, she looked so bad lately. I could see she was having problems."

Rita suddenly seemed withdrawn, worn out. Red patches appeared on her skin. It was definitely time for me to leave her alone. One last question, though, was tugging at me like an impatient child. "Do you know Teresa and Frank?"

"Sure. Teresa is Mido's cleaning lady. I believe her husband's name is Frank."

"And do you have an idea where I could find them?"

"They live on Forest Road. I don't have their address, but it's a green house, right on the corner of Geneva. Most of the times one of those monster trucks is parked in the driveway."

When I got up from the couch and wished Rita good-bye, she didn't move from where she was crouching on the floor. "You think that Mido's disappearance and your friend's death are connected to all this, don't you?" she asked.

"It's hard to say."

"What shall we do next?"

"I have an idea," I answered quickly, and much more assertively than I felt. I was possessed by the urge to keep her out of harm's way. "I'll tell you as soon as I know more. Don't worry until then. And for the moment, it would relieve me if you don't tell anybody you talked to me about these things."

Instead of a farewell Rita just mumbled, "Be careful."

Chapter 14

Frank and Teresa's house resembled Rita's and Mido's in size. It looked much less loved, though. Many sandstorms seemed to have howled over its gray facade, and the front yard was a patch of dirt spotted with flimsy brown grass. It could also have been the glossy black giant truck in the driveway that made everything next to it appear colorless and dull.

From across the street I observed the place for a while. At one point I thought I saw somebody inside pass by a window. Was it the dark curly head of the man from the parking lot? He talked with Mido about money. She wanted him to tell her where Teresa was. He had said she would come back only when he got paid. A vague plan formed somewhere in the wasteland of my brain.

After some searching around in the neighborhood, I found a street lined with many abandoned storefronts. On one corner, though, was a drugstore. I found the baby care section—a territory which was about as familiar to me as the surface of Pluto—

explored it for a while and finally bought a bag of diapers, a box of baby wipes, a pacifier, some bibs and two jars of baby food. I made sure everything was from the same company, Coocoo-Goods, and finally purchased a big gift bag with pink bunnies on it. Back in the car, I arranged everything nicely in the bag and placed it on the passenger seat.

When I caught my own image in the rearview mirror, I decided to enter the shop once more. Minutes later I was wearing dangly brass earrings and a gold scarf, which I had slung around my head in Grace Kelly fashion. To complete the picture I put on my sunglasses. I checked my appearance again and discovered that I vaguely resembled Jet Li disguised as a fortune-teller. It had to do for now.

Next came the truly exhausting part of the afternoon: to get myself into as much of a radiant mood as possible. With a fake broad grin on my face, I drove back to Frank and Teresa's neighborhood, parked the car out of sight from their house, grabbed the bunny bag and finally sprang up their front steps like the cheerful saleslady I was determined to impersonate. There was a piece of bleached tape next to the doorbell with a printed word on it: *Orlowski.*

Frank didn't recognize me when he opened the door and discovered my smiling self. He looked as if he had shrunk since Monday night. His face was serious but not unfriendly. Instead of a verbal *hello* he raised his eyebrows questioningly.

"Hi, Mr. Orlowski! I'm Shelby. I come from Coocoo-Goods and we want to present you with a wonderful collection of baby accessories so that you will be greatly prepared for the arrival of your sweet new family member."

Frank's expression remained serious. He had not opened the door completely. I couldn't see what was going on behind him. His edgy jaws twitched, and he was biting down hard.

"Maybe I could demonstrate the use of these awesome items to you and your wife. I am sure she will love them."

"My wife is not here. Are you from the clinic?" Frank finally asked. His words came out slowly.

"I only represent Coocoo-Goods. But I am sure we got your name from the clinic, yes."

"Then they should have told you that we don't need the stuff."

"Oh. I'm so sorry. Usually we only receive the names when the pregnancy is stable. But of course sometimes sad things happen." I just babbled on. Had I been a real diaper promoter, my conduct would have been a catastrophe. "Maybe you could give me the clinic's name? You know, I only carry a list of clients' addresses with me. But then I can contact them immediately and ask them to be more careful with the information they give out."

"It's okay," Frank said. His dark, deep-set eyes turned even blacker. His poker face belied an emotional storm. Whether he was suspicious, angry or even worried, though, I wasn't able to tell. "Everything's okay. We just don't need your crap."

"I understand, but—" I managed to say, then the man slammed the door in my face.

I took the freeway back to the city. The day had turned out to be gorgeous. The landscape with its thousands of pastel-colored houses scattered on the hillsides and neatly aligned along suburban streets jumped out of a real estate catalog. In the distance, the high-rises of the financial district loomed like a wizard's castle. The sky was blue and my heart was black.

I chose the exit that took me down to the ballpark and close to the Bay Bridge ramp. At the first pay phone I spotted, I stopped, took off my weird garb, pulled out the cell, retrieved the doctor's emergency number Rita had given me and dialed. "Hello, this is John," a recorded voice sounded on the other end. "I will be paged by this system immediately. You can end the call now and I will get back to you within five minutes. Please stay close to the phone."

I hung up. The voice had been low and gravelly. I had heard it before.

A loud roar from thousands of throats rose from the guts of the baseball stadium on the other side of the street. Seconds later everybody was quiet again, waiting for the next big moment, the next home run. The air was charged with suspense. A soft wind sang in the high palms. I walked back to the Pontiac, got a road map from the glove compartment and found out which route I had to take.

Ten minutes later I was crossing the Bay Bridge and headed toward Sacramento again. This time I would bypass the capital, take Highway 80 into the Sierras and follow it to Reno. I realized that John, whose voice I had heard on the clinic's voice mail, had also been one of the callers on Mido's answering machine. The last time I had heard him, he demanded some documents. He sounded much more angry than today.

I crossed the mountains during the last two hours of daylight. In Truckee I took a break, purchased a huge Styrofoam cup of coffee, a prepackaged salad and a brownie, and consumed them sitting on a bench at the sidewalk of the short main street. Dusk dyed the little old-fashioned railroad town in shades of orange. It looked like a film set, with the round heads of the mountaintops rising up from the earth like a conspiracy of sages trying to decide what advice to give those creepy little creatures crawling around at their feet. They remained silent. I thought I heard a wolf howl in the distance, aware that was wishful thinking.

Driving down the Sierra Nevada an hour later, I knew I was entering the desert, but it was already too dark to see it. Neon signs flashed by the roadside, inviting travelers to part with all their money in one of the myriad casinos along the way. Finally, a cluster of colored lights shone in the distance. It grew brighter and bigger, wiped away the stars in the sky, became the only visible entity in this landscape of shadows and fluorescence.

Reno's casinos flashed their credos at me the moment I had left the highway. *Circus Circus, Silver Legacy, 4000 slot machines, 1.3 million dollars for a quarter, $50 rooms.* The city's ferociously beating heart was small, though. The casino area was not more than seven blocks long and wide. I circled it twice, passing under the canopy of screaming neon in a state of instant hypnosis. Finally, I managed to break away and steered the car into less brightly lit areas. I soon realized that these quiet outskirts were vast, more than I expected, and decided to find a place for the night. Suddenly, the chaotic pulsing of the casino district was attractive again. It felt as if a bed in one of those big hotels would be cheap and safe in its anonymity.

Half an hour later, I stood at the window of a huge, luxurious room on the twenty-fourth floor of Silver Legacy's high-rise. Before me, the viciously grinning neon clown at Circus Circus rose up next to a giant silver dome, which grew out of the lower part of this building like a nuclear power plant.

It was seven thirty in the evening, still too early to make a call to Germany. A good time, though, to call Ethan. He picked up after the second ring.

"Hi, I hope I didn't wake your little one," I said.

"Anna! Great to hear your voice," Ethan answered. "Don't worry. Nora is reading Linda a bedtime story. Where are you?"

"In Reno."

"Oh, you were in the mood for some blackjack?"

"Kind of." My answer went unquestioned. Many people accept gambling as therapy. "I just wanted to touch base and hear if there's any news from the police," I continued.

"We found Jeff's sister's address. I tried to call her a couple of times, but so far nobody answered the phone."

"Did the cops give you an update on the cause of death?"

"They are looking for a hit-and-run driver."

"So they still consider it an accident?"

It turned out Ethan had not asked the police again since his first communication with them. I wasn't even sure if they would tell him if he called. Possibly, we would have to wait for Jeff's sister to inquire further.

In the background, Nora called for her husband. Ethan wished me good-bye. I had just hung up when my phone beeped again. The display showed a number I didn't recognize.

"Is this Anna Spring?" the woman on the other end asked.

"Uh-huh."

"This is Ruth. You asked me to call you back."

For a second I was at a loss. Then recollection set in with full force. "Yes, of course," I quickly said.

"How can I help you?"

"I am looking for a friend, Midori James. I haven't been able to get in touch with her for a while. But I know she called you a couple of days ago."

"How do you know that?"

The woman's voice was matter-of-fact, with an underlying tone of stress, but not unfriendly. A busy but helpful professional.

Again, lying was becoming too easy. "I am a guest of Mido's from out of town. She invited me to stay with her, she sent me the key to her house. But when I arrived, she wasn't there. I'm quite worried, as you can imagine. So, I pressed the redial button on her phone, and yours was the last number she called. So I thought you might know where she is."

"Mido is fine. Don't worry. She had to take care of some matters."

"Can you tell me what matters these are?" *And who are you?* I wanted to shout.

"I'm afraid I'm in no position to do that."

"How do you know Mido is okay?"

"I've been in touch with her."

"You've talked to her?" My inside tumbled like a centrifuge, blending anger and excitement. "May I ask you, *what* your position is?"

"I'm sorry, I have to check with Mido first before I can give you any more information. Let me call you back."

"Okay," I said with resignation.

But the woman kept her promise. Twenty minutes later my phone rang again. "Mido asks if you could meet her. She wants to talk to you and explain some things."

"Sure, but why doesn't she call me herself?"

"Her cell phone is broken, and she wants to keep her current landline secret. She'll explain everything soon. When you see her."

And you're sure she's fine? I almost said. Ruth's and Mido's little spy game did not exactly help me feel secure about this.

"So you're in San Francisco right now?" Ruth asked.

"No, I drove up to Truckee to stay with some other friends." I continued the lies.

"That's good," the woman said, contemplatively. "That should work just fine. Do you have time later this evening?"

"Yes."

"Can you come to Reno?"

"Sure."

"Okay, let me give you an address."

The last days had transformed my nervous system into a high-tech alarm network. "I want to meet her in one of the casinos."

People, lights, safety!

"I would be happy to offer you and Mido my house as a quiet place to get together."

"Thank you very much. But I'd rather wait for her at the Sweetwater Café in the Silver Legacy. Do you think she can make it by eleven?"

"She'll be there, I'm certain. She very much wants to talk to you. Don't go away, though, if she's a couple of minutes late. She has to drive into Reno, too."

My spirits were high after this conversation. Mido was okay, albeit in hiding. I would see her soon and maybe get some answers. It would have been sensible to sleep for a while. Instead I left my room and decided to explore the casino.

I had chosen the hotel of the Silver Legacy purely by chance. The entrance to its parking decks had suddenly appeared in front of me and I had driven in, entrusted a valet with the Pontiac and stumbled into the building like a sleepwalker. On my way to the reception desk I got lost in the maze of the place and had found myself on the restaurant level of the casino. The café I had suggested for the meeting with Mido was large, and its name had somehow stuck in my mind.

When I passed it again, I realized it had been a good choice. Tables were set up all the way to the edge of the main passageway that led through the casino. Later, I would ask the waiter for one of those tables so I could spot Mido when she arrived.

For now, I just strolled around among the blinking, ringing, beeping slot machines that lined every hall, lurked in every corner, filled out vast spaces of their own—vending machines of hope, or boredom, or just a little fun. On the lower level, which was visible from a wide gallery that ran all along the hall, were the gambling tables.

Every inch of this giant open casino space was buzzing. The restaurants were crowded, the roulette, blackjack and poker tables surrounded by gamblers, and droves of people were passing by. I walked toward a huge opening in the ceiling, the inside of the giant dome I had seen earlier from my room. It covered a sky-high ancient-looking machine. When I read the description I learned it was a 120-foot-high silver mining rig from the Victorian era, which simulates the production of silver coins.

I went back to my room. It was now nine thirty at night, which would make it six thirty the next morning in Germany, still quite early to call people on a Sunday, but Heidrun, my university friend, was an early bird and I gave it a shot. She picked up quickly, sounding fresh and cheerful. "Hey, how's it going, are you still protecting the Golden Gate from armies of invaders?" she teased me.

Instantly I felt relief and a sense of comfort. "No, I've proven to be the worst security guard in history."

"What happened?" she asked, reading the undertones in my voice like nobody else could. I envisioned her big blue eyes and the way they would narrow a bit in concentration.

"Too much to even begin telling you now. But I promise I'll update you soon. Can I just ask you your professional opinion about something?"

"Of course." Heidrun was one of the few truly patient people

I've ever met. I knew she was concerned and curious, but she could contain these feelings—very much in contrast to myself.

I summarized Rita's story for her, asked her what she made of it. Heidrun's job as a genetic counselor at a big university hospital required her to be up to date on artificial reproductive techniques and pregnancy diagnoses. I had not worked in a field so closely connected to actual human pregnancy. In my lab we had created genetically engineered mice for cancer research.

"So you're saying there was in vitro, and no amniocentesis or CVS?" Heidrun asked. "You know, the test where a tissue sample is taken from the outside of the amniotic sac. Both procedures can be used to determine certain genetic abnormalities of the fetus."

"She doesn't recall anything more invasive than ultrasound."

"Okay, it could of course be that there was no indication on the side of the genetic parents for any diagnosable condition, so they skipped the tests. Both of them contain a certain risk for miscarriages. On the other hand, in vitro itself creates a higher statistical chance of fetal abnormalities. And in a scenario with such control freaks at work as the doctors you describe, it's unlikely they didn't check for genetic conditions. My guess is they performed PGD before they transferred the embryos."

PGD is pre-implantation genetic diagnosis. This was possible only with in vitro fertilization. It meant that two cells were taken from an eight-cell embryo prior to transfer and examined for chromosomal alterations or certain genetic abnormalities. Only embryos that tested negative for any of the diagnosable conditions were then transferred.

"But that would mean that the condition of the baby for which they later wanted the abortion could not have been diagnosable with PGD, since they only saw it on the big ultrasound," I said.

"Possibly not. But PGD is not foolproof. And so far, all tests can diagnose only a tiny number of possible disabilities and diseases a baby could have. Even on the detailed ultrasound you cannot see everything that could possibly be wrong with the fetus. I usually try to warn my patients who are particularly afraid of giving birth to a disabled baby that having a child still means to hand yourself over to fate. You can try to rule out certain conditions today, but infinite possibilities remain. Anyhow, nothing can prevent your child from having an accident or coming down with whatever illness after birth. Because that's when life becomes really dangerous," Heidrun said with a little sarcastic laugh.

"So you also have no idea what the baby Rita was carrying could have had?"

"Absolutely none. I can't even speculate. You definitely need the medical records to know."

I wished Heidrun a good day at the dog school where she was heading to. She was training her one-year-old Golden Lab Barney as a search-and-rescue dog. Barney's latest little adventure, Heidrun said, had him stealing the neighbor's cat's toy resulting in a severe beating by the cat in revenge.

"Angels just like us," Heidrun said as a good-bye.

By now it was ten thirty and I gathered all my courage and dialed my sister's number. The story of Rita's lost sister had unsettled me. The devastation her disappearance had caused the family. If Sarah picked up, I would talk to her today. It wouldn't be long. I only had ten minutes before taking off for the meeting with Mido.

My twin didn't answer the phone. I left her a message. "I just wanted to tell you, I will never disappear on you. I have moved to San Francisco and don't know how long I will stay here. Right now my address is transient. But as soon as I have a more steady one I will let you know. Please call me. I promise I will pick up or call you right back."

Chapter 15

The restaurant was almost empty when I arrived. According to my wish, the waiter placed me at one of the tables by the hallway. I ordered a Virgin Mary and a grilled cheese sandwich and observed the people walking by. Constantly on the lookout for Mido's face, her athletic gait, her impish smile. But she did not show up. I ate and drank slowly. At midnight the staff was closing up for the night.

When I checked my cell phone for Ruth's number, I couldn't retrieve it. The number had been blocked from transmission. I punched *69. A phone rang. But not even an answering machine picked up. I asked for the bill, paid, and left the restaurant to the audible sigh of the last waiter who had been impatiently eyeing me for a while. The slot machines, though, never closed down. Across the hallway was a whole jungle of them. I positioned myself in front of one from where I could still view the café's entrance, began to feed the beast with nickels and brought it to its rattling, clicking and flashing life.

I was about as hopeful that Mido would still show up as I was optimistic about becoming a millionaire at the slots. But I also couldn't leave. I couldn't give up, even though I had no answers and Mido was a no-show. So I continued to watch the hallway, searching for coins in my wallet.

Somebody sat down in the seat to my right, but I saw only a swift movement. The next thing I felt was a hard punch in my back. I tried to turn, but I couldn't get far enough around. Before my good left eye could focus, the attacker pushed my shoulder back. "Do not turn round, do not try to run away, do not scream. I have a gun. You understand?"

I nodded.

"Get up. Walk over to the elevator." The man had a friendly voice. I imagined him smiling behind me. Something cold and liquid spread out through my body, invaded every vessel. I shook. The hard object in my back poked deeper into my muscles. I had once heard that somebody had taken a hostage this way by using a simple plastic pen. At the moment I didn't want to take a chance.

We neared the elevator, and I felt the man's body heat on my right side. He now asked me to pass the elevator, walk by the dome and cross the bridge over the lower casino level. My eye had suddenly become a thousand times sharper. Colors and lights were glaring, objects appeared magnified as we passed them. I managed to catch a glimpse of the roulette tables still filled with players. I wanted to hypnotize one of them—maybe the Latino in the tuxedo, or the blond elderly woman in jeans—get them to notice my distress, to call for help. In the next moment both shoved stacks of chips onto their numbers, their attention galaxies away from me.

The people around the next table were equally oblivious. Most of them stared at the spinning wheel. A man and a woman looked at each other and laughed. The man was slim with dark eyes and a very big nose, the woman petite, and she looked younger from a distance, but I knew that from personal experience. It was Susan Bradley. Big Susan.

Then we passed the bridge. "Over there," the voice behind me urged.

Over there was an unpopulated side arm of the hallway that led to the bathrooms. And to an emergency exit, which the man now asked me to open. I pressed down on a bar, which stretched the length of the door, thought I could not do it, wondered for a second if this would help or destroy me. Maybe a change in plans would confuse the man, give me the chance I needed to duck out of his range and run. Maybe his finger was tightening around the trigger right now, and the bullet would enter me before I could take my next breath.

But then the bar moved, the door swung open. We entered a decrepit alley at the back of the casino. It smelled of garbage. Dumpsters stood in a corner, walls grew up on four sides. Three of them belonged to casino high-rises. One led up to a platform which was about thirty feet high. A steel ladder was attached to it. "Climb," came the order.

It was a long climb. After every step I took he knocked his weapon against my ankle to remind me he was still there. Of course I considered making a step downward, crushing his fingers underneath my shoes, hoping he would let go and fall, but a gun has its own cruel magic: Even invisible, it corrupts your imagination, lets every escape plan go up in the smoke of a possible shot to the heart. Soon we were so high up that I knew a fall would be fatal, and if I attacked my hunter he would pull me down first.

I climbed, and eventually reached the edge of a flat roof. It was the structure out of which the dome rose. We were standing maybe ten feet away from its base. The assailant had resumed his position at my back and ordered me now to walk up to the round thing. It covered a 120-feet-high mining rig, I recalled. There was another ladder ahead of me. It followed the curve of the dome, went all the way up to the top. Suddenly I knew what the man behind me had in mind. He did not intend to shoot me. He wanted me to climb up there and then get me to fall. A suicide in Reno. Committed by a woman who was definitely troubled, whose best friend had just died, who had walked away from her country, her family, her job. It was quite a convincing scenario.

But how did my attacker know all this? Or didn't he. Had he just received an order?

My rage was doing a slow burn, but now rose it up to new heat and broke through the paralysis of fear. We had reached the foot of the ladder. If this man wanted me dead, he would have to pull the trigger, would have to go through the trouble of concealing a murder.

My muscles tensed and I whirled around, letting my arms and legs fly, punching the attacker wherever I could. He was mainly a dark shape in front of me. I could make out a baseball cap and a long jacket. Then I saw his gun; he aimed it at the sky for a moment in an attempt to get it out of my reach. It was a stout black pistol.

I ran.

The only way to get out of the sight of the gunman was to dash around the dome. His steps were behind me. I kept running, circling the entire structure. Suddenly there was the ladder again. Silence spread out behind me. I stopped.

One of the neon signs high above sent red, blue and white lights tripping over the skin of the dome, hitting and revealing a knob that protruded from underneath the ladder. I made a leap toward it. My breath was a loud surf in my ears. I waited. There was still no sound from behind me. I turned the knob, pulled it, and a small door opened a crack, hardly enough for me to squeeze through. But I was inside, facing a chaos of steel beams and cog wheels—the rig.

I pulled the metal door shut, held on to the knob, felt it twitch in my fingers. I was standing on a narrow, protruding platform thirty feet above the main level of the casino. I searched desperately for a ladder, but there was none, only the rig's firm frame. The door was being pulled open. I hung on to it with my full weight, which was not enough. So I just let go. Somebody fell back on the other side, catapulted away by the sudden lack of counter-balance.

I made it onto the mining rig, clung to a big wheel, found a hold for my foot and slowly moved downward.

It wasn't very difficult. The intricate structure offered many places on which to step. Then I looked up. The man appeared on the platform, scanned the inside of the dome. I froze, again waiting for the shot, but I couldn't see the gun in his hand anymore. His face was still a shadow, but I could see that his jowls were covered by black stubble, his lips thin, with black curls creeping out from under his cap. Finally he spotted me, watched my descent for a moment, then stepped out again through the door behind him.

I looked down. Two men were at the foot of the rig. Staring up at me. Saviors or killers? I had no idea, but I kept climbing down. The last four feet there was nothing to hold on to any more, so I jumped and landed on my butt.

"Good job," one of the guys said. He was blond and fat and spoke with an alcohol-induced drawl.

I walked away from him and his companion quickly. They followed me.

"You're a stunt woman or something?" the second man called, equally as intoxicated as the first one. "I'm sure climbing around on that thing is not allowed."

I mumbled, "I just needed a workout," trying to sound cocksure, but my voice trembled as much as my knees, and I had to struggle not to sink to the ground.

"Hey, you want to join us for some more drinks?" the second man drawled again. He was shorter than the first one and even rounder, with a pink baby face. Obviously he was convinced that just as much alcohol must be pulsing through my system as theirs.

"Another time, guys," I said, trying to sound amiable. Saviors, after all, come in interesting shapes and forms.

"Give us your room number," the first one demanded. "We'll come by later. You're a heck of a stunt girl."

I told them a room number, but they didn't notice that it was on a nonexistent ninety-second floor and strolled off.

I looked over my shoulder again and again; nobody seemed to be following me. Back in my room I locked and bolted the door behind me. Again, I had checked in under Sarah's name for safety reasons. But how much did my assailant know about me? Or the people behind him?

A violent nausea overwhelmed me. I stumbled into the bathroom and knelt in front of the toilet. After I vomited the few things I had eaten that day, I had a moment of immense, euphoric relief. I tried to get up. The nausea didn't come back, but when I was standing on jelly legs, an odd, light cloud pushed into my head. Holding on to pieces of furniture, I made it to the bed, lay down and fell into a deep, endless nowhere.

I slept almost until noon and woke up to a nasty smell. It came from my own clothes. Recollection of the last night set in. I made it through the morning routine, cleaned myself, assessed the bruises and scratches all over my body. Apart from the one on my right ankle, which had the shape of an egg and hurt when I put my shoe on, none was worth closer inspection. But I felt as if I had been shattered to pieces and put together again. Impulsively, I inserted the green mamba eye into my orbit.

I decided to keep the room for now and walked out of the hotel into the streets of Reno. It was a sunny day, hot in the sun, chilly in the shade. In the distance lay the brown hills of the desert. The big cubicle structures of the casinos looked like warehouses in the daylight, and the railroad tracks I soon crossed gave the impression of an industrial city.

I found what I was looking for down a little side street. The small, gloomy store displayed a selection of army surplus gear in the window, and I purchased a strong hunting knife in a leather case from a red-haired woman in a Stetson hat and snakehide boots. I was wearing a pair of bright blue cargo pants, and the knife found a new home in one of their many pockets.

Paranoia now full-blown, I drove the Pontiac slowly to the closest car rental place and asked to exchange it for another vehicle.

"Is something wrong with it?" the balding clerk asked me.

"I'm not sure, but the brakes reacted a bit strangely. They should be checked."

The car had behaved perfectly normally. Not knowing this, the agent just wiped some sweat off his scalp, began to fill out forms and half an hour later I was sitting in a black Escort on a tour through Reno.

I drove around the city for more than an hour, checked out neighborhoods, side roads, freeway ramps, followed the wild little Truckee River for a while. I wanted to get a feel for the city, wanted to be able to orient myself. Finally, I parked close to the casino district, but in a neighborhood that had an entirely different flair—an art museum, galleries, little theaters, restaurants with outdoor seating and blooming pots of pink geraniums by the riverbank. I walked around, found a café with the telltale computer monitors behind a window, bought a chocolate soy milk and a croissant, and punched in another Web search.

Dozens of doctors and health facilities offered reproductive services of all kinds in Reno. I scrolled up and down the search results on Google, stared at the entries, sipped at my drink and finally recognized something. I pulled out the notes I had taken during my last Internet visit—the list of AdUp's biggest clients—and compared it with the names on the screen. There it was: Green Desert Center. They promised specialized reproductive services for all fertility matters. AdUp's page had only a hyperlink to the company's own Web site and no further description. When I clicked on Green Desert Center's link, I was disappointed. There was an almost empty page with only the message: *Our site is currently under construction, please try again later.*

The Nevada phone book on the Web listed the center's number, but again no address. The café had a pay phone next to the bathroom door. After I had dialed the number, a recording informed me that I had called outside of business hours and I should try again from Monday through Friday between seven a.m.

and six p.m. "If you are a registered patient," the girlish voice added, "please call your nurse's number as listed on the registration form."

"Are you from Reno?" I asked the woman behind the counter. She was eagerly wiping down the espresso machine and hardly gave me a look.

"I go to school here," she said, rubbing a stain on the steel front of the machine so intensely that her tiny beaded braids flew around her soft-skinned face.

"Have you ever heard of a place called the Green Desert Center?"

She finally dropped her hand for a moment and slowly shook it. The beads clicked against each other. She had beautiful full lips, gleaming eyes, and in another age and time I would have flirted with her a bit. "Is it a casino?" she wanted to know.

"No, a fertility clinic."

"Never heard of it," she now said with conviction.

When I left the café she wished me "good luck." I thought I detected pity in her face, maybe worry and an iota of condescension—the whole strange makeup of sympathy.

In the car I called Information once more, this time to ask for Rita's number. I was relieved when she actually picked up in person.

"Anna," she said. "How is it going?" She sounded at once wary and glad to hear from me.

"Fine," I lied. "Listen, is there anything else you remember from your trips to Reno than what you have told me? Any landmark, any sense of direction? When you think of the streets you took after you came down from the Sierras, did you drive more to the north, or more to the south, west, east?"

"I have thought it through—what we talked about yesterday," Rita said.

I listened hopefully.

"You know, when I was in the clinic, I kind of blanked it out. But there was something about those people, Kelly and John, that

110

scared me. Maybe it was just projection because the whole situation was so uncomfortable. But anyhow, you shouldn't poke around in their affairs alone anymore. Let's inform the police."

After my adventure on the mining rig the night before, I had contemplated going to the cops. Maybe they would have believed me. Maybe they would even have taken me seriously and looked for a nondescript man with a gun who attacked single women late at night at the Silver Legacy. I doubted that they would go any further. The events in Rita's and my own life were so far still mainly connected by the wires of my imagination.

"We don't have enough information yet," I answered, "but I'm in Reno at the moment. It would be good if I could at least find the clinic."

"Promise you won't do anything stupid!"

I swore I would, but who can ever make such a promise anyway?

"Okay, I went through every detail of the trips in my head last night. I think the clinic was on the opposite side of the city from the mountains. We would drive through Reno. After we had left the city, we would turn right into a small street, I think, because the casino lights would be to our right for a while. Then we would drive through the desert and finally pass a bridge over a river—I remember that because the first time I was startled by the sound of wooden boards under the car's wheels."

"Thanks so much," I said gratefully. "That will help me find it, I'm sure."

"Wait," Rita continued. "There was an airport somewhere. I could see the lights of descending planes."

"Do you remember how the clinic building looked?"

"There were a number of flat buildings, like oversized bungalows. They were connected by covered walkways. And I think we came from the back. There was no reception area or anything. We always entered through a steel door. But I think there may have been a bigger white house in the distance."

"Is there anything you remember about Kelly and John, apart

111

from the masks? Were they tall or small, skinny or fat, what kind of English did they speak?"

"Both were about average height and weight. John was maybe six feet tall, Kelly smaller, rather petite. They appeared to be white, from what I could make out. Kelly had green eyes, John's were brown. She spoke with a slight accent. Something European, but I'm not sure. John sounded West Coast. But they didn't say that much anyway. Jane was the one who would get me ready for the procedures each time, explain things, you know."

"And how did she look?"

"She was tall, over six feet, around fifty, African American, short hair, round face, slender, she had a little piercing in her nose, her eyes were blue, kind of unreal looking—maybe she wore contacts."

I wanted to know if anything any of the people at the clinic had said struck Rita as unusual, something medical or personal that had led to her impression they were scary.

"Kelly and John never asked me anything personal," Rita answered. "I only saw John twice, anyway, and he hardly said anything. With Kelly it seemed like she had a catalog of medical questions in her head, which she would check one after the other. She even gave me a diet plan she wanted me to stick to, and then she would ask me questions about my nutrition each time. It felt as if she had bought my body. Which in a way she had, of course, or at least she was taking care of the investment the couple who wanted the child had made. During the ultrasounds she would just stare at the screen. Never explained to me what she saw. But that's not unusual too, I guess, as I was not the regular happy mom-to-be. She was weird, but I can't really put my finger on what it was."

"How about Jane? How was she?"

"Jane had this kind of professional friendliness, you know, like so many doctors and other medical people. She would ask me how I felt, but then she seemed somehow distant when I answered. But she was nice enough. Asked me if I had a partner and if I ever wanted a child of my own."

"You said she was also there during the abortion and then afterwards. Did she explain anything more about the condition of the baby?"

"I don't know if she was actually there during the abortion. I only saw her before and after. She wheeled me into the operating room where John and Kelly were already waiting, and left. Then Kelly gave me an injection that knocked me out. And you know what? After the abortion it was strange. It seemed like Jane had changed."

"Was she more compassionate then?"

"Just the opposite. It was as if she acted on autopilot. She would hardly speak to me at all, didn't even really look at me, only as long as she had to take care of the bleeding and to give me some injections. It was as if she had suddenly been exchanged for a replica, as if she had somehow completely lost her soul."

Before we hung up, I asked Rita if she had anybody she could stay with for the next few days.

"Do you think I'm in danger?"

"I don't think so," I said, trying to sound certain. "But it would make me feel better, if nobody knew right now where to find you."

She promised she would think about it.

Chapter 16

For the next three hours I explored the vicinity around Reno airport. Making sure the city was always on my right, I drove onto little country roads and dirt tracks, followed them for a while until they dead-ended or just led onto the next bigger road again. I encountered suburban neighborhoods, golf courses, upscale homes, but nothing that looked like a medical facility. Dusk was already beginning to settle in. The sky darkened from azure to a light violet and finally to the color of a deep purple bruise when I decided to quit the search. The directions Ruth gave me were too vague. I decided to wait until the next morning, a Monday, when I could call the Green Desert Center's number once more and ask for their address.

I was driving south. A big road sign proclaimed Carson City. A smaller one read Hidden Valley. I left the main road and followed the sign. My map showed a small stream ahead of me that flowed into the Truckee River. Again there were countless dirt roads leading over the desert hills into the backlands. At one point the car's headlights caught a lighter surface to my right. A rough gravel path. I turned into it and after about a mile, I reached a bridge, a sturdy wooden structure. The Escort's wheels bumped over its planks. By now, it was too dark to make out the creek beneath.

Beyond the bridge, the track continued for another mile before it ended at a metal gate. A high white fence extended from the left and right of the gate. At first sight, it looked like an oversized wooden picket fence. A closer look produced vicious-looking metal spikes protruding from its tips.

Behind the fence were a number of low, flat structures. The buildings were connected by glass walkways, illuminated by cold white light. I got out of the car, cautiously tried the gate. It was locked. There was a keypad. Somebody in possession of a secret code would be able to open the doors.

I drove back toward the bridge for a while and found a trail leading behind a low hill. The area was covered with rough giant stones on dry brown earth. I backed up the car far enough to hide it from anybody passing by on the main track, locked it and started out on foot. The last remnants of daylight made the path visible enough. I walked carefully, listening for every sound around me. The underlying music of the desert was a low purr, intercepted by the hum of faraway cars and the occasional distant scream of an animal I couldn't determine. It was quickly getting cold and I wished I had brought a sweater. A smell of dust and soil surrounded me.

Back at the gate I spotted a small path parallel to the fence. Too narrow for a vehicle but wide enough to walk comfortably. Every now and then a light from the buildings fell on the ground. I followed the trail for maybe ten minutes until brighter space opened up ahead of me. Eventually, there was a parking lot encircled by green lawns. Sprinklers hissed like snakes in hiding.

The lot was located at the side of a white building. It was designed to resemble an antebellum mansion. Its mere size, though, gave it away as a counterfeit. It was much bigger than a

Southern villa—the porch was cemented, the window panes consisted of contemporary tinted glass, and the front door was made of glass as well. A giant sign told me that this was in fact the Green Desert Center—Reproductive Clinic.

When I stepped onto the porch, the automatic door did not slide open. But there was a doorbell. A brassy-sounding female voice sounded from a speaker in the wall: "How can I help you?"

"I have some questions about the clinic."

"Are you a visitor?"

"No, a patient."

Meanwhile, I had made out a receptionist's desk in a large foyer behind the door. The woman I was speaking to sat behind it. I waved at her, smiled. Suddenly the door opened. The receptionist looked not much older than eighteen. She gave me an insecure smile, revealing her braces. Her hair was red, her face covered with freckles. "Are you checking in?" she asked, eyes glued to a computer screen in front of her, "because there are no more new arrivals scheduled for tonight."

"A co-worker told me about the center," I quickly said. "I was in the area—actually my husband is gambling with some friends in Reno—I'm not so into it, you know, and so I thought I'd just drive by and take a look at the facilities myself."

"Oh," the receptionist answered. "I'm afraid I can't show you around without an appointment. And none of our counselors is on duty. But I can try to squeeze you in with one of them tomorrow."

The determination to radiate authority let her sound more gruff than she probably was. I smiled again and said, "That's very kind of you. Unfortunately we have to drive back to San Jose later tonight. But maybe I could just ask you some questions."

"Sure," she said with hesitation.

"My co-worker said that the daughter of her cousin was treated here a while ago, and she was so happy with it. She has a very cute son. Unfortunately they weren't sure about the names of the doctors who took care of them. They only remembered their first names: Kelly and John."

The girl's eyes moved from my face, upon which she had fixated while I was speaking, quickly to the surface of her desk. She let her finger wander down a list stuck under a transparent mat. "I only work here on Sundays," she finally explained. "I'm not sure if any of the doctors is called John or Kelly. But I'm trying to find out."

"Maybe I can help you," a male voice said from a corner of the foyer.

I turned around. A rather small man walked over to me. As he approached I realized it was the mere size of the foyer that diminished him. The huge lobby was more than two stories high, painted entirely white. Blown-up photographs of desert landscapes hung on the walls, scenes of serene beauty with tiny groups of people walking in the foreground. All of them looked like families with seniors, adults, teenagers and toddlers of various skin colors and styles of clothes.

When the man stood next to me, it turned out we were about the same height. He was dressed in running gear, headphones hung around his neck, his face looked as if he had the jog still ahead of him, the forehead dry, his straight black hair was neatly combed back behind the ears. "Roy Eid. I'm the director here."

I stared at him. The man's face was almost comically unbalanced due to the giant nose that cut through its fine features like a mountain range. It was mainly for this trait that I recognized him from the previous night. He had been Susan Bradley's gambling companion. Like her, he looked older up close than from a distance. He was probably in his late forties.

"I have to apologize for overhearing some of your conversation with Alice," Eid gave the receptionist a friendly smile. "I will gladly give you any information you need."

Alice seemed relieved she was off the hook and quickly turned her eyes away from us and back to her computer screen.

"Please excuse my outfit, but I was on my way out for some evening exercise. Maybe you would like to join me for a little walk around the park," the man suggested.

"I hurt my ankle yesterday," I quickly replied. "Rock climbing.

And I don't want to keep you too long. Let's just talk on the porch." In sight of the receptionist, I thought.

"It's more comfortable in my office, then," the man said, and began to cross the hall.

I followed him, faking a slight limp, feeling for the knife in my pocket. He led me down a hallway and opened a huge mahogany door. The room contained a heavy wooden desk and some equally solid bookshelves, file cabinets, a couch and chairs. It had the feel of a corporate office. The only thing that broke the impression was a corner filled with toys, tiny blue and yellow furniture, and stuffed animals.

Eid offered me a seat on the leather couch and placed himself in a chair across from me. "So you are interested in Green Desert's services, Ms.—"

"Miller," I quickly said. "Jeanne Miller."

"Maybe we should first figure out which kind of treatment you are looking for. Then I can connect you with the perfect team to accommodate your needs. We only work with highly specialized experts here, you know," Eid added, almost apologetically.

He had a rather high-pitched but melodious voice with a faint ring of an accent, perhaps Middle Eastern.

"Actually, as I've told Alice already, I'm looking for two of your doctors who have been recommended to me: Kelly and John."

"Hmm," Eid replied. "I can assure you that all of our doctors are excellent, their expertise state of the art. I'd really advise you to look at their medical specialties and your physical needs before you make a choice. Maybe you could just tell me a bit about yourself, and I'll give you some more information about the clinic."

We could have continued to talk in circles forever. The man's weapon was definitely his benign charm. He emanated friendliness and a spirit of nonaggression that had to be a lie, at least in part, otherwise he would not be holding such a position.

"Are you a doctor, too?" I asked.

"Yes," he answered, his smile opening even a bit wider. "My job, though, is to keep this place running. A lot of organizational chores. So I let our medical experts do the actual treatment and research. But of course I can give you informed advice on any of the programs here."

"If I'm looking for a surrogate mother to carry a child for me and my husband, could you help us with that?"

"We do not act as an agent for surrogates ourselves. But we work with some agencies, let me see . . ." He got up and walked to one of the shelves. When he came back he handed me a number of brochures. "Once you've found a mother, we'll provide all the necessary medical services."

"And then John and Kelly could treat me."

He shook his head, rubbed the sides of his nose with thumb and index finger. "I understand that you are looking for doctors who have been recommended to you. I would do the same. But there must have been a misunderstanding when your friends sent you here. A John or a Kelly doesn't work here as doctor."

"Maybe they used to."

"I've been at Green Desert for almost ten years. We once had a doctor John Seymour. But he retired shortly after I started. He died four years ago."

"That's odd," I said. "Possibly my friend got something wrong. Could it be that John and Kelly are nurses?"

"We have a lab technician called John. But no nurse. And somebody named Kelly is not employed here, I can assure you."

Eid's smile began to look a bit forced. He picked a business card out of a holder on his desk, handed it to me and said, "Let me know as soon as you have found a surrogate mom. This is my direct line, I'll be pleased to introduce you to the best medical staff we have."

He accompanied me to the parking lot. I stopped in front of a row of cars, pretended to search my pockets for a key. Eid waved a good-bye and ran down the driveway.

When he was out of sight, I walked back to the sliding glass door and knocked on it lightly. Alice opened it for me without hesitation this time.

"My car doesn't want to start," I explained. "Maybe it's the dust. My husband will come over from Reno to pick me up. Can I wait here?"

"Sure," the receptionist nodded and pointed at some chairs in a corner.

Among the brochures Eid had handed me was a thick booklet promoting the clinic. During the next half hour I studied it and learned some interesting things. The photographs in the lobby had been taken by Jeff. I looked at them again, still admiring their beauty. I felt tears well up, covered my face with my hands and finally forced myself to read on.

The booklet itself had been designed by AdUp, responsible editor had been M. James, copy editor R. Shriner, photographer J. Rockwell. It contained numerous articles explaining modern reproductive techniques. Little pictures of the authors appeared at the bottom of each text. All were doctors at the clinic. I studied the faces of the men and women in scrubs or business attire. They had obviously tried to appear optimistic and assertive in the photographs. Some smiled more convincingly than others. There were nerdy-looking faces and somber ones; two—one male, one female—could have been models for a beauty and fitness magazine. Eid hadn't lied—none of them was called Kelly or John.

Pictures of the clinic's grounds, even a little map, was included in the brochure. The mansion lay at the opposite end of the park from the gate I had first encountered. It contained the clinic's administration offices and archives. In the back was a cafeteria. The flat buildings scattered across the park contained examination rooms, labs, surgical units and patient's rooms.

The last ten pages of the booklet were filled with photographs of babies held by smiling moms and dads. The babies' expressions varied from toothless grins to sullen scowls; some looked oddly serious and prematurely wise.

The brochure was concise and easy to understand for the layperson. It was encouraging without being unrealistic. One page explained how contemporary reproductive medicine was far from being a foolproof science. The success rates depended on a person's or a couple's age and fertility problems and the expertise of a clinic. It claimed that a twenty-five percent rate of achieved pregnancies after in vitro fertilization was good. The brochure didn't give its own statistics, but it did state in its introduction: *We have among the nation's highest pregnancy rates after IVF.*

It also pointed out that the clinic performed pre-implantation genetic diagnosis. And it explained that the Green Desert Center was owned by a foundation called the Sherman-Willgood Trust.

I had hoped the booklet would also contain a list of staff, but apart from the doctors' names under their articles, no other personnel was mentioned. I remembered the list the receptionist had browsed earlier and debated if I could ask her for a copy of it. But I couldn't come up with a good explanation why I needed it.

I strolled through the lobby, found a vending machine in a corner, bought a big cup of coffee and a small hot chocolate. I took the coffee over to the young woman and placed it in front of her on the counter together with some tiny packs of cream and sugar.

She gave me an astonished smile. "Thank you."

"I've worked enough night shifts myself," I said. "And there's not much going on here. That must make it even harder."

"Yeah," Alice said and sipped her coffee. "Sometimes we have late arrivals. But today everybody checked in early."

"It's still a bit odd that nobody is coming and going. I figured there would be visitors. Or do none of the patients stay over the weekend?"

"Some do. Depending on their treatment and condition. But visitors and checked-in patients usually don't come through here. They take the side entrance where the security booth is."

I resumed my position in the corner, took another look at the clinic's map. The side entrance was next to the parking lot. I had overlooked it, mesmerized by the towering mansion.

Hoping that the coffee would sooner or later have the same effect on Alice's bladder as it would have had on mine, I leafed through the brochures on surrogate motherhood. Eid had given me the material of two agencies. Their information resembled each other. Both seemed to target potential surrogate moms more than parents who wanted a baby. Clearly, it was harder to find the first.

The rules for women who wanted to become surrogates for these agencies were clear-cut: They had to be married or in steady partnerships, had to have been pregnant before, carried a baby to term and parented it. Then there were age and health requirements. The agencies stated that surrogate moms had to have a certain psychological makeup. The women should not have an unfulfilled wish for a child, so that they would not decide to keep the baby once it was born. They should also understand what parenting meant, so that they would not interfere once the child had been handed over. And they had to live in secure financial circumstances, so that the main incentive would not be the payment but a charitable wish to help a childless couple.

I wondered how many women with so much charity in their hearts and so little needs for themselves really existed. And how the agencies were able to truly assess the vagaries of the human psyche. One thing became obvious to me, however, from reading the pamphlets—Rita would not have qualified as a candidate for these agencies.

The receptionist was still as steady behind her computer screen as ever. When I had brought her the coffee, I had seen that she was playing a computer game. Who knew when her bladder would really press her enough to interrupt a game. I decided to search for a bathroom myself and found it off a hall opposite the one Eid had led me through. It was as expensive-looking as the rest of the place, with golden faucets and fake marble toilet seats. I turned up one of the hot water faucets all the way and jerked the handle as far as I could. Then I walked back to the receptionist.

"Sorry to bother you again. But I'm afraid I may have broken something in the bathroom. I can't turn off the water anymore."

Alice reached for her telephone. "Let me call the janitor," she muttered.

"Maybe if you could just take a look yourself. I'm sure it's nothing big. I don't know anything about plumbing, but I'm sure you can figure out what's wrong."

"If somebody comes, let them know I'll be back in a sec." She got up with a look of resignation over my stupidity.

The moment she disappeared around the corner, I plucked the list from underneath her desk mat. Then I quickly arranged the other papers under the mat so that the gap would not be visible at once.

When the receptionist came back I was already sitting in my corner again.

"It was just stuck," she said with a mix of pride and condescension.

I pulled out my cell phone, got up and said, "My husband should have been here by now. I'd better call him and try to find out if he's lost."

There was a big sign on a wall saying: *Please switch off your cell phones inside the clinic buildings.* Pointing at it, I waved a good-bye to the young woman and left.

Chapter 17

I truly believe that most of the time, fear is only in our minds. While I was slowly sneaking along the clinic's fence toward the back entrance, I tried to focus on this simple truth. Nevertheless, my heart banged against my chest uncontrollably. Only the darkness provided protection here, but it could also hide surveillance cameras, security guards or lurking attackers.

I encountered none of these, though, and I made it back to the Escort safely. I immediately locked the car doors behind me, quickly rubbed my goose-pimpled arms and drove off.

On the way to Reno I stopped at a steak house, realizing I was craving a big chunk of medium rare meat. After having devoured a huge sirloin steak, two baked potatoes, chocolate fudge cake and an espresso, I felt strong and strangely human again.

Back in the city I looked for a drugstore, bought some packages of hair dye and makeup, and changed the color of my hair from black to a silvery blond in the hotel room. It took three rounds of dyeing, and my scalp felt as if it was about to peel off. For the first time I realized the tortures a fake blonde has to endure. The rest of the evening I spent studying Green Desert's list of employees, comparing their names with the data in my head and trying to figure out what to do with the discoveries I made.

Early the next morning, I drove out to the airport. I was wearing my brown eye, eyeliner, some rouge, and bright red lipstick. Originally, I had thought of buying and wearing a dress but had discarded the idea as too impractical. Instead, I had put on the most inconspicuous uniform of all—blue jeans and a white T-shirt.

The Avis clerk at the airport rental car station looked at me out of tired, bored eyes, checked my file in their system and said, "You exchanged the car only yesterday."

"I'd like to upgrade today. Do you have a minivan available?"

I was not becoming particularly popular with the rental car agents, but half an hour and dozens of sighs from the clerk later, I drove off in a green Windstar.

After some searching, I found the road that led to the main entrance of the Green Desert Center. I picked a spot in the parking lot where I could overlook most of the area as well as the path to the side entrance. And then I waited. The van's windows were tinted. I was wearing my sunglasses and hoped that I had achieved a state of incognito.

The grounds were much busier than last night. Every few minutes a car came or left the parking lot. Behind the fence there were people walking through the park in which the clinic's bungalows were located. Some of the people were wearing scrubs and looked as if they were in a hurry. Others strolled around in civilian clothes.

A dark blue Mercedes parked two spots down from me. When the driver exited, I finally recognized one of the faces I had seen in the clinic's booklet. It belonged to a blond bespectacled man. He didn't look as nerdy as in the picture. There was something wholesome about him. I imagined him with a farmer's hat and a guitar, singing "Rocky Mountain High." He quickly disappeared behind the mansion.

Then a couple walked over from the side entrance. They were holding hands and exchanged a quick kiss. When they came closer I could see that both were women. One was short-haired and sturdy, in gray business pants and a matching gray jacket, the other tall and thin, with a brown ponytail and dressed in a long, elegant dark blue skirt and white blouse. The shorter woman with the black hair looked Caucasian, the tall one was probably Latina. Their car was parked next to mine, and before they could enter it, I jumped out of the van and walked over to them.

"Good morning," I greeted them. "How are you?"

"Fine," the tall woman said. "And you?"

"I was wondering," I said. "Are you clients here at the clinic?"

The shorter woman nodded. The tall one jingled her car keys, then unlocked the little red Mazda sports car.

"I'm a bit desperate," I continued. "Green Desert Center is something like my last hope. I've had bad experiences with some other facilities, them promising more than they could keep. I've tried to become pregnant so often already. And now I'd like to hear somebody's firsthand experience, before I sign up for treatment here."

The black-haired woman looked at her partner, who had one leg already in the car. An impatient racehorse, wanting to take off. She said, "Nothing to complain about. But we have to leave now. You should just talk to the doctors here. They are very helpful."

"We have to be back in two hours for treatment," the shorter woman explained. "We just wanted to get some breakfast in Sudden Springs. If you want to join us, we could tell you a bit more."

Her partner gave her a resigned but tender look. "You will have to drive in your own car. Ours has only two seats."

"No problem," I said. "And thanks!"

I hummed a little nonsense melody while following their car. What unbelievable good fortune that the two women were willing to talk to me, a perfect stranger, about such a personal matter. But then there was the solidarity of people sharing the same fate. A solidarity which I had no right to. I decided to take the women's helpfulness as a good omen for the quest I was on. Little did I know what still lay ahead of me.

To my astonishment, a purely vegan bakery and café was located on the main shopping street of the next little town. It had three tables and seemed to make its profits mainly with German-style breads it sold over the counter. I sucked in the delicious flavors of freshly baked whole grain yeast bread and ordered a small breakfast consisting of two slices with strawberry jam and a cup of coconut soy milk. Rachel, as the smaller woman introduced herself to me, and her partner, Melissa, went for the big breakfasts, which came with all kinds of other condiments, one being a soy paste with mushrooms.

Not that bad, I thought, when I tried the first bite. Maybe I could become a vegan for breakfasts. Then I wondered if that could really redeem my health or my conscience.

"They don't offer vegan food at the clinic. One of the few setbacks," Melissa said.

"And the others?" I inquired.

"It's quite a technical environment," the tall woman answered again. "Not exactly the warm, wholesome surroundings you'd like to make your baby in."

"I know," I said, faking a sigh. "Don't you sometimes envy all the couples who can conceive naturally?"

"Not exactly," Rachel said, with a vicious little grin.

I grinned back. And as if a confidential code had been confirmed, the two women suddenly became more open with me.

"So are you going for it without a partner?" Melissa wanted to know.

"Yes," I said. "I haven't found anybody yet who wanted to have a baby so badly, too."

"Did you try inseminating yourself?" Rachel eagerly asked.

"Of course," I answered. "But it didn't work. And so far not even in vitro has been successful. But I've heard Green Desert is really good at it."

"We're trying it, too," Rachel confessed, her round, boyish face flushing a bit. "My ovaries are kind of clogged. So the doctors said it would be the best."

Melissa's intense eyes had narrowed while we were talking. Of course I didn't ask why she wasn't considering getting pregnant if her partner had physical trouble conceiving.

"Do you like the doctors at the clinic?" I wanted to know.

"They're okay," Melissa said. "Some of them are very friendly. Others more detached. You know, the way physicians sometimes are, when they see your body more like a machine or an interesting study object."

"Come on," Rachel intercepted. "Dr. Willgood is a nice guy. He's treated us with a lot of respect."

"That's what I said," Melissa responded irritably, her forehead creasing up. "Some are nice, others not so much."

"I talked to a number of people from the clinic on the phone yesterday," I quickly said. "I forget right now what everybody was called. But there was a man with a rather deep, gravelly voice. Do you know who that could be?"

"Dr. Willgood has a deep voice. Even though he looks rather like a teenager," Rachel said. "Funny contrast."

"That's good to know," I replied. "Because it seems as if he will be my attending physician, too. And then there was a woman who had a slight European accent."

Melissa and Rachel looked at each other, shaking their heads in unison after a moment. "Doesn't ring a bell," Melissa finally said. "But anyhow, we've mostly dealt with Dr. Willgood and some of the nurses."

"Was any of them called Jane?" I asked. "Because I'm pretty sure I spoke to a Jane yesterday."

"Not this time," Rachel said. "Last year. When we went through the second cycle of in vitro there was a woman called Jane. Remember, Mel? A tall, black nurse."

Melissa shook her head. Obviously the details had not burned themselves into her brain the same way they had into her partner's.

"It's good to know that you like and trust Dr. Willgood. That relieves me already. So, how many cycles of IVF have you already been through?"

"Six," Rachel said. Her eyes suddenly lost their focus. "And you?"

"Four," I lied, feeling truly terrible about it.

"The hormones you have to take are the worst, don't you think? And then the waiting after the transfer. Before they can tell you if it has worked. Or not . . ."

"Uh-huh."

"Have you ever considered adoption?" Melissa asked. She reached for Rachel's hand, avoiding her gaze at the same time.

"No."

A friend of mine in Germany had put herself through a similar ordeal as Rachel. When I had once asked her Melissa's question, she had said that she desperately wanted her own child. I must have looked puzzled or disbelieving. I had never had a particularly strong wish to have children at all. My friend had then described her wish like the desire to fall in love—one of these inexplicably strong feelings that can absolutely consume you. But I also knew that I would never give up wanting to fall in love. After my friend's third unsuccessful in vitro cycle—in Germany the health insurance paid for three attempts—she began to borrow money to pay for the next rounds of IVF. As far as I knew, she was still at it.

In reaction to my answer it seemed a little triumphant glow had settled in Rachel's face. Melissa stared out the window.

"It's difficult to adopt at all," Rachel explained. "And as a lesbian couple it's even harder."

"But it would be a child that has already been born that's really in need of parents. What is it about a baby having to be your own that is so important that you want to go through all this?" The question now broke out of Melissa. She looked at me accusingly, avoiding Rachel's eyes, which filled with tears.

"It's . . . it's hard to explain," I said, and then gave her my friend's little analogy comparing wanting your own child and wanting to fall in love.

"But can't you fall in love with an adopted child?" Melissa asked, spinning the gist of the story.

Big tears were now running down Rachel's round cheeks. I tried to tell myself that it wasn't the first time the two women had been at this point.

"Well, thank you so much for the information. I'll keep my fingers crossed for you," I said, pulling out my wallet to pay for the breakfast.

"We have to go, too," Melissa said. She put an arm around Rachel. "Dr. Willgood wants us there in half an hour, sweetie."

Rachel blew her nose, smiled at Melissa as if everything was okay again and said, "I have the feeling today it will happen."

Melissa just nodded.

Rachel pulled out a credit card. I would have liked to treat her and her partner to breakfast, but first I needed to take a closer look at the Visa card that was displayed in front of me on the table. I had just deciphered the woman's last name when the waiter came and took away the piece of plastic and with it my chance at showing a little generosity.

Chapter 18

It wasn't so easy to hide the long knife under my jeans. I ended up buying a piece of Velcro in a shop not far from the vegan café, and strapped the weapon onto my calf in the back of the van.

The security guard at the clinic's side entrance gave me a friendly look when I walked up to his booth. "How can I help you, young lady?" he asked me.

The man was not older than me, possibly younger, a skinny, pale guy with acne craters and eyes that were glazed over by whatever chemical substance he had pumped into his metabolism. Possibly just alcohol, I thought, as the strong telltale smell of menthol seeped out of his booth.

"I'd like to visit Rachel Lewis. She's a patient here."

He didn't even look at a screen or a list, just buzzed me in through a whitewashed steel door. When I looked back at him, he was staring into the distance again, at peace with the world, waiting for the next apparition to show up at his doorstep.

I had memorized the map of the clinic's grounds the night before. I first walked to the cafeteria at the back of the mansion, which was accessible from the park via a short flight of steps. The room had the ambiance of a greenhouse, with high windows facing the park and huge potted plants standing among the tables. At closer look though, the plants were as fake as the antebellum charm of the place, their artificial leaves covered with a thin layer of dust. Nevertheless, the wicker chairs created a kind of southern atmosphere, despite the linoleum floor and the Formica food counter.

Six of the ten tables were occupied. The conversations of the patrons and the whir and sizzle of the coffee makers and refrigerators reverberated in the big space and created a rather loud background noise. At its bottom was a song, coming from hidden speakers: an elevator version of "Imagine."

Behind the counter a lonely woman with very high blonde hair was reorganizing pieces of cake on a tray. I walked up to her and ordered a cappuccino.

"One minute, honey," she replied with a soft, sweet voice, as reminiscent of the grand old South as the mansion hopelessly attempted to be. She moved swiftly over to an espresso machine.

"I was wondering," I said, when she set the cup in front of me. "I'm looking for a nurse who works here. A tall African American woman with striking blue eyes and a nose piercing."

"You mean Jane."

Jane Abdel Farragh. The only Jane on the receptionist's list. Her name had been crossed out, neatly, with a fine-tipped pen and a ruler, still perfectly readable. I hadn't dared to assume that Rita's Jane had in fact used her real name.

"Jane Abdel Farragh," the woman repeated musingly, almost as if she was singing a lullaby. "She doesn't work here anymore."

"Oh, I didn't know that."

"Yeah, she left some months ago."

"Do you know why?"

"Some kind of health problem."

"Do you have an idea where I can find her? A friend, who also used to be a patient here, asked me to give her a present."

The woman moved her pudgy face closer to mine. "You can leave it with me. Jane sometimes comes by at the other job I'm working. At Wendy's. When I see her, I'll give it to her."

"Maybe, if you could give me her number, I could just call her."

"I don't have her number."

She sounded close to being offended and I quickly said, "I have the gift in the car. I'll bring it to you later."

I left her a three-dollar tip and took the cappuccino to a table. Most of them were now vacant. An Asian family—mother, father and a boy of about five years, who was quietly playing with a toy Porsche—sat next to me. Another table was occupied by a woman clad in a white doctor's coat. I could only see her back. Her auburn hair fell to her shoulders in shining waves. Something about her posture interested me. Her back was extremely upright and small under the big head of hair, radiating a sense of fragility and determined strength at the same time. The woman had positioned herself close to one of the windows. There was no possibility to catch a glimpse of her face.

The cappuccino tasted good, and it infused me with the caffeine missing from this morning's healthy soy milk. My next step led me to the mansion's foyer. I only had to follow the signs to the bathrooms. They guided me through a glass door, behind which I landed in a corner of the big lobby, quite far away from the front desk. Today's receptionist also seemed completely absorbed by her computer screen. I only caught a glimpse of a clean-cut blond pageboy haircut and quickly walked on. In one of the bathroom stalls, I pulled out the knife, stuck it into the pocket of my jeans and let the T-shirt cover it as much as possible.

The elevator was a couple of steps down the same hallway. On the second floor I encountered another hall, cutting from one end of the building to the other. The purloined list had revealed that Ruth Shriner's office was in room No. 34. She was the only Ruth listed in the staff directory. An R. Shriner had also been named in the clinic's brochure. According to the map of the clinic, room No. 34 should be at the end of this hall.

Most doors were closed. Whenever I had to pass an open one, I dashed by quickly. I reached the very last of the open doors. A sign underneath the number 34 read *PR Department.*

Without knocking I stepped across the threshold. An obviously startled man in a wheelchair shot around, knocked over a pile of papers he had been stacking on the floor, and yelled, "Holy mother of Jesus Christ Superstar." He stared at me, regained his composure and said, "Hi, do I know you?"

"Maybe I'm not the right person to ask that. But if it helps, I don't know you," I replied quickly.

He laughed, big white teeth showing in a huge, full-lipped mouth. His skin had the deep bronze tone you cannot achieve through sunbathing but must have inherited. He looked like he combined a whole lot more ethnicities in his heritage than I did.

"I'm looking for Ms. Shriner," I said.

"Sorry that I'm such a disappointment to you," the man replied. His smile had retreated into his eyes, where it was throwing a happy mischievous party.

"Oh, not at all. If your first name is Ruth, I have found who I've been looking for."

"As I said, my lot in life: to disappoint. My name is Rashid."

"Rashid Shriner?"

"Rashid Jackson," he continued the nonsense conversation, which under different circumstances I would have enjoyed more.

"Sorry," I said and grinned. "You are a disappointment. But only when it comes to name and gender."

"I wouldn't know about the second," he replied enigmatically.

"Let's get into that in another lifetime," I said quickly. "Ms. Shriner works here, doesn't she?"

"Sometimes yes, sometimes no."

"And today?"

"No."

He pointed at the desk opposite his own. "Empty!"

"Will she be out the whole day?"

"She called in sick. Hasn't been in for a couple of days. I don't know when she'll be back. Hopefully soon. I love her."

This man was a serious oddball, but an endearing one. "That's great," I said. "Are you two the public relations department?"

"The one and only. Ruth and Rashid, the voice of Green Desert to the world."

There was a stack of the clinic's promo booklets on his desk. I pointed at them. "This is a great brochure. I've seen that Ms. Shriner's name is in there. And I wanted to talk to her about the collaboration with the agency involved. Have you worked on it, too?"

"I only started here a month ago. Maybe on the next edition."

The first completely reasonable sentence from his mouth. I had to seize the occasion: "Since when has Ms. Shriner been out of the office? I've tried to call her the last days, you know, but only her voice mail picked up."

"Since Wednesday."

I had left the message on Tuesday.

"By the way, who are you?" Jackson now asked me.

"Sun Manudo. I work for an advertising agency in San Jose. I've seen that your Web site is not online."

"And now you want to win us over as a client."

"Exactly."

"Take me out to dinner and I'll help you." Good old Master Joker had moved back into his face.

"Tomorrow night?"

Now he looked honestly astonished. I left him my phone number and asked him to call me the next day and let me know where to meet him.

"How shall I explain to my boyfriend that I'm going out with a pretty woman?" he finally said in mock despair.

"Tell him my girlfriend will beat you up, if you make a wrong move."

"That's truly comforting!"

The night before, after my little Sunday evening trip to the clinic, I had called the number listed for Ruth Shriner in the clinic's directory using a pay phone. I had only heard the message once before, but it was clearly the answering machine I had reached Tuesday from Mido's house: "Ruth's office. Leave a message after the beep." This time I didn't. I had planned to confront Ruth in her office today without warning. In my deluded imagination I had envisioned me threatening her to reveal why she had lured me into the trap in the casino, where Mido was, and what lay behind everything that had happened.

Sitting on a bench in the clinic's park, I now pulled out my cell and called Ruth's office number once again. I tried to recall the voice of the woman who had phoned me Saturday night and compare it to the recorded message. The "Ruth" who had invited me to meet Mido, had sounded softer, friendlier, with a different timbre in her voice, I was now pretty sure.

With my next call I tried to find out Jane Abdel Farragh's number from Information. But it turned out she was not listed for Reno, Carson City or Hidden Valley.

A number of people had passed by the bench. None paid me any attention. Another cluster of voices now approached. I quickly looked away when I recognized the man from the parking lot. After my meeting with Rachel and Melissa I had checked out Dr. Willgood's picture in the booklet. He was the blond man I had spotted that morning. His first name was Dan.

He was now passing right by me, speaking loudly and very seriously with the people around him. "I need the lab results this afternoon . . ."

His voice had the quality of a growl. Dan Willgood was definitely the "John" from Rita's emergency hotline and the caller on Mido's answering machine demanding certain documents back.

At the next crossing the group split up. Two men in scrubs disappeared into the closest building. Willgood continued down the path with a woman. And again I could only catch a glimpse of her from the back. Her curls gleamed like planet Mars in the noon sunshine.

Willgood and the woman walked to the very last of the box-shaped buildings, the one closest to the clinic's back entrance. I followed them with enough distance to remain undetected. *DNA Lab*, read a sign next to the door through which they had entered. Although the buildings were all connected by the enclosed walkways, each had an individual entrance as well. Apart from the DNA lab, this one contained the genetic counseling department as well as three of the doctors' offices, as some smaller writing on the sign informed me. One of the doctors was Dan Willgood. The others were Lamont Snipe, M.D., and Dr. Marie Bruno.

Dr. Snipe had authored an article entitled "Genetic Counseling on the Path to Your Healthy Child" in the clinic's booklet. His picture looked as if it had been cut out from a fashion magazine—high cheekbones, strong jaws, determined eyes, ebony skin. Willgood's contribution was titled "Finding Out in Advance: Is Pre-implantation Genetic Diagnosis Indicated for Your Pregnancy?" I didn't recall an article by Dr. Bruno, nor a picture with her name underneath.

The door to the building had closed behind Willgood and the woman. When I tried it, it was locked, another keypad to the side.

"Do you have an appointment?" somebody asked. A thin-haired man with hectic movements rushed up to the door and started to quickly punch in a long sequence of numbers, his body completely covering the keypad.

"Yes, with Dr. Snipe."

The man let me in with him and pointed at a waiting area right behind the door. "It's easier to enter the lab tract through the patients' building," he said, and explained. "The one opposite the cafeteria. Its door is open all day. From there you just have to follow the signs and eventually you'll land here."

He winked at me and ran down a flight of stairs toward the DNA lab, which was located in the basement, as another sign with an arrow pointing down indicated.

I followed the hall into the core of the building. It had an institutional feel—gray doors, white walls, blue linoleum, spiced up by an assembly of framed pictures. Children's drawings of ageless people with teddy bears and rainbows over slanted red roofs alternated with photographs taken through a microscope—the well-known monochromatic pink or blue shots of a round human egg cell before fertilization, then with a single little tadpole, a sperm, breaking through the membrane.

All the doors I passed were closed. Some of them had signs marking them as examination rooms. One was the door to Dr. Snipe's office. I had almost reached the end of the hall where a window showed a view of the last unnaturally green strip of park and the white fence that cut it off from the desert. There were two doors left. I was just about to study the little name tags when the right one slowly opened. A woman's voice, whose muffled sound I had heard through the walls for some seconds, suddenly became very loud. The door hid her from my view. "Nobody will compare the DNA," she said. "We should just let it go."

"But the deformations are suspicious," Willgood's rasp came from within the room.

"They are indistinguishable from spontaneous mutations. We've talked about this often enough."

It was really quite weak. But when you listened for it, it was clear: The woman's flawless English was flavored with a French accent. Distracted by this peculiarity of her language, I missed the chance to escape before the door was fully opened, and the doctor with the auburn hair stepped into my sight and discovered me.

Chapter 19

The woman's features were much less remarkable than her hair. Underneath all that red-golden glow lay a finely structured face with small eyes, thin lips and a narrow nose. She had the light, paper-thin skin of a redhead but without any freckles. At first glance she looked very frail. However, the firmness of her gaze and the determined tension of her mouth contradicted this impression.

"Are you looking for somebody?" she asked.

"I'd like to talk to Dr. Willgood."

Now she gave me a closer look, quickly assessing my hair, my clothes, my sunglasses, and said, "I believe he is not expecting anybody."

"I'm here for genetic counseling."

"Why don't you come into my office." She opened the door to my left. She was at least five inches shorter than I, petite as a sparrow, her gait hard and wide, her heels clicking loudly. *Marie Bruno, Dr. Med. Sorbonne*, was printed on her door tag.

The room was your typical doctor's office. There was an examination table adjacent to a wall, white vertical blinds, a white desk behind which Dr. Bruno now placed herself, and a plastic-cushioned, metal-legged chair, on which I sat.

She stared at me for a few seconds. I stared back, finally took off my sunglasses. Then her stare melted, as if a neurotic ghost behind her eyes had suddenly retreated. "Well, why don't you begin and tell me your story," she said almost lightheartedly, filling her voice not with friendliness but at least a seasoned charm.

It was clear that she knew who I was and even derived a strange joy from our sudden encounter in her territory. I inhaled deeply, forcefully suppressing the impulse to jump up and run.

"I've been pregnant once," I replied, ready to play. "I was already in the second trimester when the doctor found out the baby was disabled. I had an abortion."

"What was the baby's condition?"

"I'm not sure."

"Do you know of any hereditary disease you or the child's father may carry?"

"No." Had I really sought genetic counseling, this would have been misinformation with regard to my own DNA.

"Then we need your medical records."

"They didn't give them to me."

"I can request them, when you tell me your physician's name."

"He won't reveal them."

"It's the law, he has to provide them."

"He will say he has never seen me."

"That is very odd."

"I suspect he has something to hide."

Bruno's expression didn't change. Her hands remained calm on the desk; she didn't show a single physical sign of nervousness, while I had to concentrate to keep my leg from doing a quick nervous twitch.

"Did you conceive naturally?" she asked.

"No, through in vitro."

140

"Do you know if your embryos were genetically examined before the transfer?"

"I'm not sure."

"Was there an amniocentesis performed during your pregnancy?"

"I don't think so."

"You don't give me much to work with."

She asked me all these questions without ever taking her eyes off my face.

"Maybe I should just look for a surrogate mother," I said, breaking free of her gaze, taking a look at her hands. A delta of blue veins shone through the white skin. Her fingers looked stronger and shorter than I expected.

"There's no reason for that, as you were able to become pregnant the last time. The condition of your baby is connected to the quality of the egg and the sperm cell and the genetic makeup of both parents. If there's a problem along that line, we can try to prevent it by testing the embryos and selecting only the strongest and healthiest ones for the transfer." She sounded as easygoing as if we were talking about a flaw in a cake recipe.

"But the abortion was so traumatizing."

"I would nevertheless advise you to try it again. Surrogacy won't be a substitute for your own pregnancy and birth experience."

"Don't you work with surrogates?"

"If our patients wish."

"Can you tell me what the legal situation is, considering surrogacy?"

"That's something the surrogacy agencies will advise you on."

"And if I don't go through an agency?"

"Then you should talk to a good lawyer."

She remained perfectly calm despite my grilling, displaying not a single sign of agitation or impatience. And I was sure she had a busy schedule.

"You do abortions here too, don't you?" I now probed.

141

"I'm only involved if there is a medical indication in one of my patients."

"Can you tell me a reason why a doctor would want to cover up the reasons for a second trimester abortion after an in vitro fertilization?" I asked. "Are there circumstances under which he—or she—could be sued for malpractice if the fetus develops abnormally?"

"Unlikely," was the prompt answer. "All our patients sign a consent agreement, stating that they have been informed of the inherent risks of any pregnancy, and of the impossibility of predicting the fetus's development in the womb, even after pre-implantation diagnosis. And I don't know of any physician in his right mind who would not make such a contract the prerequisite of his treatment. We practice reproductive medicine, not acts of divine power."

She was as convincing as a hypnotist telling you to jump from a high building with a tiny parachute, promising you will not get hurt—if nothing goes wrong. In a different lifetime I would not have doubted a word she said, even though she had just contradicted her reassuring lecture from half a minute ago.

"And how about the new law regarding so-called late-term abortions?" Suddenly a newspaper article I had read a couple of weeks earlier in a state of angry yet detached interest popped up in my mind.

"That's a very troublesome matter. But there are pending court cases. It will take years before the ban can be enforced."

"So if I need another abortion in the near future, it will at least not be a legal problem," I said, not able to keep the sarcasm from my voice.

"We'll put all our knowledge to work to prevent that. You shouldn't look at things so pessimistically." Bruno rose from her chair and reached for one of the desk drawers.

Her unexpected movement made me shoot up. Like the sudden realization that the fascinating hyena in front of you has the power to tear your guts out, it hit me again who I was trapped with in this tiny office. The hard contours of the knife in my pocket had pinched me while I was sitting down. Now I dug for it, grabbing the handle.

There was a knock at the door.

As Bruno pulled the drawer open, loud voices entered the room. "My number, if you have any more questions," she said, taking out a business card and handing it to me.

A little boy of about four walked up to her followed by a pregnant woman and a man carrying a toddler. The last of the group was Willgood. "Look who wants to say hi to you, too," he announced.

The boy gazed shyly up at Bruno, and the man and the woman gave her big smiles.

"The ultrasound looks great. You and Dr. Willgood will soon become godparents for the third time," the stout man with a moustache said.

The pregnant woman looked exhausted. She pulled back the boy who was grabbing a small bronze model of the familiar DNA double helix from the desk. Nevertheless, she radiated contentment and gave me an encouraging smile.

Bruno's smile was much more forced. She sent a quick look spiced with anger to Willgood. He looked back, smiling apologetically but also with a hint of provocation, reminding me of a dog who had brought his master back a stinky piece of carrion instead of a pretty ball he was supposed to retrieve.

Bruno had recognized me the moment I took off my sunglasses. Maybe she had just made the connection seeing my eyes, because somebody had told her about my special feature. There had been this instant of mutual recognition, though. I felt I had seen her before, but I could not pin it down.

It was high time to leave the clinic's grounds, but first I had to wrap a present. I quickly walked back to the mansion and asked the receptionist for a white piece of paper, a pen and some tape. After

I had told her that I was a patient and needed to stick a note to one of the doctor's doors about his missed appointment with me, she had given me the requested material with a wink. "Yeah, they can be chaotic," the woman said. Her perfect blond pageboy surrounded a face as brown and weathered as the desert outside.

Again a bathroom cubicle served me well as hideout and workspace. I drew a picture reminiscent of the children's art I had admired in the hall of the lab building. I could never draw a human shape. The stick people's arms were dangling at their feet, their heads were bumpy instead of rounded and they had overlong, crooked necks. On the back of the paper I wrote: *Dear Ms. Abdel-Farragh. Please give me a call in an urgent matter. Everything will remain confidential.*

I added my cell phone number and wrapped the sheet around the DNA model I had taken from the little boy's hand in Bruno's office.

The woman in the cafeteria was still on duty. She accepted the neatly taped package and smiled at what was visible of my picture.

"My friend's daughter made it," I explained. "Ms. Abdel-Farragh helped her into this world. In every sense of the word."

"I'll give it to Jane. I'm sure she'll be happy to hear from your friend and her daughter," the woman said and dropped the present into a tote bag behind the counter.

Chapter 20

The concrete underneath the minivan was dry. Nevertheless, I repeatedly stepped on the brake to see if it was still working, while I was driving away from the clinic. Everything seemed okay. Still, the car didn't feel safe. But then, my own skin didn't feel like a safe place to live in anymore. I took the minivan back to the airport, returned it to the rental car agency and flagged a taxi into Reno. I asked the driver to drop me off at the entrance to Circus Circus; I wandered through the maze of the casino via a connecting mall to the Silver Legacy. Back in my room I changed my hair color once more, this time to a bright blue, switched on the cell phone and dialed AdUp's number. Today was Monday, the day Mido had said she would be back at the office. The man who picked up the phone, though, could only inform me that Ms. James was not in.

"Did she show up at the agency today?" I inquired.

"I haven't seen her, but that doesn't mean that she hasn't been here earlier."

"May I speak to Peter, Ms. Bradley's assistant."

"What's your name, please?"

"Anna Spring."

"One second."

My scalp itched. I rubbed it absentmindedly while staring at the bright pattern of the hotel carpet—blue, yellow and red spirals were chasing each other across the floor. Maybe the design had been thought up by an expert on the subconsciousness of gamblers. Maybe it spiraled itself right into your brain and made you want to lose everything.

"Peter is in a meeting. But he told me to let you know he hasn't heard from Mido. And you should please call him if she contacts you."

There was one new message on my phone. Not from Sarah, I noticed with a sharp sense of disappointment, and not from Mido. It was Ethan who had called me earlier that day. The police were releasing Jeff's body. Jeff's sister had still not gotten in touch with Ethan. He was worried that she and her family were on vacation. He wanted to talk to me about what we should do concerning the funeral.

I tried to bring myself to dial Ethan's number. Instead I kept staring at the hypnotic carpet. For a fraction of a second, Jeff's face appeared in the crazy pattern, and once more the realization that I would never actually see him again hit me like a blow to the chest. I jumped up, frantically collected my belongings from the room and stuffed them into the duffle bag, rushed to the elevator, rode to the lobby and checked out.

In the café in the arts district, the same waitress with the beaded braids took my order and gave me a sweet smile. It had the effect of physical relief. I chatted with the young woman while she prepared my drink—it was called a Death Wish—with whipped cream. She said that she liked studying in Reno, that she majored in architecture, but that she would be happy to leave this place when she graduated and move somewhere more exciting. When I asked her which city she dreamed of, she answered, "Las Vegas. I'd love to be involved in the construction of a new casino there."

When my complicated order was finally completed—the potion consisted of four shots of espresso in a double hot chocolate, infused with chocolate fudge and topped with cocoa powder—a line of people had formed behind me. As I balanced the cup through the café, I spotted a man with dark curly hair at a table close to the computers. He looked up from his newspaper for a second. I had not seen him before. I chose a monitor that would hide me from him and once again drifted into the Web's worldwide confusion.

There were hundreds of Google hits for "Marie Bruno." The name was quite common, and most entries had nothing to do with the doctor whose publications I was searching for. It took me hours to browse through all of the search engine's results, to access the contents of medical periodicals—fortunately I was still a subscribed online user to some of them—and to assess my findings.

Dr. Marie Bruno had been born in 1958 in La Rochelle, France, as I learned from a short biography published with one of her articles in the *Journal of Medical Studies*. After she had received her doctorate from Sorbonne University in Paris in 1982, she had come to the United States for postdoctoral studies at Stanford. The biography was dated 2002, and her current position at Green Desert Center was not mentioned.

I found publications by Bruno from 1992 onward on the Web, but I was sure there had been more before. In most of the articles Bruno appeared as one of two or three authors. But two articles, one from 2000 and one from 2001—her latest ones, according to the search engine—she had authored alone. The first was titled "Undifferentiated Stem Cells in Adults: The Search for Locations." The title of the second article was "Culture and Transfer of Blastocysts." The first text appeared in a journal I could not access online, but the second one described a state-of-the-art IVF technique where the embryo was allowed to grow beyond the eight-cell stage before implantation, which was supposed to help increase pregnancy rates.

I found a short bio for Dan Willgood as well. He was born in 1960 and received his medical doctorate from Reno University in 1995. Since then he had worked at the Green Desert Center. On the Web I could detect only one article he wrote. It was about the success rates of IVF, and its gist was that Green Desert Center's rates were much higher than comparison figures from international studies; Willgood roughly described the methods used, pointing out the center's outstanding facilities, as well as the top-notch résumés and expertise of its staff. The article was more political than it was scientific. It was published in 2003.

I punched the words "Sherman, Willgood and Trust" into Google. One of the links belonged to the clinic's Web site, still inaccessible and supposedly under construction. The other link led to the page of a law firm in San Francisco—Sherman, Spencer and Oaks. There I read that Mrs. Lila Sherman had been the senior partner of the firm until she passed away in 1999. Now Peter Spencer and David Oaks headed the firm, which took care of the trust's businesses.

I also learned that Lila Sherman's parents, William and Denise, were self-made millionaires. They had founded a company that produced lab equipment in the 1920s. By the sixties, their little firm had grown and earned them a fortune. They sold it to a big medical corporation and set up the trust, which their daughter, Lila, successfully managed until her death.

It had been the wish of the Shermans that the money from the trust would go into medical research. They left it up to their daughter to determine which projects to fund. In the early 1980s Lila had drawn the trust's assets and concentrated them in the founding of the Green Desert Center.

Lila had been married to Daniel Willgood Sr. and they had two children—Dan Jr. and Julia. Behind Julia's name was a little cross, indicating that she had passed away. But it didn't say when Dr. Willgood's sister had died.

I had made notes of all my findings and purchased two more Death Wishes when I noticed that the waitress was wiping down the tables and counting the receipts for the day. It was dark outside and the big wall clock showed ten minutes to seven. The man at the other table had left. When, I didn't know. I had forgotten all about him. I wondered now if I would forever be afraid of nondescript guys with dark curls.

"Do you want me to leave?" I asked the friendly young woman.

"I have to wait for the manager to lock up, anyway," she responded with a tired smile. "She'll be here maybe in twenty minutes. Surf as much as you want until then."

Hurriedly I made a search for Roy Eid. Like Marie Bruno, he had published many articles on reproductive techniques in the 1990s. And like Bruno's, his publication career seemed to have come to a sudden stop in the last few years. After 1999, his name did not appear in connection with any medical studies again. Instead I found his name now mostly linked to marathons all over the world. He had run four in the last two years, including New York and Berlin. In Germany, he actually finished among the top ten runners of his group.

A low murmur came from the café's counter. The manager had arrived. I performed one last quick Web search, found what I was looking for, paid for my drinks and the computer use and wished the ladies a good night.

The dark evening sucked me in like a vacuum. Walking into it meant stepping into utter loneliness. I had given up car and bed for the night. It wouldn't be difficult to obtain both again, but for the moment, I needed this empty space I was drifting in.

The blinking lights of the casinos grew in front of me like a psychedelic cloud. I ventured toward it, soon spotted a cab, flagged it and gave the driver an address. He was a nonverbal hippie who drove me through the city to the music of the Eagles— "Desperado, why don't you come to your senses . . ."

The taxi took me to a quiet suburban neighborhood at the southern outskirts of Reno. Ranch-style bungalows stood in vast

149

gardens. The lights from the windows fell on dusty lawns and dried-up clusters of thick-leaved succulents. The facades consisted of off-white vinyl clapboards. The house at 14 Carson Drive was as nondescript as all its neighbors.

I gave the driver three twenty-dollar bills, more than triple the amount on the meter, asked him to wait for me, and handed him a scrap of paper with my cell phone number. "If I'm not back in fifteen minutes, could you call me? If I don't pick up, you can leave, but call 911 then and send the cops around."

He nodded without surprise or actual acknowledgment of my wish. I walked up the driveway, carrying my duffle bag over my shoulder like a prodigal daughter who has finally made it home. I breathed in deeply and pressed Ruth Shriner's doorbell. There had been only one entry in the online phone book under her name in the whole of Nevada. And it had listed this address.

A light had automatically turned on when I entered the property. I peeped through the window next to the door. The hall was unlit, but I could see light from a lamp in one of the back rooms. Nobody approached. The only sound I could make out was faint music, but I couldn't tell if it came from the taxi or the house. Then my cell phone beeped.

"Listen, I have to go. A call came in from display," the cabbie said. "I'm sure you'll be okay."

Before I could answer more than "Uh-huh," he hung up. When I turned around I saw the taxi disappear down the street.

I cursed to myself and rang the bell once again. The music came from the dark guts of the house so low I could not figure out what kind of music it was—a clarinet, classical maybe. After a few minutes, I dialed the number I had retrieved together with this address. A phone rang inside the house. Nobody answered it.

I followed the music. A wide concrete path led to the back of the house and ended at the steps of a huge porch. An orange cone of light fell on the ground. Staying close to the wall, I snuck up to the glass door. A blind was pulled almost to the floor. I knelt and glanced through the narrow gap. All I could see was the edge of a floral-patterned couch, a side table with a can of V8 on it. A leg was dangling from the couch. Clad in green sweatpants, it was a heavy leg, ending in a bloated foot.

The music was louder here. I identified it as a clarinet concerto by Hindemith—I once owned the record myself.

I gently knocked at the door. Neither the foot nor the leg moved. I pressed my face closer to the gap, trying to make out the rest of the person. Now I could see the shape up to the chest. It was a rather big woman. Her other leg was fully stretched out on the couch. Again I knocked and called out, "Ms. Shriner."

The body was too still. Did her abdomen move with the motion of her breathing? Then I caught the smell. It was weak but unmistakable. I pushed against the door. It didn't move. The stench made me panic, as if I had to hurry, as if helping was still an option.

The only item on the porch was a raggedy garden swing. In a corner of the yard I spotted some small rocks. I ran there, picked up the biggest one, ready to smash in the door with it. But before I could make it back, a new sound mixed in with the clarinet. A slow shuffle. It approached the porch. Only when it had almost reached the corner of the house, I realized it was the sound of steps in rubber-soled shoes on the concrete path. I pressed myself flat onto the grass and held my breath.

There was the clanking of keys, the turning of a lock, the little creak of hinges. The next thing I heard was a woman say, "Ruth! Oh my God!"

I recognized the voice and inhaled deeply. The smell began to invade the air around me, and with my second breath the sweet, the absolutely nauseating odor of decomposing flesh exploded within me. The person who had entered the house stumbled back onto the porch. Certain that she would spot me in the next moment, I stood up. But the woman was leaning with her back against the railing, facing away from me. There was no doubt—it was Mido.

Chapter 21

I couldn't shake this strange sense of déjà vu. So desperately had I anticipated finding Mido, for so many days had I felt both rage and anxiety over her disappearance that it was now no surprise that she was really there—and no relief. My first reaction was suspicion, then an odd tenderness. I wanted to walk up to her and hug her, but at the same time I didn't want to get too close.

I softly called her name. She turned around and stumbled a few steps backward when I climbed the two steps up the porch.

"Anna?" Mido finally whispered when I came closer. "Anna, what in the world . . ."

"She is dead," I said.

Mido nodded. Her eyes were the deepest spots in the center of dark craters, her cheeks were sunken in, her hair uncombed and much less golden than it appeared the last time I had seen her. She was wearing beige jeans and a once white shirt, both stained in various spots.

"What happened to your hair?" Mido finally asked.

I quickly brushed my hand through it, asking myself for a demented instant what she could mean, and answered, "Reno."

She smiled very quickly and suddenly began to sway. I stepped toward her, caught her just before her legs gave in and guided her to the swing. We both sat down. Mido leaned forward and buried her face between her knees.

Thousands of questions stampeded through my head, and I desperately wanted to let them free. Instead I stood up, walked over to the still wide open door, stepped into the room. Flies were circling above the dead woman's face. The smell itself seemed toxic, able to kill you if you took just one more breath. But somehow it stopped bothering me. I breathed through my mouth and studied what was left of Ruth Shriner.

Over the sweatpants she had worn a checkered blue and yellow blouse. Dark greenish spots covered the skin of her face and arms. She was a very big woman, and decay had bloated her even further. But her features still looked strong and angular. A long nose pointed at a square chin. The arcs of her brows stretched high into her large forehead. Thick white hair streamed around her face. Her eyes were closed. Even dead she radiated a certain benevolent determination. To my layperson's eye it didn't look as if she had struggled. She could have just fallen asleep and never woken.

Mido appeared at my side. "What shall we do?" she said. Her own edgy energy appeared to have been eradicated in the days since I had last seen her.

"Call the police," I said. Then it occurred to me that I had no idea what to tell them when they would ask me why I was here.

Mido only nodded.

"Did Ruth call you Saturday to set up a meeting with me?" I had to find out.

"No," she answered. "She hasn't called me in days."

Another look at the body told me that Mido was telling the truth. I was no expert, but the degree of decomposition seemed too far advanced. Ruth must have died before Saturday. As I had already suspected, somebody else had called me and lured me into a trap.

The room in which we were standing was an extension of a long hall, which connected to the front wing of the house. Apart from the couch there were two floral chairs, a television set and a stereo system. The clarinet concerto had just begun all over again. The CD player was obviously set on repeat. I wondered if I could turn it off, or if it was necessary evidence for the police.

I dialed 911 and gave the dispatcher Ruth's name and address.

"And she's dead?" the woman on the other end said. "You're absolutely sure I shouldn't send an ambulance."

"Yes," I only answered.

"And who are you?"

I told her my name. It was only seconds before sirens screamed in the distance.

"Listen," Mido quickly said. "Let's tell the police as little as possible for now. I'll explain to them that you are a friend of mine and that we wanted to visit Ruth tonight. Then we found her dead."

"You are really her friend, aren't you?"

"Not a close one. But we've been through a number of things together lately. She gave me the keys to her back door a while ago. Said I could drop by whenever I wanted when I'm in Reno. I tried to call her many times in the last days. But I could never reach her and she didn't call me back."

The doorbell rang. I went around the house to the front. Greeted the cops, guided them to the porch. As soon as the two men in uniform caught the smell, they looked at each other. The taller, heavier one of the two stayed outside with Mido and me, while his colleague entered the room. He was back with us immediately. "Coroner," he merely said and the other officer pulled out a radio.

"When did you find the deceased?" the smaller one wanted to know.

"Right before we called you." Mido repeated roughly what she had told me about her friendship with Ruth Shriner. She added

154

that she and I had been on a road trip to Mexico and on our way back we had planned to stay overnight at Ruth's house.

The officer listened. He asked us for our names and addresses, had us show him our IDs, and explained that we would have to wait for the medical examiner.

For the next twenty minutes Mido and I sat silently on the swing, while the officers leaned against the porch railing, smoking and chatting about baseball.

The medical examiner, a middle-aged woman with cropped brown hair and a macho demeanor, came to the back porch without first ringing at the front door. She hardly stopped to greet the officers or us, following the smell like a cadaver dog right into the house. The smaller officer joined her. His broad-shouldered companion, who had by now taken off his cap and revealed an oily, slightly disheveled Elvis hairdo, walked over to us. "Not a nice sight, huh?" he said. To my recollection he had not even taken a quick look at the body yet.

"It's not too bad," I answered gruffly, wanting to embarrass the man with his obvious fear of dead bodies.

Suddenly I felt Mido's hand quickly touch mine.

"It was a shock," she said to the police.

This answer made him nod in a fatherly way. "So you just came back from Mexico, huh?" he asked. "Hot down there?"

"Actually it was raining," Mido answered. "But we've only been to the north."

"Yeah, they've had some bad weather there lately," the officer said. "Just talked to my brother yesterday. He lives just south of Tijuana. You've got family there, too?"

"Friends," Mido said.

The medical examiner and the other officer stepped back outside. Both drawing deep breaths. "Looks natural," the woman said. "I'll order an autopsy, then we'll know more. But my guess is sudden heart failure. It's a risk factor of obesity."

Please be thorough, I wanted to say to her. Check for needle pricks, potassium chloride, an insulin overdose—every possible way a medical professional could induce a natural-looking death. Of course I kept quiet. Uttering suspicions would only draw attention to me and lead to never-ending questions to which I had not even remotely reasonable answers.

The next minutes passed with the officers checking the windows of the house, the locks on the doors, finally touring the inside of the building. Two people in coveralls arrived with a stretcher and carried off Ruth Shriner. The medical examiner went with them after the officers had informed her that they had not found a sign of forced entry into the house nor anything extraordinary on the inside. Eventually, they even turned off the unbearable clarinet music.

"Where can we reach you in the next days?" the officer wanted to know.

Mido and I gave him our cell phone numbers. The police locked the back door, kept Mido's key and walked with us to the street. "Do you need a ride?" Elvis asked us.

"No thanks," I quickly answered and Mido nodded with determination.

The cops drove off and she said, "How did you get here?"

"Taxi. And you?"

"My car is over there."

She pointed at a red Accord. The bandage around her hand, with which I had last seen her, was gone, but when she unlocked the passenger door, gesturing for me to get in, I could see that she was not using her left hand. A closer look revealed that it was still swollen and marbled by yellow and violet bruises.

"Shall I drive?" I asked.

Her answer was to just sink into the passenger's seat herself and hand me the keys. I chauffeured us back to the city, entered the driveway of Circus Circus this time, and fifteen minutes later Mido and I stepped into a room with two queen-size beds on the nineteenth floor. At the reception desk, I asked her if she wanted her own room, but she shook her head and I shyly requested a double room for us. When the clerk inquired if we wanted one king-size or two queen-size beds, I quickly answered "two" without checking with Mido again.

Now she was lying on the bed closest to the door, while I was puttering around, checking out the hotel's brochures, discovering that there was all-night room service—by now it was almost eleven—and realizing that I hadn't eaten anything since the vegan breakfast light-years ago.

"What would you like for dinner?" I asked Mido. She was motionless, could have been asleep but for her wide-open eyes staring at the ceiling.

"I'm not hungry," she said.

Neither was I, in fact my stomach seemed to have turned into a sharp-edged, heavy lump. I ordered turkey and ham sandwiches, nevertheless. Waiting for the food to arrive, I took a shower. This one time I would have liked to keep my artificial eye inserted, but the socket was too irritated. When I came back into the room, wearing a green patch and one of the two soft white hotel bathrobes, Mido was standing by the window. I walked over to her.

Our room looked out over the quieter areas of downtown. No hectic neon signs were visible, just a carpet of yellow and white glowing dots.

Mido turned around, looked at me, said, "Just what I need, too," and went into the bathroom.

By the time she came back the food had been delivered. She was wearing the other robe, which was too long for her, and we both had to giggle when she walked across the room holding it up like a princess holding her silken train. She looked less worn out now, more animated.

We sat down in two chairs by the window, a small round table between us. This hotel favored rather inoffensive colors for its interior design—rose and beige bedspreads and a light brown carpet. We both chewed on sandwiches, staring at our plates, avoiding each other's eyes.

"Why did you just disappear like that?" I finally asked, trying hard not to sound reproachful, but unsuccessfully.

Mido put the last piece of her sandwich back onto the plate. "And what are you doing here?" she asked instead of answering, her voice as chilly as a December rainstorm.

Aggravated by her tone, I said, "Jeff was killed. We were worried, tried to find you, and then somebody hit him with a car."

"What?" Mido said, with such horror that I was instantly convinced she had no idea what had happened while she was away.

"Have you really been to Mexico?" I inquired.

She nodded. "Searching for a friend."

"Teresa?"

"Yes."

"She is in New York." I told her how Jeff had found the postcard in Mido's mail.

"Why would she go to New York?" Mido mumbled. "She doesn't know anybody there. And she doesn't even have the money for one night at a hotel."

I confessed that I had lost the card but that Teresa had written Mido should not worry, she was just trying to get away from her husband.

"That doesn't make sense. Angelica would have known about it," Mido said to herself. "Her sister," she then explained to me. "You shouldn't have looked for me, Anna," she finally said, her voice husky with rage—or despair, I couldn't tell. "I'm not good for the people I love."

"Neither am I."

Chapter 22

"Tell me everything!" Mido demanded.

And I did. Her eyes narrowed when I confessed I had entered her house. For a moment I was tempted to apologize for my intrusion. But then I had to recall the night Jeff was killed. And my story took on a life of its own, crawling out of my mouth while I stood in a corner of the room, far away from Mido. I knew my own face was tense and pale. Mido's skin was glowing pink as if she was developing a fever.

Finally I had made it through this part of my account and found myself at the table opposite Mido again. When I came to the events in Reno—my encounter with the gunman, the trips to the clinic and eventually the decision to pay Ruth Shriner a visit—I didn't know if I had lost Mido's attention, she looked so withdrawn.

But as soon as I had stopped talking, she fixed her eyes on me and said, "They killed Ruth, too."

"If that's true," I replied, "let's hope the autopsy can prove it."

"I would never have thought Dan would go that far," Mido said with despair.

It wasn't easy to make clear sense of what she told me in the next half hour. She was beyond exhaustion, full of self-loathing, incoherent in her account of the events, but finally a more complete picture evolved.

The Green Desert Center had for many years taken care of its own public relations matters. Ruth Shriner was the payroll accountant and had also dealt with the clinic's advertising. But the center was growing. They wanted a state-of-the-art Web site and expensive new promotional material. Roy Eid was a friend of Susan Bradley's, and asked her if AdUp would be interested in the account, so Big Susan brought Ruth and Mido together as the responsible managers at the working level. Their first mutual project was the beautiful booklet I had gathered so much information from. In the course of processing the material for it, Mido met Dan Willgood. He made it clear early on that he was an influential person at the clinic, that he basically owned it, and that he was the one to decide if the relationship between AdUp and the clinic was to continue.

"Why isn't he the director of the center if he has so much influence?" I asked Mido.

"He told me, he is not interested in the paperwork but wants to focus on his research."

Considering this, he had become quite involved when it came to Mido's and Ruth's work, I thought.

Actually, the two women did not get along very well in the beginning. Ruth seemed not particularly interested in her job; she was detached, even quite cynical when it came to the clinic. So Mido pulled things through mostly on her own. When the booklet was published, everybody in charge was very satisfied, and the new Web site was being planned. Again Mido was at the clinic often, and quite frequently Dan Willgood asked her to have coffee with him and finally invited her out for dinner.

First Mido thought he was trying to date her, but soon she realized that he was as uninterested in her on that level as she was in him. After her original relief, she found out he in fact had plans for her that she found much more disturbing. On the first occasion—a dinner at an expensive restaurant in Reno—he told her about a couple who were desperately seeking a woman to carry their baby. Because they were high-profile people who wished to keep their identity hidden, they did not want to involve an agency. Willgood was hopeful that Mido would agree to help them.

Mido was so stunned by this request that she did not even turn it down right away. She said she would have to think about it. She secretly hoped that Willgood would not mention it again if she just pretended it never happened. She felt he had definitely gone too far, considering the nature of their relationship, and actually did not want to embarrass him by talking about it again.

"I should have just lied and told him I was infertile," Mido mumbled at this point of her story.

"Who would think that such a trick could be necessary, when it comes to such an intimate request," I answered.

But Willgood had been much more serious and much less fussy about it than Mido thought. The next time he asked her—only a few days later over a cup of coffee in the cafeteria—he already employed outright extortion. He would see to it that the television commercials the clinic planned to launch would also be assigned to AdUp if Mido was willing to help him. She still did not budge. But the idea that her friend Rita, who was in a difficult situation, would possibly be more interested in the whole thing, started to develop in Mido's head. She still discarded it at that point, still thinking that Willgood would realize he was asking for too much.

But the good doctor pushed. A few days passed, and he said that he was not sure if the clinic would continue with AdUp at all, considering the lack of engagement on Mido's side. The contract for the development and future maintenance of the Web site was almost signed. AdUp's art directors had worked on the drafts for weeks, Web designers had been consulted and the clinic's computer network had been assessed. The Green Desert Center wanted the site not just to serve as promotion; they also had plans of connecting their research database to a huge international medical information service this way. Huge sums of money would be involved in the near and far future. This was an immensely important account for AdUp, which was trying to expand its internet activities. If Willgood pulled the clinic out at that point, stating his dissatisfaction with Mido's work as the reason, it would have been a disaster for her and the agency. At least that was how she perceived it then. And suddenly the idea to help her friend Rita to a nice sum of money without having to become pregnant herself seemed like a feasible plan.

"She sold her body, and I was her pimp," Mido said, rubbing her eyes with her palms as if she wanted to squeeze them out of the sockets.

At this point, the story Rita had told me added the missing link. And in fact, after Rita became pregnant, Willgood left Mido alone for a while.

Mido felt protective of her friend, though, and asked him why there was no surrogacy contract in which the conditions, especially the financial ones, were spelled out. But Willgood told her such contracts were not considered valid by the courts anyway and that Rita could trust him and the potential parents. He even asked Mido never to reveal his own identity or even the clinic's name to Rita. He felt it was best if she knew as little as possible, to protect the child's parents and herself. The less she knew, the easier it would be for her to forget everything once the task had been achieved.

"By then I felt as if I had been brainwashed," Mido whispered. "Dan was so enthusiastic that Rita had become pregnant and that everything was going great."

But then Rita's pregnancy had been terminated. Willgood informed Mido that there had been a problem with the fetus that rarely occurred, but the odds that a future baby would be healthy and the pregnancy carried to term were very high.

"He said that Rita would certainly become pregnant again easily, that the baby would be all right this time, the parents overjoyed, and my friend a rich woman. The sum she would receive for success would be doubled if she tried again. I knew she was depressed and thought it was a bad idea to ask her. But I also felt it was not my decision to make, but hers," Mido said.

"But she had already refused when Bruno called her."

"Dan didn't tell me that anybody had spoken to her. Otherwise I would never have asked her. When Rita told me a woman from the clinic had already called, and she had said no to a second try, I backed off instantly."

I wanted to know what Mido's experience with Marie Bruno had been, but she said she had never talked to the woman. Her only contact had been with Dan Willgood.

After Rita had finally pulled out of the game, Willgood's pressure on Mido began once more. By then, however, she said he did not have to push so hard anymore. She was almost at the point where she finally would have agreed to become pregnant herself. "Just to see the success, you know," she tried to explain.

I recalled how Rita had described her old friend as an overachiever even in childhood.

However, just as Mido was ready to try it herself, her cleaning woman Teresa had one day broken into tears. Mido had told her that because she was out of town so much, she would only need her service once a month from now on. It turned out that Teresa and her husband Frank were in deep financial trouble and about to lose their house. Frank had caused an accident with his monster truck. People had been injured. Frank's insurance covered only the minimum, and he was left with more than ninety thousand dollars he had to pay out of his pocket, more money than he and Teresa could ever imagine making. Teresa felt she needed every hour of work she could get. Mido had always paid and treated her well, and Teresa became desperate when she heard she would lose this portion of her income.

Mido said that she couldn't pass up the opportunity to help

Teresa earn two hundred thousand dollars within nine months through a pregnancy and birth, and make an infertile couple eternally happy. Not only that, again it would get herself off the hook.

Teresa was initially doubtful that she would be able to part with the baby once it was born. Mido explained to her what she had learned from Willgood, and again she was more than honest and did not paint anything in unrealistically bright colors. She told Teresa there would be no way she could change her mind and try to keep the child. California courts granted the genetic parents custody in surrogacy cases, even though they did not acknowledge surrogacy contracts. Willgood had told Mido that the rich couple also had their residence in California, and although the woman could not carry a child, her egg cells and the man's semen would be used to create the embryos in vitro. The baby Teresa would have in her womb would be rightfully the other couple's child.

Teresa wanted a baby of her own badly. But so far Frank had always been against it for financial reasons. Mido pointed out to Teresa that the money she would make would be her very own. She could pay their debts and still have more than a hundred thousand left—definitely enough to convince Frank that they were not too poor to have their own child.

So Teresa agreed and two months later became pregnant. As with Rita, things looked bright for the first months. Mido continued her work for the clinic, Willgood left her alone, and she had in fact even felt quite good about the outcome of the whole affair.

"I was so naive," she said.

The time of innocence was soon over. One evening, about twenty weeks into her pregnancy, Teresa came to Mido once again in tears. Somebody from the clinic had called her. They said the last tests had shown that the baby was not okay. It had to be aborted. Teresa would be picked up the next afternoon and taken to Reno for the procedure.

"I was stunned when I heard that, you can imagine," Mido said. "I called Dan, wanted to find out more, but he just said it was confidential information, none of my business. When I said that

Teresa had given me permission to learn about her medical state, he only replied that the genetic parents already had custody of the baby in Teresa's belly and they did not want to disclose information on the condition of the child."

"I wonder if that's legal," I said.

"I have done some research on it since," Mido said. "As far as legalities, surrogacy is the most wishy-washy business you can imagine. Teresa would have had to challenge the whole issue in court to find out if she had a right to the child's medical records. Instead she decided to disappear. She wanted to keep the child. Her suspicion was that the other couple just didn't want a baby with a disability. She said she didn't believe what the doctor—a woman named Kelly—who telephoned her had said: that the fetus would die in her before it was born, that her own health would eventually be in danger.

"Kelly was Marie Bruno," I added.

"It looks like it," Mido said, "after what you've uncovered. Anyhow, I called my own gynecologist the next morning, asked her to examine Teresa, to find out what was really wrong. But when I went to pick Teresa up, she was gone. Dan called me later that day, said she hadn't been there for her pickup to the clinic either. He was furious, accused me of hiding her. When I talked to Frank and wanted to know where she had gone, he just said she was in a safe place. She would only come back when the clinic paid the promised amount of money. The full sum. Not just what they wanted to give her in the case of an abortion. I tried to find out her sister's number in Mexico, but information didn't have it, and Frank didn't want to give it to me."

"And so you called the police." The events in the parking lot spread out before me again.

"Yes. I got more and more worried. And Dan kept calling me. I drove up to the clinic to talk some sense into him. I said that if Teresa's life would eventually be endangered by the baby's condition, it was time for him to disclose the records. But he just repeated his old threats all over again. To be honest, at that point I

165

couldn't care less about AdUp losing the clinic's account. In the end I basically ran out of his office, steaming, and bumped into Ruth in the park."

Ruth Shriner had had her very own experiences with Dan Willgood. And she was set and determined for revenge, as Mido soon found out. Ruth must have sensed that behind Mido's rage and confusion was the same force that had driven her for the last eighteen months. When Mido practically ran into her arms that day in the park, her until then so distanced colleague Ruth just asked her if she had trouble with Willgood. When Mido nodded, Ruth said, "Did he ask you to be a surrogate?" and Mido felt like a secret agent who had finally found her crucial informant.

Willgood had asked Ruth's daughter Stacey to become a surrogate. She was only eighteen at the time. Ruth, who had raised her on her own, had sometimes brought her to Christmas parties when she was a teenager, and so she had met the doctor. Stacey had undergone IVF and was already in the third month of pregnancy when she told her mother about it.

Ruth was equally furious at her daughter and at Willgood. She found the whole idea crazy and had a falling out with the doctor as well as with Stacey.

At first, Stacey just laughed in her face. She had been accepted by a prestigious but expensive university on the East Coast. The baby would be born just a month before the beginning of her first semester. She planned to finance her studies with the baby reward.

Ruth found herself powerless to argue with her daughter, who was not a minor anymore and already pregnant. But then came the moment when Stacey learned that the baby had to be aborted. After the operation, the situation between mother and daughter became more strained. Ruth tried to comfort Stacey, but too many angry words had been said, and the daughter refused to speak with her mother. She packed her things and moved to Massachusetts long before her classes began. Since then she had called Ruth only every couple of months and had never come back to visit.

"Ruth could never believe that her daughter was the only

woman Willgood had persuaded to become a surrogate," Mido said. "She was also sure that there was more behind the whole operation. And when I told her about my friends, she felt she was proven right."

Something puzzled me. "But why did she think that there was anything fishy, apart from the unorthodoxy of surrogacy as such, about her daughter's pregnancy? It doesn't sound as if Willgood had to use any blackmail in her case."

"Ruth was not so sure about that," Mido said. "He definitely threatened her, told her she would be let go if she didn't keep very quiet about the whole affair. Ruth obeyed, but not because she was really scared to lose her job. Mainly she wanted to remain in a position where she could snoop around. She observed his patients while they stayed at the center, attempted to talk with them. But she didn't find another woman who would disclose that she was being used as a surrogate by him.

"Ruth is . . . was . . . a strange person. On the one hand she was very matter-of-fact and levelheaded. But when she became enraged, she was a fury from hell. Willgood had seriously pissed her off. She and Stacey had been really close before the pregnancy. Her daughter's refusal to communicate with her anymore afterwards was eating at Ruth beyond description. I think she originally just became obsessed with Willgood as a scapegoat for her misery. But now it looks as if she had her ear right at the heartbeat of his enterprise."

"Do you have any idea what this enterprise might be?" I asked her.

"That's where I told Ruth you could possibly help us."

Duncker, ask Anna—those words jumped up in me, and I suddenly knew Mido was sharing my suspicion.

"I think they are using these women as test animals," I said.

Chapter 23

"Did you ever speak to Mrs. Duncker?" I asked Mido.

"No. She was never there when I wanted to. And when I tried to call her, nobody picked up."

I told Mido about my two visits to Sacramento. "It looks as if Mrs. Duncker has already tried the surrogacy thing a number of times. A neighbor boy told me she was pregnant more than once and lost the babies."

"Mrs. Duncker is no surrogate mom," Mido answered. "She can't even become pregnant. She lost her uterus."

For a second I was very confused. Mido continued, "It looks as if the Dunckers are the couple for whom Dan has tried to hire a surrogate mother. They are the secret money-givers."

In my heart I had no longer believed that the mysterious couple existed at all. Mido's revelation shed a new light on my whole theory. "But Mrs. Duncker looked quite pregnant when I saw her," I said.

Mido got up and searched through the big tote bag she had brought to the room, her only piece of luggage. She handed me some crumpled pieces of paper. It was a computer printout containing charts and tables. I recognized the symbols on the last page immediately—the bar code pattern of a DNA test. I quickly looked through the other sheets. They were parts of Horatio and Mindy Dunckers' medical records. The last page was incomplete, the text broke off in the middle of a sentence. The first page contained a description of Mrs. Duncker's reproductive condition, and as Mido related, it mainly stated that she wasn't able to carry a child because her uterus had been removed because of a tumor when she was in her early twenties. It also mentioned that her ovaries were intact but that the quality of her egg cells would have to be tested.

Blood work had been done for Mr. Duncker but not for his wife. He had been checked for hereditary conditions with negative results. The author of the records, whose name did not appear on any of the pages in front of me, listed the gene disorders Duncker had been tested for and stated that the patient did not carry any of them. The DNA chart with Duncker's name at the top still made no sense, because it did not reveal anything about genetic abnormalities he might carry. It was the kind of DNA analysis necessary to establish paternity.

"Where did you get these from?" I asked Mido.

"Ruth e-mailed them to me. After you told me that you are a geneticist, I called her right away. She had already prepared herself for quite a while to hack into the clinic's computer network in order to access Dan's account. And she finally managed to get some records. I started to print them out, but then Dan called again. Somehow he had found out about Ruth's mail to me and said he was sending somebody to get the records back. I decided to go into hiding for a while, packed some things, and then these guys were already banging on my door. I panicked, jumped out of the window and ran. These are the only pages that had already been printed out. Do they tell you something?" she asked hopefully.

"I'm not a physician. But these records confirm that Mrs.

Duncker can't become pregnant herself. How did Ruth find out about the Dunckers?"

"As I told you, she was observing Dan's patients. One day she spotted the Dunckers with him. Later she saw Mrs. Duncker in the cafeteria on her own. She seemed very unhappy and Ruth saw a chance to chat with her. She found out that the Dunckers were trying to have a baby through surrogacy. When Ruth asked how they were going to find a mother, Mrs. Duncker just mumbled that her husband and Willgood were taking care of that. Finally she must have almost begged Ruth not to tell anybody that she had even talked to her."

"But it's not certain that the Dunckers are actually the owners of Rita's and Teresa's fetuses?" I asked and cringed for a moment under the cold cruelty of my own words.

"Mrs. Duncker is the only patient of Willgood's that Ruth could find who even mentioned the word *surrogacy*. Isn't there anything in the records that can tell us more?"

"The records are not complete," I said. "But they look quite regular at the first glance. The only thing that seems a bit odd to me is the DNA chart." I explained to Mido what such a chart was usually used for. "This kind of DNA test on its own is actually quite useless if there is no comparison test from another DNA sample. In forensics you would need it to see if DNA left at a crime scene matches DNA from a suspect. In family matters you would take a sample from a man and one from his potential child and compare the patterns."

"So maybe Duncker doesn't trust Dan and wants to make sure the baby from the surrogate mother will actually be his own." Mido was guessing.

"But the DNA test was done by the Green Desert Center's lab, as the letterhead shows. If Duncker distrusts Willgood so much, he should have used an independent lab. Or another doctor altogether."

I racked my brain for another explanation for the chart. But as long as I didn't have the comparison DNA analysis, I wouldn't be able to come up with a reasonable guess. "I need to see more records," I said. "Do you know what else Ruth e-mailed you?"

"I'm not sure. These were the first pages. I was hoping she had also been able to get Rita's and Teresa's and Stacey's records. But as I said, I had to run before I could find out."

"Can you access your e-mail on the Web?"

"The files had already been downloaded to my computer, so they've been deleted from my Web mail."

"And your computer is gone," I uttered, full of frustration.

"What kind of experiments do you think Willgood and Bruno are performing?" Mido wanted to know. Her voice told me that she believed in this theory, too.

"Maybe I am wrong." I tried to stay grounded. "Now that it seems there actually is a couple who wants a baby via surrogacy, it could be that Willgood and the Dunckers just had a streak of bad luck and somehow the embryos the doctors transferred always developed abnormally."

"Isn't there a way to find out if an embryo is healthy before it is put into the womb?"

"Pre-implantation genetic diagnosis," I confirmed. "But it's also not foolproof. You can only check for certain genetic disorders. There are so many other mutations that could occur, even far into the growth of the embryo in the uterus, it's hard to say what happened in these cases."

"But let's say they are experimenting. What could they want to find out? What consequences would that have for the babies? And what would the Dunckers' role be in all that?"

I didn't even want to imagine the implications of Mido's questions. The problem with medical science is that you can only prove that something works, when you test it in human beings. You can try out your theories with mice, dogs, even chimpanzees, but you will still never know if your stem cell therapy, your genetic treatment will ever work in humans if you don't have a human guinea pig.

When it comes to reproductive treatment the complications are even bigger. All the world speaks about genetically engineered humans. But if one wants to find out if a genetically altered embryo will ever develop into an altered and still healthy human being, it will first have to grow within a woman.

Mido had begun to walk around in the room, while I was lost in my thoughts. Finally she pressed her forehead against the window and stared at something out there in the dark distance. "What a miracle we are," she said in a low voice, "and what a mess."

There was a little hot plate in the room. I prepared two cups of instant coffee and set them down on the table. It was four o'clock in the morning. But I could not imagine ever being calm enough to go to bed. "So Mrs. Duncker is just faking her pregnancies," I said, continuing an earlier line of thought.

Mido didn't answer.

The moment the coffee was not scorching anymore, I lifted my cup and swallowed the horrid-tasting liquid in one gulp. Mido's cup remained untouched and sent little clouds of steam into the air between us.

"Did you tell Susan Bradley any of this?" I wanted to know.

Again Mido didn't react.

"Do you think she knows what Willgood is up to?" I continued. "Eid is, after all, her friend. Possibly they are both covering for him. A scientific sensation at the Green Desert Center will be good for his career as well. And your Big Susan will have a client who will become truly famous in the human reproduction scene." I let my head sink into my hands in frustration. When I looked up again, Mido was lying on the floor.

She is dead, was all I could think for the first instant. But the next moment she tried to push herself up with closed eyes. Only now I realized that her red-hot skin, her shallow breath and apparent weakness was more than just utter exhaustion.

"I'm sorry," she whispered, her eyes now wide open, feverish.

I helped her to the next bed, wishing I could have just lifted her up and carried her. When she was lying under the covers she was shivering despite her high fever. I asked her if she was thirsty, if I should call a doctor, if there was anything I could do for her. But she shook her head and said, "I guess I just need some sleep."

I didn't dare let her out of my sight, still fearing she could just be dead from one moment to the next if I didn't watch over her, and so I crouched on the floor next to the bed and waited for the morning to come.

Chapter 24

Mido's breath sounded like the rasping of a file on hardwood. I was convinced she needed a doctor and called the hotel reception desk. The night concierge suggested we drive to the nearest hospital emergency room and gave me a lengthy description of where to find one. I didn't have the heart to drag Mido out of bed and into the night and wondered if her condition was serious enough for immediate attention and an ambulance. I kept my watch over Mido from the floor next to her. I must have fallen asleep, only realizing it when I woke to a gentle touch on top of my head. Somebody was stroking my hair. I looked up. The room was still lit by the lamp next to the window, but the world outside sent a mild orange glow into the room.

Mido was lying on her side. She pulled her hand back from my head. "How do you feel?" I wanted to know.

"Strange," she said. "It was a strange night."

I nodded in agreement.

"You should leave, Anna," she continued. "Do me a favor and get out of all this, before you get hurt. Go back to your life."

I reached for Mido's hand dangling over the side of the bed. I did what I had wanted to do that first day with Mido in my kitchen. I stroked it with every bit of tenderness I possessed. "Remember that morning when I drove you home?"

A smile reached Mido's eyes for the fraction of a second. That was the answer I needed, but I still asked the question. "When you said you wanted to see me again, was that because you already knew you would want my scientific advice?"

Her fingers tightened around mine. "Things were different even then," she finally said. "I still thought I could find some sort of explanation soon. An answer that would help Teresa and Rita to find justice, that would give some comfort for Ruth. Now I know there will not be comfort. Not after what happened."

"And that's why I cannot stop," I just said.

Our hands would not release. I did not dare move because I couldn't risk losing the warmth beneath my fingers. Then Mido started to cough.

The sun had fully risen now. I called the hotel desk once more and reached a different concierge this time. He told me there was a doctor who worked at the casino during regular business hours and said he would send her to our room. Ten minutes later there was a knock on the door. A shy Asian woman of around fifty with a heavy Chinese accent introduced herself as Becky and entered.

When the doctor saw Mido she became all business. She took her pulse, checked her chest with a stethoscope, asked her to breathe deeply, cough a couple of times. Then she took her temperature and said, "Bad bronchitis." She gave her antibiotics and syrup for the cough, and asked us to call immediately if the fever should rise even higher.

Before Becky left, she promised to come back in the afternoon before the end of her shift and told Mido to drink as much water as she possibly could and stay in bed for at least three days. "My services will be charged to the room," she said instead of a good-bye, gave me a last intense look and then uttered gravely, "Vitamin C!"

The moment the woman left I had to laugh. Mido was grinning too, interrupted by a mean coughing fit. I tucked her in, found some bottles of water in the mini bar, opened them all, and set them on the table next to her. Then I went to the bathroom, put on street clothes and told her I was going out to quickly make some purchases.

There was a small supermarket around the corner, and I bought all kinds of vitamins and fruits, threw bagels and donuts and other provisions into the basket and paid. Back at the hotel I placed myself in a chair in a corner of the lobby. I wanted to check my voice mail without bothering Mido. Again, no message from my sister. I decided to call Rita and find out if she was okay. But her phone rang through, and I could only hope she had kept her promise and was safely staying with a friend.

I was still trying to make up my mind to call Sarah once more when I looked up for a second and spotted a lanky but muscular man with a head full of dark curls standing at the reception desk. Before any conscious thought formed in my brain, my gut drove me out of the chair and into hiding behind it. The tiny blond concierge was checking something on a computer screen, shaking his head.

The curly-haired guy pushed some dollar bills over the counter. But the concierge just shook his head again, and the other man took the money back and walked away. When the receptionist turned his back to the lobby, I slipped out and dashed to the elevators.

By the time I had reached our floor, I wanted to give up this whole lunatic investigation. At that point I didn't know exactly why, but it had something to do with the bitter taste of fear and what it can do to your heart. Walking toward our room, I was ready to wake Mido, ask her to get ready to leave and drive back to San Francisco. *But where shall we go?* was my next disturbing thought. Nothing had changed since we had both fled from the city. We still knew too much to be safe but not enough to put an end to all this. Again I could only hope that the anonymity of the huge hotel and checking in under my sister Sarah's name would provide some protection.

Mido was not asleep as expected, but she was sitting up, talking to somebody on the phone. A violent cough was shaking her. When she was able to speak again, she said, "I know that you have no idea where she is. This is serious, Frank. You have to finally report Teresa missing." She coughed again, slammed down the receiver. "He just hung up," she said, her red-rimmed eyes dark with anger. "I'll call him again." She pressed the redial button and waited, but in vain. Frank didn't answer. Finally Mido gave up. Then she bent forward, coughing so much I thought she would break into pieces.

I decided not to tell her about the man in the lobby. It looked as if he had not yet found out we had a room in this hotel, otherwise the concierge would have accepted the money. Moving to another place would only leave new traces.

Mido's cough calmed down again. She sank back into the pillows, sweating and trying to catch her breath. I unpacked my purchases and asked her if she wanted anything to eat. Of course she declined, and it was clear that all she wanted was to go back to sleep. I persuaded her to take some of the vitamins and took her temperature. It was still below what the doctor had warned us about.

I stretched out on the empty bed, trying to figure out what to do next. Usually I have my best ideas in a state close to sleep. But today my head was in tight knots, and my body twitched and ached in various spots. In between there were Mido's coughs.

"How did Ruth get those records?" I finally whispered.

"I'm not sure," Mido said so quickly that I knew she had been lying there awake, pondering the same questions as I.

I pushed myself up. "You said she e-mailed you the documents. Maybe they are still on her computer."

"I don't think so. Remember, Willgood caught her somehow. I'm certain he deleted everything."

"She was in the office when she sent out the records, right?"

"Yes. I called to let her know I had met you and you could maybe give us more information. She was very excited and told me she had managed to get something that could be the key to our questions. Then she hung up and sent the e-mail."

"You said she broke into Willgood's computer account to get them."

"Yes, at least that's what she was planning. She read books about the software for the clinic's server, even asked hackers in an anonymous Internet chat for help."

"Did she have a computer at home, too?"

"No, she did everything from her office. She often stayed until late at night. I remember she told me that she would have to do the actual hacking from the office computer anyway because it was the only way she could hook up to the clinic's server. She didn't have access rights for the medical files, but at least she was already behind the internal firewall."

Computer files are fragile but also sticky—you can delete them in an instant, but often they leave traces wherever they have been stored. I wondered if Willgood had managed to delete every remnant of the records Ruth had gathered from her computer or her server account. Not that I was a particular data whiz myself. Still, I wanted to surf a bit within Ruth's personal cyberspace.

My cell phone beeped. A number I didn't know blinked on the display.

"You wanted me to call you," said a clear, strong female voice on the other end.

"Who are you, please?" I inquired.

"I could ask you the same."

"Let's not play games. Just tell me your name."

The caller hung up.

For an instant I was just annoyed. Then I pressed the call-received button. I saved the number and called it back. It rang forever. I was about to throw the cell phone out of the window. Mido was lying on her side and gave me a questioning look.

Finally somebody picked up. "Jane here!"

"This is Anna," I said. "Ms. Abdul Ferrer?"

"Abdel Farragh," she corrected my incompetent memory.

"I didn't expect you to call me so soon," I tried to explain. "Actually I didn't know if you would call me at all."

"You want to talk about the clinic and Dr. Bruno?" she cut off my babbling.

"Is there anything to talk about?"

"You can meet me tonight at work."

Chapter 25

Jane Abdel Farragh asked me to come to the Wonderland at seven that night. "Look for table nineteen," were her instructions.

Mido's fever had risen in the last several hours. I called the hotel doctor again. She came and gave her something to lower the temperature and some codeine, promising some sleep for Mido. And so it happened. Shortly before it was time for me to leave, Mido had finally calmed down and was breathing evenly.

At about twenty minutes before seven, I wrote Mido a note, explaining that I would be back as quickly as possible and leaving her my cell phone number. When I walked toward the Wonderland, I was wearing my black cap and sunglasses. I had cut one of my eye patches into a shape that was almost covered behind the lens. The sun was still up over this city of artificial illumination, but the shadows were already tall and the air cold, as cold as my sad new friend the knife, stored in easy reach in a pocket of yet another pair of cargo pants I wore.

The casino space of the Wonderland consisted of one large room with a maze of slot machines through which one had to navigate to get to the gambling tables. It was crowded and dimly lit, lacking the glitziness of the Silver Legacy. Many of the players had a disheveled, homeless look. They stared at the spinning wheels, mesmerized with the kind of hope that is as destructive as a disease. I felt oddly at home among them.

At Table 19, blackjack was being played. The dealer was a tall, muscular woman with cropped, curly hair dyed yellow. Not only her nose carried a bright diamond stud, but each of her earlobes were weighed down by at least ten silver loops. She gave me a quick look when I approached. Her irises were bright blue, matching Rita's description of Jane Abdel Farragh. I kept my distance from the table, indicating I did not want to play. She focused on the lone gambler in front of her again. The old man took one more hit and lost with twenty-three points.

Another woman in the brown uniform of the casino's staff took the dealer's place behind the table. Abdel Farragh signaled me to follow her and reluctantly I walked behind her to the back of the room. She opened a metal door. I stopped in my tracks.

"What's the matter. You're afraid I'm going to mug you?" the woman said with an impatient smile.

Much worse, I thought to myself, but I walked through the door and down a neon-lit hall into a small windowless room. It stank of sweat and smoke and mold. Rusty metal lockers covered the walls. A beige Formica table occupied the center of the space. It was surrounded by five orange plastic chairs with crooked chrome legs.

My host pulled a pack of Lucky Strikes out of one of the lockers, sat down and stretched her long legs. She pointed at another chair and I placed myself on it.

"Smoke?" she asked.

I shook my head.

Abdel Farragh lit her cigarette and inhaled. It could have been the quick relaxation of her mouth while she was blowing out the smoke, or the fleeting little smile that formed in the outer corners of her eyes. I felt an unexpected sense of trust.

"I need your help," I found myself saying.

"I'm not particularly talented at altruism," was the answer. "Guess that's why I switched careers."

"You once must have felt differently when you decided to become a nurse."

"People change. What happened to your eye?"

I took off the sunglasses, answering, "Hereditary retinoblastoma." Hereditary retinoblastoma is a genetically linked cancer of the eye that sometimes breaks outas early as in the womb.

"Oh," Abdel Farragh said. "You would have been discarded by my former boss already as an embryo."

"I know," I said. "And my twin as well."

"That must have been hard for your parents. Two little ones with a dangerous tumor."

"My sister didn't get it."

"She's not maternal?"

"She is."

"I've heard that the gene doesn't always express. Interesting to meet somebody who is living proof." Abdel Farragh gave me a penetrating stare. "Do you think your mother would have wanted to have you if she had known you carried the gene?"

"I'm not sure," I answered, my voice as cool as hers. "I'm the first known case in our family. Maybe she would have undergone amnio, maybe she would have said yes to an abortion. After all, there was the possibility of losing us both or of having to raise two blind children. But maybe she would have wanted to give us a chance. I never asked her. Would you have?"

"No," Abdel Farragh replied. "No woman can answer such a question when her child asks it."

"Do you think a woman can answer it when she is pregnant and a physician asks?"

"That's why doctors don't often ask. They suggest. Or persuade. Illness and disability are natural enemies to medical personnel. Something you want to beat and kill."

182

"Quite a simplistic approach, don't you think? Particularly when killing the condition means killing the patient."

"Absolutely. I have proven to be a coward before that enemy and deserted my troops."

"That's why I'm here. Why did you quit your job at the Green Desert Center? Or did they fire you?" Abdel Farragh had set the tone. I didn't feel she was a big fan of unnecessary tact.

"And who are you?" she asked sarcastically.

"Somebody who switched careers as well."

"What did you leave behind?"

"I was a geneticist."

Abdel Farragh lit another cigarette and sent a high whistle through pursed lips. "And now you're a little private eye for a big compensation lawyer."

"No. Even though I do think some of your ex-boss's patients deserve a pretty big compensation. All these surrogates, for example, who had no idea what their bodies were being used for."

If eyes could shoot arrows I would have dropped dead now instantly.

"What do you want to know?" Abdel Farragh finally asked.

"They are experimenting, aren't they?" I probed.

"I'm not sure," she said, her voice lower now, calmer. "How did you find out about this?"

"Let's say I've heard about the unorthodox protocol Bruno and Willgood apply when it comes to surrogates. And there has been this series of second trimester abortions in a number of women who were hired by them to carry other women's babies. Your name came up when I talked to one of the surrogates. Also, somebody has been trying to get rid of me—for good. And I think they already killed a friend of mine."

"You think?"

"I need more information if I want to prove it. That's why I'm here."

"I don't know much. When I asked Dr. Bruno once what was wrong with one of the fetuses she aborted, she just brushed me off, said it was confidential information. She and Willgood always performed the procedures alone without a nurse or an anesthesiologist. Marie claimed that she was board certified in anesthesiology too, so I wasn't completely astonished about it at first, but it made me wonder." Abdel Farragh stubbed out her half-smoked cigarette and lit a new one. "I felt bad for the surrogate mothers, even though they were prepared to give the babies away once they were born. But abortion is always hard. That's why it's so crazy of these pro-lifers to assume women would do it out of neglect or carelessness. I've worked in a Planned Parenthood clinic before. Women do it out of deep distress, and I've never seen one who has gone through it unscathed in one way or the other. When the baby could already be able to live outside the womb, it makes it worse."

Abdel Farragh was on a crusade now. I knew it would not be wise to interrupt her.

"There is a certain madness about working in the human reproduction field," she continued. "Green Desert has the philosophy that they offer all stages of care in one place. If you get fertilized there you can also give birth at the clinic, or have an abortion if something goes wrong. On the one hand doctors and nurses put all their knowledge and effort into keeping alive premature babies who weigh hardly a pound. The price for this is very often a more severely disabled baby—even more so than the ones other doctors advise women to abort. I asked Dr. Bruno once what she thought about this contradiction. She just answered, 'If I couldn't deal with the controversial demands of my job, I better quit.'"

"Bruno can be very charming."

"She can. And now I'm not kidding. She is a passionate researcher. She's always trying to enhance the methods of in vitro fertilization to heighten the pregnancy rates. And she's brilliant. I used to love working for her."

"And for Willgood?"

"Marie is the scientist. Dan is the bully."

"What kind of relationship do they have?"

"Let's not get into that. It would take a whole department of psychiatry to analyze them. Dan hired her a couple of years ago.

He loves and uses her; she loathes and plays him. That's my theory. He had hardly any scientific merits before. That's why he never made it higher in the ranks of the clinic. Do you know that it was founded by his mother?"

I nodded.

"Legend has it that she established it after the death of her daughter who tried to have a baby over and over again and eventually committed suicide after her tenth miscarriage. Dan thought the clinic would be his personal playground, and he never doubted he would become director immediately after he finally managed to get his degree. The foundation, however, demands outstanding contributions to science from the head of the clinic."

"And Roy Eid has that?"

"He had the big name. I don't know what happened to him, but somehow he lost interest in research once he had taken over the post. I once suspected Dan's talents at applying pressure had something to do with that, too."

"And then he won Ms. Fabulous Physician Bruno as his teammate."

"Yes. And from what I've witnessed, it must be part of their agreement that she has absolute freedom of research by any means necessary, as long as the findings are published under his name."

"They both haven't published much since she started there." I recalled the slim article by Willgood and the total lack of publications by Bruno in the last years.

"I think she is working on something real big." Abdel Farragh looked at her watch, then rose from the chair. "Back to the coal mines," she hummed.

"Please," I begged. "I need some more information. Where are the medical records stored in the clinic?"

The former nurse asked incredulously, "Are you planning to break in?"

"I only know I need to find out what was wrong with those babies. Or what Bruno and Willgood did to the embryos before transfer."

"The records are all on the computer. The attending physicians make printouts and keep them in their offices together with the ultrasound pictures and other documents. But the records for the surrogates we're talking about are not in the general database."

"You've tried to get a look at them yourself!"

Instead of an answer Abdel Farragh left the room. She did not hold the door for me, and once I managed to open it and step out, she had already vanished from the short hallway.

I found her by the blackjack table chatting with the dealer who had replaced her. While I was passing them, Abdel Farragh grabbed my hand, pushing something into it. "Try this. I've watched Dan punch it in often enough. He's not good with numbers. Maybe he hasn't changed it. On Wednesday nights, Willgood and Eid always play tennis in Carson City. That may be a good time."

Out on the street I unfolded the note. It contained a handwritten ten-digit code.

Chapter 26

Wednesday night, Abdel Farragh had said. Tomorrow. Again I felt that strong urge to trust the woman. It would be great to have a full night and a day to recover and plan the next move. The gift of a break, handed to me by the powers which had the ex-nurse from Wonderland go to Wendy's the same night I sent her a message via the woman from the Green Desert Center's cafeteria. Was this a chain of events too good to be coincidental? Was I again being lured into a carefully laid out trap? Or was it a hint from the goddess of chance herself, telling me she was on my side?

When I came back to the hotel, I found Mido still asleep. It was ten past eight. Her peaceful image made my limbs melt. I wanted to lie down beside her, feel her close to me and dive into the innocence of unconsciousness. I told myself, I should stay in the room for her sake. She was still severely ill, would maybe need me later, and would certainly be worried if she woke up and found me gone. And above all, there was the matter of the curly-haired man who might by now have learned we had checked into this room.

I would not have been able to explain even to myself why I did not listen to any of these arguments. I just wrote Mido yet another note, telling her I would meet a friend in a restaurant close by and she should call me when she needed me. Only when I stood again in the elevator did I think about the mess of lies and evasions that had so far been the foundation of our brief acquaintance.

Today it was easy to find the little back road to the clinic, and I slowly steered the Accord Mido had rented down the gravel path and over the wooden bridge. Again I parked along the same hidden trail, out of sight from the center's grounds. The desert was covered in darkness lurking all around me, invisible and all-knowing.

The park looked empty when I scanned it through the fence close to the back entrance. I memorized the code Jane Abdel Farragh had given me. I thought about trying it out at the keypad of the back gate but decided against it. Who could say what kind of alarms would be triggered by using it.

I followed the path along the fence, avoided the well-lit parking lot and crept up to the clinic from a darker angle at the back of the security booth. Behind a little window, the broad shoulders of the guard on duty were visible. He was slouching in his chair, staring at a cluster of small screens. Only one of them showed movement—a football game broadcast on a portable TV. The surveillance monitors all showed lifeless views of the clinic's grounds.

Suddenly the guard swung around on his chair. I managed to throw myself onto the ground before he could spot me. But I had seen too much of his face already—it was the man from the hotel, the man from the dome, Mr. Curly-headed Gunman.

There was no way I would try to get by his booth and into the entrance he was guarding.

Crouching low, I retraced my trail. Now I had to risk it and see if the code worked—and if it would set anything off.

I punched in the ten numbers and pushed against the iron gate. It opened noiselessly, and I slipped through. I was standing behind the last of the clinic's low buildings. This was the way they must have smuggled in Rita and possibly the other women.

Avoiding the paved paths, I moved toward the mansion, sneaking from one dark area to the next. The bungalows closer to the front were well lit. Occasionally someone exited or entered the first building whose entrance lay only a few yards away from the security booth.

In the shadow of the big staircase, I studied the windows of the fake villa. Most of them were dark, including the one to Eid's office on the first floor. Only behind the last one to the left a weak light shone—in Rashid Jackson and Ruth Shriner's office.

The clinic's purloined phone directory was still in my wallet, and I found Rashid's number with the help of the lit display of my cell phone. I crouched behind the bench I had sat on the day before, hoping it would muffle my voice.

"Jackson."

"Hi, this is"—for a second I had to search for the name I had used with him yesterday—"Sun. I've stalked you already yesterday. Now I'm sitting in this restaurant in Reno feeling lonely. Didn't we agree to have dinner today?"

"You are truly up for trouble," he giggled. "Remember I promised you a beating by my boyfriend?"

"I told my girlfriend about it and she is just warming up with her coach. She has a pink belt in Burmese boxing."

"That sounds great! Tell me which restaurant you're at."

"Sweetwater Café. Silver Legacy."

"That's nasty. I have to rescue you from there immediately. Don't go away. The prince in brass armor is on his way."

"Don't forget to bring your boyfriend."

"I'm afraid he's too scared already."

"You don't deserve such a coward."

"That's love."

After I hung up I felt bad for a moment. For chasing the man through the night, for lying again. "Self-pity is the starting point of mental decay," I mumbled to myself and decided to really treat Rashid to a great meal one day—if he didn't turn out to be one of the bad guys. Then it suddenly occurred to me: *How did Willgood learn that Ruth had gotten hold of the Dunckers' records?*

After a while the light behind the window vanished. I waited another fifteen minutes and then walked up to the cafeteria door. It was secured with yet another keypad. And again my code worked. I threaded quickly through the clusters of chairs and tables. The connecting door to the lobby was unlocked, the reception desk empty. A second later I stood in front of the elevator about to press the button when it lit up.

I barely had time to slide into the narrow corner between elevator and wall. Then the elevator door opened and Rashid rolled out. My stomach nearly jumped out of my throat. Fortunately the man in the wheelchair was fast and did not look back. The stairs were a safer option, but I had no idea where to find them, so I took the elevator up. In the long hallway on the second floor all the doors were closed. I peered out of a window overlooking the parking lot. Rashid got into a car and drove off.

There was no possibility to enter a code for his office door. At first disheartened, I touched the lock in the dark and found that it was one of the complicated modern security models. Not that I could have picked even the simplest of locks. My grand spy plan had come to a premature end. In frustration I pushed against the door, rattled a bit at the knob, and it turned.

The lights from the park sent a weak, cold glare into the room. There were two computers in the office—the laptop on the desk Rashid had occupied the day before and a desktop on the opposite table. Deciding that this was most likely Ruth's work computer, I turned it on, turning the back of the screen to the window and reducing the monitor's brightness as far as possible.

It was a simple Windows setup. Ruth had used Outlook Express as her e-mail software and Explorer to surf the Web. I checked all her e-mail folders, and they were in fact all empty. Even the folder for deleted e-mails did not contain any documents, and neither did any of the Windows folders. I performed a number of system searches trying out various possible filenames. I searched for the word *Duncker* in full and abbreviated spellings, and tried the same with the words *records, Willgood, Bruno, Marie, Daniel, Stacey, Rita, Takahashi* and so on, until I exhausted the possibilities and gave up.

Maybe Ruth had ingeniously hidden the file somewhere on her computer, but if so I had no idea how to find it.

There was one more possibility. I started her Explorer and looked for bookmarks and favorites. None had been selected. Without much hope I clicked on the "history" button and discovered the trace of a user. The last clicks on the Web had been made on Tuesday, October 14, Ruth's last day in the office. The opened link was a GMX account.

GMX is a German free mail provider. I recognized it only because I had an e-mail address there myself. The site was exclusively in German, so its user must have known the language. I opened the GMX start page and the request to fill in the user name and password appeared. Sometimes, if the settings are right and you type in only the first letter of the user name, the system adds the rest automatically. A lucky star had risen above me. I typed "r" and the address *ruthy2543@gmx.net* appeared before me. The password had been saved as well: a row of asterisks appeared in front of me, and with my next click, the Inbox of the account appeared. It was empty.

Navigating GMX had always been a bit tricky. When I first opened my own account there I had had to search a little to find the Outbox—in German it was called Gesendet. I hastily opened Ruth's and had to suppress a triumphant little yell. There was one item in it: an e-mail with an attachment to JamesMi@earthlink.net.

The attachment contained the Dunckers' medical records, the first pages of which I already knew. I searched for more records, other attachments, but without success. Then I pulled Mido's printout from the pocket of my pants where I had put it and compared it to the contents on the screen. There was no second DNA chart that would have explained the existence of the first one, but merely a continuation of the text I was holding in my hands. The physician who had authored it—the last page on the monitor displayed his or her undecipherable signature—described Mr. Duncker's reproductive abilities. It said that his sperm count was quite low. And there was a short addendum: *The possibility that the patient will be able to naturally fertilize is low. With IVF the use of the ICSI method is recommended.*

The ICSI method calls for a single sperm injected directly into an egg cell in vitro. If a male's sperm count is very low and his live sperm are rather weak, this heightens the chances of a successful fertilization. The condition of Duncker's sperm could have explained why the fetuses had developed abnormally with such frequency, I realized. Weak sperm is sometimes connected to other genetic problems that cannot be diagnosed easily. But the ICSI method was nothing unusual or experimental, nothing that Bruno and Willgood and the Dunckers would go to so much trouble to hide.

I made one more attempt to find out how Ruth had gotten into possession of these records. There was a button that promised to connect me to the clinic's intranet. But when I clicked on it, a message popped up informing me that it had been disabled.

Jane Abdel Farragh had mentioned printouts of files in the doctors' offices. Was it plausible to assume that Bruno and Willgood had gone to all the trouble of hiding the surrogates' data and mere existence, and would then let their records lie around somewhere on their desks or in a file cabinet? *I'm here*, I thought, and I decided to go and check.

Again I made it through the park undiscovered. And again the code worked. Within seconds I was inside the gloomy, lifeless hall of the building containing Bruno's and Willgood's offices. Light strips, like those on planes, pointed where to walk. Ten inches above the ground their effect vanished, and darkness took over.

Encouraged by my earlier success I snuck up to Bruno's door. I had checked her window before entering the building and had made sure the office was empty. When I touched the doorknob a silly Pavlov reflex let me now expect it to be unlocked, but I had run out of luck. It was tightly secured. And around the window I saw the wires of a high-tech alarm system: no chance to crawl in that way, either.

And of course Willgood's office was equally secured as was every other door along the hall.

Then I encountered the staircase which led downstairs to the DNA lab. A little itch of intuition persuaded me to descend it. A keypad greeted me at the door. I hesitated for a moment. What if somebody was inside working late? I looked around and spotted a bathroom opposite the lab door. It was open and had a nice strong lock on the inside. I quickly punched in the ten magic numbers, opened the lab door, then dashed into the bathroom and locked myself in. Then I listened hard. All was silent, and when I eventually dared to peek out, the lab door was still open and undisturbed, the space behind it dark.

The familiar lab smell enveloped me, resembling the stench of a toilet bowl freshly bleached with gallons of chlorine. I had a strange sensation of momentary comfort and familiarity when I saw the lab equipment gleaming quietly in the room.

Somebody had forgotten to switch off a halogen lamp over a counter at the far end wall, and I followed its beam through the rows of tables carrying microscopes, petri dishes and trays of test tubes. A door with a sign read *Sterile Room*. It was locked, as I quickly found out, but my interest was in a small section of the main lab divided off by a glass wall and holding a desk and office equipment and a series of filing cabinets. I opened one after the other. They contained alphabetically arranged paperwork and, more luck, a copy of the DNA analysis for Mr. Duncker.

Test records are as a rule kept in a lab. According to Abdel Farragh, Bruno and Willgood had managed to avoid leaving a paper trail on the surrogates in the clinic's database, but I was pretty sure they kept some kind of records on them. They would want to be able to document their procedures in case of success— whatever that might mean—but they would not want the documents to be available to anyone but themselves. I was not very hopeful when I leafed through the letter "T."

However, I found a slim manila folder with the name *Takahashi,*

R. printed on it. It contained only one sheet: another DNA chart, the same kind as Duncker's.

I held Duncker's chart next to it. It took me a moment to understand what I was seeing. There was not only a close resemblance between the DNA analyzed, as if Duncker and Rita had been related. But, from what I could make of the charts, Duncker and Rita had the same DNA. Like Sarah and me. Their DNA analyses made Rita and Duncker identical twins, or at least the DNA analyzed in both cases belonged to the same person.

There must have been a mixup by the lab or by the doctors who had provided the DNA samples. I looked for Stacey Shriner's file and found another chart and a similar result. How odd, I thought for a moment and then, finally, understood. The DNA analyzed had of course not been Rita's or Stacey's but the DNA of their fetuses. Comparing them to Duncker's chart, I was in fact looking at the results of identical twins, only these twins were more than a generation apart. Bruno and Willgood were cloning humans.

I had of course read and heard of scientists trying to create a human clone despite legal bans in many countries, but so far none had been able to show proof of success. Inserting the nucleus of an adult cell into an egg cell in vitro and waiting for an embryo to develop was an idea so beautiful in its simplicity that of course it created a temptation for scientists. And then there were the successes with cloned animals. But in order to create Dolly, the infamous sheep, almost two hundred embryos had been transferred and had developed abnormally. The problem with adult nuclear cloning was the reprogramming of the genome, a procedure that more often than not goes wrong. I had sometimes marveled about the motivation of the women who were willing to have a cloned embryo transferred into their womb, be it their own or somebody else's. Naively, I had assumed they were always informed about what they were doing.

I put Rita's and Stacey's charts back where I had found them. It would be more convincing if the police could retrieve them from this official location than if I, a thief, handed them over. At the moment they did not prove much. Bruno and Willgood could always claim there had been a mistake made by the lab and that everything I asserted was a wild, crazy fantasy. The only way to prove there had been experiments was to find Teresa and convince the police that the DNA of the child she was carrying should be independently analyzed and compared to Duncker's, something I was more than pessimistic about. How should we find Teresa? And was her baby even still alive? And on top of all this, why should Duncker ever agree to giving a sample of his DNA?

Chapter 27

There was a noise at the door of the lab. I slid under the desk next to me. I could hear footsteps moving through the room. I concentrated on the clicking of the heels, trying to synchronize my breathing with their slow staccato. The person did not turn on the ceiling lights. At first I was relieved that it remained relatively dark, then I realized that a harmless visitor would most likely have reached for the light switch immediately.

The steps came closer, stopped, moved away, stopped once more, approached again, down one aisle of the lab and up the next. The person was systematically searching for an intruder. I pulled out the knife. The steps came closer, stopped.

My cell phone vibrated. I had turned off the ring tone, but in this looming stillness even the little hum from my pocket sounded like a siren. I shot up from underneath the desk. Marie Bruno was standing two yards away from me. She spotted the knife and froze. I fumbled for the phone, tried to switch it off. The next thing I saw was a gun in Bruno's hand. She had stepped back and was now blocking the opening between lab and office.

"I knew I would find you in here," the doctor said calmly. She looked taller today, dressed in a long dark coat. "Little lab rat that you are."

Mesmerized by the small revolver in her hand, I just nodded. Already during our first conversation I had felt she knew who I was. Besides my address, the stolen personnel files from Carlos's office had also contained my résumé.

Bruno pointed at Duncker's DNA chart still lying on the desk. "What do you make of it?" she asked.

"I've seen the other charts as well. So it's not hard to guess."

"The other charts?" She sounded astonished but not agitated. "Dan always promises more than he can deliver. He said there would be no copies."

The weak light disguised Bruno's features; her beautiful hair was just a shadow around her small face. But this image suddenly let a suppressed memory reverberate and I realized where I had seen her before. Not seen, but I had sensed her, felt her, possibly caught a glimpse of this dark halo while I was cowering behind a palm tree next to Jeff's dead body. I was now certain Maria Bruno had sat in the car that killed my friend.

"Your fetuses have developed far," I said. "Do you have a new method?"

"Yes," the doctor answered with a smile. "And as you will not be able to tell our secret, I will enlighten you." There was sincere pride in her voice now and only a hint of sarcasm. "A newly discovered source of stem cells in the brain," Bruno revealed.

"You've extracted cells from Duncker's brain?"

"I've been fortunate to find him. Actually Dan found him. Mr. Duncker absolutely wants a child who is biologically related to himself. And his sperm just doesn't do it."

"What about his wife's eggs?" I asked.

"You don't understand. He wants *his* child, not hers. And he is a supporter of science, somebody as interested to break through a frontier as I am."

With a little click she released the safety catch of her gun and, at the same moment, switched on the glaring ceiling light.

Abdel Farragh had been only partly right about Willgood's and Bruno's individual talents. Sure, he was a bully and she a brilliant scientist. But she was also a killer, and one who was fascinated by death. Her eyes now wandered over me like automatic cameras, and I could sense the processor behind them scrutinizing and analyzing how somebody feels and behaves in the instant before she will be shot.

I shivered; the knife in my hand was twitching. "What were the conditions of the babies?" I asked, mainly to keep her talking.

"Fetus and placenta were much too large," Bruno answered, contemplatively. "I am looking for a way to control their growth. And there were various other problems . . . with the lungs . . . one fetus was visibly disfigured." Her gaze became unfocused for just a fraction of a second.

That was my chance. I stepped to the side, lunged toward her and reached for her right hand. She pulled her arm upward. A shot fired, hitting the ceiling; flaky dust rained down on us. I dropped the knife, trying again to wrestle the gun from her. Bruno's arm and hand were waving wildly and I could not get hold of the weapon. She fired another shot into the ceiling, and a third. How many rounds did one of these tiny revolvers contain?

Frantic from the pops of the gun and the unexpected physical strength of Bruno, who was punching and struggling in my arms like an experienced fighter, I pushed her aside, dashed past her and ran. I was certain the next sensation would be a breathtaking hit to my back and then the incredible weakness after the shot. The shot came, but it hit me in the right leg. It felt as if somebody had kicked me in the back of the knee. I fell forward, expecting the pain, but it did not come.

Somehow I managed to get on my feet again and make it out the door and halfway up the staircase. A tall, broad shape suddenly appeared before me. I rammed the man, actually throwing him off balance, and he rolled down the last couple of stairs. "Go after her, for heaven's sake!" sounded Bruno's angry voice.

I stormed out of the building, toward the back gate. It was not locked from the inside. I darted out and into the night.

My hope was to make it to the car. But there were running steps behind me. They came closer. My only refuge was the pitch darkness of the desert. I left the path, ran through the thorny underbrush, up the next hill and down again in complete darkness. I stumbled over the rubble. There was a moment of relief; the steps behind me had vanished. I could not see even the ground before me, but I was sure I had become invisible as well.

Then suddenly the pain set in like a pinch to my knee and accelerated to a piercing stab. I made the next step, hit an obstacle, and it felt like my leg broke in two. A sword of pain was being rammed into my body from the knee upward. I fell heavily on my side and lay there, wishing I could faint, but nothing happened, only this gigantic, crazy pain.

"She ran over there!" A male voice came from the left. Not very close, but near enough.

"Find her!" Bruno yelled from farther away.

"She can be anywhere here. We have to wait until dawn. You said you hit her. She won't get far."

"We cannot let her get away! Don't you have a flashlight? And call for backup!"

"We need searchlights!"

"Then hurry up!"

"Where in the world do you think . . . ?"

I was panting, my breath pushed out loudly. I tried to hold it back, but the pain grabbed for my throat. I bit on my lower lip, desperately suppressing a whimper. The voices trailed off.

I waited, listening to the low noises of the desert, the humming and crackling. I expected the voices to return, but nothing happened. I made one vain effort to stand but fell down immediately, attacked by another stab of pain. A long time passed until the pain subsided. Eventually, I tried to orient myself, to push and shove my lower body slowly in the direction where I thought the car was.

Prickly plants and hard-edged rocks blocked my path. I moved around them, still biting on my lip, trying to stay focused, conscious, sane. Dust covered the inside of my nose and the back of my mouth. It didn't taste bad—it was earthy—but it made breathing even harder.

Time vanished. I had no idea how long Bruno and the man had been gone, it could have been minutes or hours. I just pushed and pulled and moved, finally cresting a hill. I knew I had to get down the other side. Maybe the car was there. Or maybe I was moving in the wrong direction, pushing myself farther out into the desert.

Going downhill proved to be more difficult. Gravity helped me with the pushing and pulling part, but I struggled not to roll over and tumble down the hill. Under different circumstances I might have gone for this quick method of descent, but now every uncontrolled move seemed to tear off my injured leg.

The sound of an engine in the distance ripped the silence. I stopped, lay down flat, and expected powerful searchlight beams to blanket the area, blinding me like a rabbit about to be run over by a car. It remained dark, though. Suddenly there was a whisper, the clicking of a vehicle door being closed, and a cough. It was muffled at first, transforming into a wild fit like the ones that had knocked down Mido during the previous day.

The sound became weaker. I listened intently, wanting to be absolutely sure. Somebody walked by not more than ten yards away. "Mido," I called, my voice only a whisper. I tried it louder. "Mido!" An instant of quiet caught my breath, and then just one word—"Anna!"

"I'm over here."

"I'll find you. Just keep on talking."

Mido practically fell over me. "Anna! I was so worried, when I called you and then just heard all those sounds. There was a shot!"

The cell phone! In my attempt to quiet the thing I must have picked up the call.

Mido later told me that she had known immediately where I had gone. She had called a taxi and ordered it to drive her to the clinic's back entrance.

She helped me to the car. It was a long haul with the backdrop of Mido's coughs and my groans of pain, which we both tried to hold back without success.

Finally we made it into the Accord, and Mido started the engine. She steered the car toward the gravel road. We had just turned around the bend, when behind us a massive beam of light cut a path into the desert.

Chapter 28

White flakes swirled all around us. The Sierras greeted us with the first snow of the season. We had pulled over at a gas station to have chains put on the tires and were now crawling in an endless line of cars across the mountains.

Mido was driving. It was late morning the day after our night-time adventure at the clinic. My right leg was wrapped in a tight brace from the thigh down to the ankle. Huge amounts of painkillers were circulating in my system, and I was high as a kite.

My escape from Bruno was replaying itself in my drugged mind. Mido had rescued me at the very last moment. Had we gotten into the car only seconds later the powerful searchlight that had flashed up behind us would have hit us, making us easy prey for the doctor and her henchman.

Mido had hit the accelerator of the Accord as if she were steering at a Nascar, taking off down the desert path in rally fashion, and we made it back to the main road without anybody at our tail.

She then took me to the emergency room of a small hospital in Carson City. I have no idea how she found it. The drive there was a blurry, strange dream. A broad-faced, friendly doctor introduced herself as Immaculata Santafernanda and added with a smile that made her look tired, "But everybody calls me Dr. Imma."

Dr. Imma cut off my pant leg, inspected the knee, pumped something wonderful and soothing into my veins immediately, and took X-rays.

"Okay, sweetie," she said. "Now tell me exactly what happened."

I mumbled something about an accident during a walk in the desert, and Dr. Imma replied, "It's clearly a gunshot wound. Through and through. Fortunately it only scratched the tibia and didn't tear anything precious."

"It didn't hurt so bad right away," I said.

"The fracture could have occurred later. The bone was weakened and then you made a wrong step."

Dr. Imma explained to us that she had to inform the police. It was the law with gunshot injuries. While we were waiting for an officer, the doctor sterilized the wound, applied the provisional brace, gave me crutches and said I would have to see an orthopedic specialist as quickly as possible to find out if the fracture needed surgery.

Dr. Imma also checked Mido for her cough and pronounced she was over the critical stage of her bronchitis.

"Spontaneous healing through adventure travels," was Mido's dry comment.

"You should still take it easy the next couple of days," our Samaritan said with another one of her tired but amiable smiles.

The police arrived in the form of a stocky man in his sixties with thick white hair and the face of a pug dog—Sheriff Carmichael. The interview took place in an empty examination room.

"So you were shot, young lady?" the sheriff started slowly. His watery eyes took in my torn, stained clothes, the dirt-encrusted skin, the eye patch. There was a hint of disgust in his expression. He gave Mido a similar look when she started to cough again. Her hair was matted, she was wearing the same, once light-colored clothes as the day before, freshly patterned with desert dust and my blood.

"It's difficult . . ." I began, clearing my throat a couple of times. And then I told the sheriff that Mido and I had decided to watch the sunset in the desert. That we stayed out there until it became dark. When we were walking back to our car, I suddenly felt the pain in my leg and only then heard the reverberation of a shot. We were both in shock, hid behind a big rock, and when we finally dared to glance in the direction of the attack we did not see anybody.

"Did you trespass?" the sheriff asked immediately.

"Not intentionally, but maybe without realizing it," Mido said.

The man wanted to know the exact location of the incident, and I claimed it had been close to one of the many dirt roads off the highway to Carson City, but I was not sure where exactly.

The sheriff assured us he would take care of the matter and then said with grumbling authority that we should not talk about it to the press. He jotted down our personal data, took a couple of notes and left. "Let's only hope we don't have another one of those God-forbidden snipers," I heard him mutter to somebody in the hall.

Mido and I could not stop talking. We had by now almost made it across Donner Pass. The snow was still whirling around the car like the veils of an Arabian dancer, and we tried to come up with possibilities of how we could tell the authorities what Bruno and Willgood were up to. Teresa was the key, and Mido was very worried about her whereabouts. She could not believe that Teresa had traveled to New York on her own. Teresa's only relatives were her sister Angelica and Frank, and both clearly had no clue where she was.

"We'll drag Frank to the police station at knifepoint," I finally said, and I was beyond joking, "to make him file a missing persons report. He has to tell them her pregnancy may turn dangerous. Then they can check with the airlines, see if she has flown to the East Coast recently . . ." I had no idea what could be done after this point.

Mido nodded contemplatively. "Why has Bruno become so lethal?" she then asked. "Wouldn't there have been other ways to defend her research?"

"She's scared of malpractice suits by the surrogates," I guessed. "Big compensation claims. Punitive damages and so on. She will lose her reputation if this comes out." I also suspected that the strange dynamic between her and Willgood, the air of blackmail and favoritism he spread among the clinic's personnel, had corrupted whatever professional ethic they once possessed. And there was this aura of imagined omnipotence wafting about Bruno. Science could be a religion of its own, the illusion of controlling chance, where the successful researcher becomes an infallible deity and the goals pursued are not assessed for necessity or potential harm anymore. After all Bruno had had very real power over life and death.

"And she was defending her baby," Mido now philosophized. "Do her experiments have any therapeutic value?" she asked a little later.

"If she were cloning embryonic stem cells, yes," I said. "But since she is trying to create a cloned human being, no. There are of course people who say clones could be used as organ donors for their sick DNA-counterparts."

"Wow," Mido answered. "What crazy questions all this genetic stuff creates. Is a baby worth less than an adult? Would a clone really be just a copy of the person whose DNA was used? Would it still have its own human rights? Its own personality?"

"It would," I said. "You'd just have to meet my twin sister to find that out."

Mido looked puzzled for a moment. Then she grinned. "There is a second one like you somewhere? Don't scare me!"

205

I smiled back. "Yeah. You'd better be scared. Sarah is quite something."

"Do you resemble each other?"

"Of course. A lot, physically. We are maternal twins. Our DNA is identical. We are even more perfect clones than the ones Bruno is trying to make. We share the same mitochondrial DNA, developed at the same time in the same womb, grew up together . . ."

"But?"

"It's hard to explain," I started. Then I fell quiet. Talking about Sarah still felt like a betrayal. After all, we had been raised to the credo of our mother that we were privileged. As twins we had a person closer to our self than non-twins could ever wish for. If we wanted to understand ourselves, we would only have to study the other and discover amazing things.

Despite my mother's assertions, though, Sarah remained more of a mystery to me than most anybody in my life. We shared a room while we were living at home, a small studio while we were at the university, a big apartment after we found our first jobs. For Sarah this closeness had gone without saying. But the older we became, the more I continued to live with her only because I felt a strange sense of responsibility related more to guilt and a misled ideal of family loyalty than anything else.

In the last years I had become more and more afraid that Sarah was drifting into mental illness. She had made up things from an early age, telling stories that were not true about celebrities she had met, travels to interesting places with wonderful friends that did not exist. When we were children and later teenagers, these tales amused me. After all, I could understand the desire to create an alternative reality. While I kept my own fantasies completely to myself, Sarah shared them with everybody.

She had always been a good storyteller, so people often believed her. As a child, this just made her laugh forever over the gullibility of people, but as she grew older, she took it more for granted that even her wildest tales were going to find believers. Once we were in our twenties, she would get annoyed when I doubted the adventures she had clearly concocted. She was telling me about boyfriends who did not exist; wild nights that could never have taken place because she had been in her bedroom alone at the time, as I knew because I had been at home, too; and wedding plans with fairy-tale princes. On the one hand I was glad these guys were not real, because they sounded like complete jerks, and on the other hand, I wished one of them would just walk through the door and prove to me that my sister was not stepping over sanity's edge and into a delusional world.

I had tried to share my worries with our mother. Mom, though, was not willing to admit a problem. She claimed that I always had been a dreamer myself. That I was making too much of Sarah's stories. At one point she said that since I had come out, I had become more irritable and critical of my sister, and maybe I was just unbalanced. For our mother it had been difficult to accept that I am a lesbian. Not because she was particularly homophobic. It just damaged her neat twin theories, after which Sarah and I were supposed to be so similar in the most decisive personal matters. Mom is one of the leftover believers in genetic determinism.

I contemplated daily how I could have Sarah admitted for psychiatric treatment, but I did not know how to follow through without her consent. She was getting into trouble at the lab where we both worked—she became erratic during team conferences and lagged behind in her work. I tried to cover for her as much as possible, secretly hoping on the other hand that somebody else would notice her trouble, that her condition was revealed and had to be dealt with.

Eventually I convinced myself that the only way to end the situation was to leave. I told myself that this would hopefully trigger some kind of catharsis involving my mother and Sarah, maybe opening Mom's eyes. Deep down I knew of course that my main motivation was just to be left alone, to throw off the weight of responsibility. What I could not cut off, I had realized in the last week, was the love for my sister, the mysterious tether that bound me to her, be it due to heredity or genuine fondness.

I did not tell Mido any of this. After a period of mutual silence, she coughed a bit and some time later asked, out of the blue: "Do you want children?"

"No," I said without hesitation. "And you?"

"Yes."

The inexplicability of our wishes now cut a breach between us and we drove on toward the Central Valley in deep silence. At one point I fell asleep. When I woke up again we were already passing Sacramento. There was no remnant of snow anywhere, just bright blue sky and the familiar clutter of strip malls and gas stations along the freeway. The trip over the Sierras had become not more than the memory of a strange arctic fairy tale.

"What happened to the snow chains?" I wanted to know.

"I had them taken off half an hour ago," Mido smiled.

"I didn't hear anything, I'm sorry. You must be dead tired, too, and I just snored away here."

"I had a lot of sleep yesterday. Don't worry."

Another hour later we crossed the Bay Bridge. Mido and I had a little discussion about our next destination. She wanted to take me to a hospital right away. I persuaded her it would be early enough if I went the next day. I just wanted to clean myself up, go to the police, convince them they should launch a search for Teresa, and get some sleep.

We had left Nevada without picking up our things at the hotel in Reno. We would have to call there later, check out, and arrange for our bags to be stored. Mido and I finally agreed that we would risk quickly stopping by my apartment to get some fresh clothes and then check into yet another hotel.

For the first time I was grateful for the stinky, tiny elevator in my building. It provided just enough space for Mido, my crutches and me. The door to the apartment looked undamaged. The heavy and somehow damp air of rooms that have not been touched in days greeted us.

Mido rushed under the shower. I checked my closet for something that would fit her or could at least be fixed in an acceptable way, and found a pair of black jeans that were rather tight on me and could be rolled up fashionably. A wide white shirt would complete her outfit. Finding something for me was a problem. The cumbersome brace would not fit under any pants I owned. It was tightened only by Velcro bands, but Dr. Imma had warned against taking it off on my own.

Finally I found a ridiculous but practical piece of clothing—a bright red pair of thermal pants I had brought to San Francisco only because people said it would get really cold here. It had not been cold enough, so far, for me to put on these things, but they had long zippers down the sides of both legs and could be adjusted over the brace.

I got a pair of scissors from the kitchen and cut the remains of my cargo pants off my body. Sitting on the bed, I awkwardly put on the thermal gear, cursing when my leg, which behaved like a foreign object, did not want to slip in.

Suddenly there was a knock at the door. I froze instantly. In the bathroom the water was still gushing. I knew it could be heard in the hall. There was another, louder, more vigorous knock.

I tried to calm myself—somebody who wanted to attack us would probably not knock. And then there was a familiar loud voice. "Come on. I know you're there. I saw you come back with your friend. Open up!"

Martha! I struggled to stand up, grabbed the crutches and hobbled to the door.

My neighbor pushed her wheelchair in, looked at me, said, "Did you try to jump off a cliff?" She dangled a piece of cardboard before my eyes.

I recognized it as Teresa's card. "Thanks," I said, relieved that this important object was returned but also annoyed that I had let it fall into my neighbor's hands.

"It's not addressed to you. I was thinking of sending it on to the correct receiver. But as it was sticking out from under your doormat, I thought I should first let you know that there's a code in the card. Make sure to tell the rightful owner."

Mido appeared from the bathroom wrapped in a large blue towel. Her hair was wet and spiking in all directions, and she smiled mischievously when she saw my fancy pants.

"A code?" I asked incredulously. "Good news," I then explained to Mido. "Martha has found Teresa's card."

My neighbor grabbed the card back, moved over to Mido and let her sausagelike finger wander over the back of the card. "See these letters. They are drawn a little bit thicker than the others."

"Martha is a retired police officer," I told Mido.

"If you read them together they form the word *piloto*," Martha continued.

Mido looked puzzled, but quickly her eyes grew wide with recognition. "Pilot," she then said.

"Oh no," I whispered. Images of my two encounters with Mido's neighbor began to flash before my inner eye like a video being fast forwarded. Donald Mayer, as he had introduced himself to me, in his movie star uniform, with his little moustache twitching, constantly on the watch over his female neighbors. I remembered his grin as he was trying to ask me out for dinner, the sudden dark rage in his stare when I refused. I remembered my impulse to get away from his porch. A sharp-edged stone began to roll around in my stomach as the implications of Teresa's message resonated within me.

We have to call the cops, I mouthed to Mido.

"Why don't you just call my friend Julia," Martha sounded. "She's looking for you anyway."

"For me?" I asked sheepishly, consumed by the revelation in Teresa's message.

"Detective Wayne. She called me an hour ago. Couldn't reach you on your cell. She noticed we have the same address. So she asked me to tell you to contact her immediately should I spot you. She's somewhere in Reno. Here's her mobile number."

210

Chapter 29

The police had found the owner of the car that struck and killed Jeff. A tiny flake of lacquer from the front bumper stuck on Jeff's clothes had told them the brand and year—a 2001 Jaguar S-Type in cinnamon red, fortunately a rather rare color. The cops had searched some databases and discovered that only three of these cars were registered in California. Two belonged to people who had been out of state on the night in question. The third caught Detective Wayne's attention because the owner had been mentioned in her interview with me: Horatio Duncker.

Wayne and her partner had shown up at the Dunckers' residence in Sacramento but learned from Mrs. Duncker that her husband was in Reno at the Green Desert Center. The detective called her colleagues in Nevada and together they paid the clinic a visit. They found Duncker in the park, obviously in the middle of a heated argument with Willgood and Bruno. When the officers attempted to take Duncker into custody, he claimed he had sold the car to Willgood a week ago. Willgood admitted the Jaguar had been in his possession the night of Jeff's death, but he said he had left the car at the clinic and had no idea who could have used it.

The police were now questioning Duncker and the doctors. Detective Wayne had tried to reach me because Bruno said that I had stolen the car and used it to kill my friend. After all, I had broken into the clinic as well and threatened her with a knife. Bruno even produced the weapon, saying they should search it for my fingerprints.

On the phone with Detective Wayne, I could give only a nutshell version of what had happened. I was astonished that she was less skeptical than I expected. I was sure Bruno could be very convincing, but Wayne told me Willgood's, Duncker's and Bruno's statements were just too incongruous to make any sense. My acquaintance with Martha probably helped my credibility, too. While I was still explaining things, the detective received a message from the other officers that Duncker was hinting at experiments being performed at the clinic. He was losing his nerve and blowing the whistle.

Of course Wayne now wanted to know in more detail from me what I had discovered there, but I convinced her to first listen to the story of Teresa's postcard. I could practically hear her impatience crackle through the phone, but she let me talk and finally said, "Stay where you are. I'll arrange for an officer to come over and then I'll have you brought to Reno to shed light on a few things here."

Martha, Mido and I waited impatiently. Mido paced from the kitchen to the living room window and back to the kitchen again. Martha tried to milk me for every detail of our adventures, and I was sitting sullenly on the bed, trying hard not to yell at her.

Fifteen minutes later Detective Sergeant LaFleur—an elflike, blond woman who looked like she was eighteen but radiated the determined seriousness of an experienced cop—arrived.

We gave her the postcard. Mido told LaFleur about Teresa's pregnancy and her disappearance. Martha pointed out the code

212

once more. The highlighted letters screamed out the more you looked at them, and then the detective said, her round forehead wrinkling with concentration, "You actually believe this pilot—"

"Donald Mayer," Mido interrupted her.

" . . . Mr. Mayer is holding your friend captive."

"What else could this mean?"

LaFleur explained that the card and our suspicion were not hard enough evidence for the police to storm the house. "Even if we find Teresa there, we have no probable cause, and with the right lawyer, the man could get off and we'd be in trouble."

She studied Mido and me with compassion and concern. I was about to hack my crutches into pieces when Martha interrupted and laid out a number of possibilities for a plan.

When I arrived at the Market Place Restaurant in the ferry Building at ten to six that same evening, the maitre d' looked at my outfit with dignified astonishment. I was not wearing the red pants of horror but had hastily purchased a long, black skirt and a matching jacket at Macy's on Union Square. Nevertheless, there was still the issue of the crutches, my eye patch, and the glazed-over look of my good eye due to the painkillers I had just taken.

Donald Mayer would not be very attracted to me, I was certain. Trying not to think about what the pilot's original motive for inviting me to dinner had been, I was glad that I could take him up on the offer when I called him earlier. My main task would be to hold him in this restaurant until I got a message from LaFleur.

The host guided me to a little table for two in a corner of the restaurant. It was too small to fit my stiff leg underneath; I had to stretch it out into the aisle. A lanky man in a brown suit winked at me from the opposite table. LaFleur had insisted a police officer be on the scene, and I grinned back at the guy nervously. If he was called into action tonight, he would later claim he had been in this restaurant coincidentally.

The plan Martha had suggested to LaFleur would let the police off the hook. Even though the police could not storm Mayer's house on the basis of the flimsy evidence of what we thought was Teresa's code, they could go in if a neighbor called and claimed she heard somebody yelling in distress inside.

"If he's there we have to ask him for permission to enter," the detective answered.

"Then we have to make sure he's gone!" was Martha's response.

This had been my clue for a suggestion. LaFleur looked doubtful at first but agreed after Martha said, "Chicky knows what she's doing."

I wanted to slap and hug her at the same time. Instead I called the pilot. He picked up after the seventh ring. I explained who I was and apologized for my rude behavior the other day.

"Already forgotten" was the man's nonchalant but cautious answer.

"You know, I was in a really bad mood, things on the job were a mess. And then I took it out on you. And all you were was friendly and hospitable. If you are still up for dinner, maybe I could ask you out. I'm sure you're not too old-fashioned to accept such an offer from a lady."

He hesitated. Maybe I had overdone it. But then Mayer answered, "I'd like that. Usually I have to pay for the ladies. It would be a nice change."

The time until dinner passed excruciatingly slowly. At the very least, I mentally prepared myself, trying to create a mind-set to keep me from throwing up when I saw the man.

Mido was prepared to call the police the moment the pilot left the house. She would complain of terrible cries for help from his premises.

Mayer did not appear at six. A waiter brought a bread basket, small plates and two glasses of ice water. I grabbed a piece of bread, intending to nibble on it. Without realizing it, I began to tear it into little pieces instead and drop them into the water in front of me. My watchdog at the next table was eating a salad, not paying any attention to me, apparently completely absorbed with trying to get the huge lettuce leaves into his rather small mouth.

Ten minutes past six the pilot entered the restaurant. He was wearing a dark blue three-piece suit and looked strangely over-dressed, even for this formal surrounding. He took one long look at my scratched-up self, produced a tense little smile and apologized profusely for being late because he could not find parking. I forced a smile, too.

Mayer hid behind the menu. His strangely sweet scent I had already so disliked at our first encounter crept across the table. I asked him about his last flight. He answered in an overly patronizing, utterly annoying tone. The only thing that worried me at this point, though, was how to keep the man at the table as long as possible. So I continued to marvel about the wonders of flying.

"You're really steering one of those big planes? How does it feel to have the lives of three hundred passengers in your hands?"

"I'm used to it."

"And how fast does such a bird have to be for takeoff?"

"That depends."

"On what?"

"That's too complicated to explain."

Mayer did not seize a single chance to brag about his abilities. When the waiter came to take our orders, the pilot asked for merely a soup. I ordered a three-course dinner—salad, soup and steak—hoping this would buy me time with Mayer. But the man let his eyes wander through the restaurant, checking out the other patrons, staring at the women. I found it impossible to make him focus on me and our conversation and I realized I could not possibly keep him in the restaurant very much longer. Involuntarily I cast a glance at my watchdog at the next table. Mayer followed my gaze. My nervousness was becoming too palpable.

Fortunately the waiter appeared with our bowls of soup. I stirred the creamy white substance, forced myself to eat a spoonful, tasted nothing. Mayer practically created a tsunami in his bowl, moving his spoon with such high frequency and velocity between the surface of the soup and his mouth.

"Do you have to eat the same horrible airplane food as the rest of us?" I tried to continue our one-sided conversation, desperately wishing for my brain to shake off its inertia and come up with a subject fascinating enough to grab the pilot's attention. Again the man didn't react to my last question.

"I'm sure you're dying to know why I really asked you out for dinner," I finally said.

Mayer looked me in the eye, for the first time since he had arrived. "Sure," he answered cautiously.

Only something truly crazy would work now. "I wanted to ask you for help in the matter of the disappearance of a friend."

"Why do you think I could help you?"

"I know that you take a keen interest in your neighborhood. I thought you might have seen something of importance."

"Who is this friend?"

"Her name is Teresa."

Mayer stopped eating. He let his spoon sink into the bowl but didn't release his grip on it. "Sorry, I don't know anybody with that name," he said.

The muscles of his face performed a strange little quarrel, as if amusement and rage were fighting with each other. His eyes were immobile, uninhabited, their gaze fixated on my forehead.

"Maybe you've seen her around. She is Ms. James's cleaning lady."

"I don't think so."

"But she has told me about you. She has certainly seen you."

"Then the pleasure was one-sided."

"Teresa is pregnant. It is likely she will have complications. I am very worried. She might die if she doesn't get medical attention."

"I'm sorry I can't help you." Mayer sounded as if he was talking to a seriously disturbed person—patient, persuasive, somewhat absentminded. His lips under the little moustache looked moist and fleshy, his smug smile moving in. "Anyhow, I have to say good-bye. I have to leave earlier than expected, to take over a flight from a colleague who called in sick. Thanks for the invitation." The pilot began to rise.

I had lost, had to accept that I could come up with nothing more to hold him back.

But then shadows fell on the white tablecloth. Mayer charged up from his chair, to be pushed down by strong hands. Two uniformed officers and a plainclothes cop were hovering above us. "Donald Mayer. You are under arrest for the abduction of Teresa Orlowski. You have the right to remain silent, anything you say can and will be used against you in a court of law . . ."

One of the uniformed police cuffed Mayer and escorted him away. The pilot's face turned a vicious red. He stared at me—disbelief, contempt, despair, rage all pulling at his features, transforming them into an ugly mask. He tried to lunge at me and stumbled over my injured leg. He would have fallen if it hadn't been for the officers holding his arms. When he had regained his balance, Mayer again fixed his gaze on me. I was still trying to regain control over the rising pain in my leg when a sharp whisper escaped from the man's tight lips—"Bitch!"

Chapter 30

"People really take all the fun out of having kids," Martha ranted. "First they become pregnant without sex, and then they want their babies to look and behave like their ugly old selves. I always thought the reason why you go through all the stress of raising a child is because you're up for the ride, you want to see somebody new and unexpected grow up."

"Clones won't be copies of their parent," I answered.

"Then why even bother?"

"Maybe because it's hard to embrace the unexpected, and people need the illusion that they have control over their lives," I said.

"And then they hand over all the control to a bunch of crazy doctors. It makes no sense, chicky, people make no sense, I'm telling you."

"Haven't you ever fantasized about reviving somebody, getting somebody back who is dead?" I said, playing devil's advocate. But I thought of Jeff, and a corner of my soul held a very real longing to do just that.

My remark had achieved the unthinkable. Martha fell quiet for at least thirty seconds, contemplation digging a furrow between her brows.

"Did Detective Wayne tell you who actually drove the car?" I changed the subject.

We were sitting in the donut shop on the ground floor of our building. Martha had lured me in here with the promise of news from the Green Desert Center.

It was three weeks after the events in the clinic, after the arrest of Mayer, after the rescue of Teresa. The police were still trying to piece the stories together, and every now and then Detective Wayne let some details leak out to Martha, who happily passed them on to me—if I was willing to spend an afternoon with her over gallons of coffee and tons of pastry. A plate with three chocolate donuts sat in front of me. So far I had not bitten into the first one, though; I was too anxious to hear what she had found out.

"The security guard, this Lester Smith guy, claims it was Marie Frankenstein Bruno herself."

Lester Smith was the name of the man who had attacked me at the Silver Legacy. Before their whole enterprise blew up, he had been a devoted servant to Willgood and Bruno. Once he realized his masters were trying to frame him for quite a bit of their foul play, he decided to turn the tables.

"Smith said that the plan was only to scare your friend Jeff, maybe give him some bruises, a little concussion, deter him from snooping around. Obviously Duncker had informed the doctors immediately after your first visit to Sacramento. Bruno and Willgood didn't know where to place you then, but they knew Jeff because he had taken photographs for the clinic's promotion booklet. They told Smith they wanted him out of the game for a while—until they had taken care of all matters pending. The attack on Jeff was also supposed to lure security away from AdUp's offices so that the thugs Smith had hired could break in. They should wreck Mido's office and get the medical records in case she kept copies there. But then sweet Marie insisted on driving herself, and Smith says he was shocked when she accelerated and hit Jeff at high speed."

"So shocked he had no problem threatening me with a gun a day later and trying to get me to jump from the roof of a casino."

"He's denying all of that."

"I know. And trusting that his lawyer will claim I'm too visually impaired to identify him beyond doubt."

"Cheers to the world of the disabled," Martha joked and raised her coffee cup.

My leg was still in a cast, and the crutches good friends to lean on. I had not been taken to Reno for questioning after the incident in the restaurant. Instead, the undercover officer from the next table, a goofy guy named John Brown, realized I was in pain and drove me to UCSF Hospital. The orthopedic doctor there had set the bone and kept me at the clinic for the night. Julia Wayne picked me up the next day and took me to the Hall of Justice, where she interviewed me for many hours. Mido had to go through the same procedure in an adjacent room, we later found out. Detective LaFleur interrogated Mido.

Even to this day, Wayne was furious with me for snooping around on my own, particularly for breaking into the lab. "A pity that the clinic decided not to press charges," she grumbled.

Bruno had pleaded for our encounter in the lab to stay off the books. This way her assault on me with an illegal deadly weapon, as police lingo had it, would be dropped. Her original self-defense claim did not hold up after it became clear that I was shot from behind. Willgood was now asserting Bruno was solely responsible for all scientific experiments, as well as for the treatment of the surrogates. Of course, testimony from Mido, Rita and Teresa would shed a different light on that, but Bruno's former allies, Willgood and Smith, were trying to dig a very deep hole to bury her.

Of all of us, Teresa endured the most horrific ordeal. I got my first glimpse of her at the hospital the night after her rescue while watching the television news in the waiting room. They were showing an old snapshot of her and Frank. Both were smiling into the camera. Teresa had a chubby face, melancholy black eyes and thick brows. She looked happy but insecure. Frank looked relaxed and self-assured on the television screen, very different from how he came across when I had encountered him, and different also from how the news cameras caught him the night of the rescue. There he smiled, too. But it was a forced smile, a grimace, put on out of embarrassment, reflex or a sense of obligation to appear happy now that his wife was safe.

Then they had shown Teresa being carried to an ambulance on a stretcher. Had it not been for the medical equipment, the tubes, drips and oxygen mask, it could have been the image of a dead person. Her face was white and bony, and she was motionless.

It turned out Teresa had been acquainted with Donald Mayer for a while. He had seen her come to Mido's house to work and had talked to her. From then on they would sometimes have tea together and talk for a while. A few times, on weekends when Frank was away to one of his monster truck shows, Mayer took Teresa on a flight in his Cessna. When she worried that her husband might find out about it and throw a fit, Mayer assured her that he respected her marriage, and everything would remain a secret. And he really never made a pass. Teresa wasn't happy with Frank and told herself she deserved some fun and friendship. If she had been a different person, maybe she would have left Frank for Mayer. And if the pilot had not been who he was, maybe that would have turned Teresa's destiny for the better.

Teresa originally did not tell Mayer about her pregnancy. In those first months she could still easily hide the signs under baggy clothes. And then "Kelly" called and demanded that she have the abortion. She did not understand why. She felt good, the baby seemed fine, and the only reason given her was that it had a mysterious disability and the parents who had ordered the pregnancy did not want the defective baby anymore. But she was not prepared to

221

give it up. Frank, however, wanted the money, and not somebody else's possibly sick child. So Teresa and he fought. Bruno and Willgood also kept calling and pressuring her. Teresa was frightened and furious, and in her distress she confided in her good friend Mayer.

Mayer seemed extremely compassionate. He even invited her to hide in his house until she was ready to give birth. Teresa declined. She just needed somebody to talk to, maybe to give her advice. She no longer trusted Mido—after all, she had gotten her into this situation.

When the police questioned Teresa later, she stated that she and Mayer were sitting in his living room, drinking tea, when she lost consciousness. The next thing Teresa remembered was being in a windowless room, nicely furnished with a white bed, a couch, a nightstand and a fridge filled with muffins, cheese and orange juice. When she tried to open the door, she realized it was locked. She screamed for Mayer, but nobody responded. Only what she believed to be more than a day later, he entered her prison a completely different man. When she demanded to be released, he beat her, raped her and locked her up again.

Later that day Mayer came back to continue the torture. And the next day and the next. Sometimes he would show up every few hours, sometimes he was gone for days in a row. He forced Teresa to write two New York postcards, one to Frank, one to Mido. Teresa dared to highlight the letters. Mayer's flight schedule later showed he had in fact been in New York when the cards were mailed. Even though Mayer always stocked up the fridge, Teresa hardly ate. She was wounded and scared out of her mind, and then she went into labor.

After many hours of pain she gave birth to a dead baby. She held it for a long time, finally wrapped it in a blanket and placed it in the freezer. She wanted to preserve the child, to give it a decent burial once she was set free. Teresa never gave up hope of being rescued.

But during the delivery she lost a lot of blood. When Mayer

came back he must have seen the traces and could have known that she had had a miscarriage, but he never asked. He did not even give her fresh sheets—just continued to rape her. When Teresa was finally discovered, she was near death.

Teresa's suffering made me brood once again about the merciless workings of chance. Why of all people did she have to turn to the pilot in a time when she was so vulnerable? Why couldn't she have met somebody truly compassionate and helpful? But then I had to accept that while coincidence did play a crucial and cruel role in Teresa's horrors, it was merely an assistant to the destructive forces of human perversion. It had been exactly her vulnerability that let the monster that Donald Mayer was seek Teresa out and attack her.

When the police later searched Mayer's house they found evidence that Teresa was not the first woman he had kept and tortured there. They had not yet disclosed what exactly they discovered, but it was clear his other victim had not survived.

Horatio Duncker volunteered to give a DNA sample, which had been compared to the DNA of Teresa's baby. The results showed that it was in fact his clone.

Willgood's and Bruno's attempts to cover up their experiments were still a mystery to me. Why had they gone to such lengths to stay anonymous to Rita and Teresa, but approached women like Stacey Shriner and Mido, who knew exactly who they were? Jane Abdel Farragh's role in the whole scenario was also a puzzle piece that did not fit. She had suspected something, and Bruno must have known that. Still, Bruno and Willgood let her take care of the surrogates after the abortions.

When I laid out these questions to Martha she just said, "Politics."

I looked at her in wonderment and she explained, "The more people you involve, the less you can control it. I don't know if Willgood did it on purpose or just out of arrogance—he does not strike me as a mastermind criminal—but in fact he used quite a common political strategy: create confusion, spread fear, lie about the facts, but tell different lies to different people. Take the doctor's whole corny little spy game with the fake names, for example. No one could seriously believe they could hide their true identity this way from somebody who was set on finding out who they were. But wearing the masks did intimidate the surrogates. Had one of them decided to go to the police after all, it would have discredited her that she didn't even know the doctors' names nor the address of the clinic. And then the warped paper trail. Bruno and Willgood needed documentation of their procedures in case one of their clones in fact had been born alive and kicking, and they would have wanted to shout out their success to the whole medical community. And they knew they could not use the clinic's facilities without creating records. So they simply decided to hide and spin whatever possible, making it nearly impossible to draw connections. A loaded little vigilante geneticist like you showing up there was the worst-case scenario, something they never really counted on happening."

The clinic's security system had recorded my entry with Willgood's code. When some time later Bruno called the center looking for her partner in crime, she received the information he was on the premises. She had driven there only to receive a call from Willgood when she was already in the parking lot, and learned he was in fact in Reno. She decided to search for the intruder, who she had correctly guessed was me.

The forensic experts were still looking into Ruth Shriner's death. The lab results were incomplete, and it was not clear if there was any evidence that she had been yet another victim of the doctors.

Roy Eid and Susan Bradley both claimed they had no idea about any of their staff's escapades. Big Susan asked Mido to tell her the whole story from her point of view. After Mido finished, the lady billionaire just said, "You know I encourage ambition. I want AdUp to succeed. But there was no reason to go that far to earn me more money."

And the great moments of the enigmatic ladies in my life continued. My mother called to let me know that Sarah had begun treatment as an outpatient in a psychiatric facility. During the last months my twin's behavior had become alarming even to Mom. Sarah, she said, was stalking a colleague. It was mainly unwanted phone calls and love letters, but when he contacted Mom—they knew each other from conferences—the embarrassment had led her to nag Sarah on and on about seeing a specialist. My twin finally agreed. The term *borderline personality disorder* had been mentioned by a psychiatric expert and Sarah was now receiving medication and psychotherapy.

On the phone, Mom asked in her flighty way, "I wonder if I was wrong about you. What do you think, is Sarah maybe suppressing the fact that she is really a lesbian?"

I struggled hard not to break into tears and laughter at the same time. "You better just focus on decoding our genes, Mom, and let the other experts mess up our minds," I joked.

I started up from my musing because Martha was wildly waving one hand in front of my face and the other in the air. When I turned, I saw Mido enter the donut shop. She came to our table, gave my neighbor a hug and kissed me on the cheek. As usual I had to fight the urge to just give her a kiss on the mouth. So far, all the caresses we had exchanged were fond, friendly, but terribly casual. In my dreams I made all kinds of plans of how to change that. Unpredictable reality took over, though, and crushed my self-image as a brazen lover along with the courage I had managed so easily to muster in my imagination.

"Hey, chicky, you're gone again." Martha's voice made my skull quake.

"I'm back, I'm back," I quickly assured her, biting into a donut, pushing the plate over to Mido, who had just come back from the counter with a cup of coffee.

"If you weren't such a dreamer, you'd actually be the ideal business partner for the little company I have in mind."

"No thanks," I said spontaneously.

Martha did not look hurt at all. "Just listen first. You won't have to spend your days with me, don't worry."

I shook my head wildly.

"Just tell her what you have in mind," Mido said and covered my mouth with her hand.

"I've had this idea for a while to open up a private investigation firm," Martha said. Suddenly there was a spark in her onyx eyes that conveyed that this tough cookie had dreams, too. "On my own it would be quite difficult though, accessibility issues, you know. But with your legs, chicky, and my experience and brain, we could do it."

"Why thanks," I said. "And don't forget to count my one eye."

"I think I have a name for your firm already." Mido smiled.

"Yeah, maybe we can employ you to do some advertising, to get us started," Martha said. "Of course I already have a lot of contacts."

A castle in the skies for this woman's self-confidence, I prayed to myself.

"Let me know what you need," Mido replied. "Actually, Rita and I are thinking about opening our own business, too."

"You want to quit your job?" I asked.

"I already have," she replied. "Half an hour ago. AdUp is history for me." She devoured the donut and gulped down her coffee. "Are you ready to go?"

I nodded and pushed myself up on the crutches.

Fog was flowing into the void between the blue sky and the green earth at the cemetery in Daly City. Jeff's sister, who Ethan had finally tracked down, wanted a traditional funeral service. Mido had offered to drive me to the ceremony. The next hour passed as a blurry vision of silhouettes of people forming into groups, shuffling and whispering, bending their heads and lifting them to smile at somebody they knew only to quickly lower their chins again, possibly afraid their own behavior might be considered inappropriate. Some of the visitors were wearing black; many others had shown up dressed in bright colors, carrying vibrant bunches of flowers. I had come empty-handed. Mido stayed at my side throughout the service, nodding to former colleagues, pressing her shoulder against my upper arm as support.

Getting away from the cemetery felt like an escape. We did not say good-bye to anybody. The day before at Ethan's house I had talked to Jeff's sister—a tiny brunette with tight skin who did not resemble her brother in the least. It was the short, anxious conversation of two strangers who had met under circumstances where one was not up for talking to a stranger. I told her how much I had appreciated her brother, what a great person he was. She looked at me, trying to understand, I guessed later, what I had seen in Jeff, a brother she had apparently never felt close to. She did not seem to blame me for anything in connection with his death, and when I tried to tell her about his last day, and how he had helped me search for a missing friend, she interrupted me. "I can't hear any of this. Stories of blood and crime disturb me, always have. I get nightmares. I'd rather not know how he died." Her features hardly moved when she spoke. I could not tell if that was due to extreme self-control or a real lack of emotions.

I asked Mido to drop me off at Pier 3.

"Shall I wait, or come back to pick you up later?" she wanted to know.

We were sitting in the Infiniti in the lot across from AdUp. She would soon have to return this car to the company, I thought, suddenly realizing the change in Mido. There was something softer about her today, as if a glossy but hard outer layer had thawed and fallen away.

"It's okay. I'll take the streetcar."

She pointed at my cast.

"Or a cab," I said with a mixture of gratefulness and impatience. "Don't worry."

"What's there not to worry about when it comes to you," she teased me gently.

"Ditto." I smiled.

And then I did it. I stroked her cheek with the back of my finger, pushed a short strand of hair behind her ear. She closed her eyes and let it happen. As she finally bent over to me, her lips touched the corners of my mouth, moved a little bit to the side and found the right place. They were unexpectedly hot, sending their warmth through my veins and into my whole body immediately.

The kiss passed in a unit of time measured by the flap of a wing or a trip to the edge of the universe. When it was over we did not look at each other. Mido leaned back in the driver's seat, her eyes still closed.

I opened the passenger door, arranged my awkward limbs and got out.

"I'll come back for you," Mido said. "Just give me a call." Then she drove off.

I stopped by the coffee shop where Jeff and I had first met, and purchased his favorite drink, black coffee, a mocha for me, and a chocolate muffin. One of the staff carried the cups to a table outside by the bay. It was already dark. The fog had descended onto the water like a down comforter. A fat white seagull was watching me from a safe distance. I broke a piece off the muffin and dropped it on the floor. The bird quickly hopped over and gulped down the treat in an instant.

Then it was my turn to bite into the moist, sweet, comforting chocolate dough.

The gull inclined its head without taking its eyes off me. It opened its beak and let out a very polite low *creeeeeeeeeee*.

I fed it another morsel of pastry and sipped my mocha. The cup of coffee sat in front of an empty chair on the other side of the table, steam rising from it like warm breath into icy air. I did not believe that Jeff was there with me. That was not why I had purchased a drink for him. If the dead were reborn into another world, I figured, they would be busy enough over there trying to get their life together. If not, well, then they were gone for good. But the legacy my friend had left me was the memories of him, which had now merged with the molecules of my self. I was happy when Jeff and I shared our moments of understanding and a warm drink by the bay during the few months I had known him. And I felt the traces of this happiness now, sitting here again, remembering him.

The seagull let out another shy *creeeeee* and looked as incredulous as a bird possibly can when I fed it the big remaining chunk of muffin. It was not a typical seagull. *Try to multiply*, I thought. *Maybe your gentle ways will infuse the gene pool of your species with a whole new peacefulness.* "Dream on," I then mumbled and took one more sip of mocha. The bird watched me for another ten minutes, obviously hoping I would magically produce more food, and finally took off, lifting itself into the misty air with a loud, screeching, final *creeeeeeeeeeeeeeeeeeeeee.*

THE NEXT WORLD by Ursula Steck. 240 pp. Anna's friend Mido is threatened and eventually disappears . . .   1-59493-024-4 $12.95

CALL SHOTGUN by Jaime Clevenger. 240 pp. Kelly gets pulled back into the world of private investigation . . .   1-59493-016-3 $12.95

52 PICKUP by Bonnie J. Morris and E.B. Casey. 240 pp. 52 hot, romantic tales—one for every Saturday night of the year.   1-59493-026-0 $12.95

GOLD FEVER by Lyn Denison. 240 pp. Kate's first love, Ashley, returns to their home town, where Kate now lives . . .   1-1-59493-039-2 $12.95

RISKY INVESTMENT by Beth Moore. 240 pp. Lynn's best friend and roommate needs her to pretend Chris is his fiancé. But nothing is ever easy.   1-59493-019-8 $12.95

HUNTER'S WAY by Gerri Hill. 240 pp. Homicide detective Tori Hunter is forced to team up with the hot-tempered Samantha Kennedy.   1-59493-018-X $12.95

CAR POOL by Karin Kallmaker. 240 pp. Soft shoulders, merging traffic and slippery when wet . . . Anthea and Shay find love in the car pool.   1-59493-013-9 $12.95

NO SISTER OF MINE by Jeanne G'Fellers. 240 pp. Telepathic women fight to coexist with a patriarchal society that wishes their eradication.   ISBN 1-59493-017-1 $12.95

ON THE WINGS OF LOVE by Megan Carter. 240 pp. Stacie's reporting career is on the rocks. She has to interview bestselling author Cheryl, or else!   ISBN 1-59493-027-9 $12.95

WICKED GOOD TIME by Diana Tremain Braund. 224 pp. Does Christina need Miki as a protector . . . or want her as a lover?   ISBN 1-59493-031-7 $12.95

THOSE WHO WAIT by Peggy J. Herring. 240 pp. Two brilliant sisters—in love with the same woman!   ISBN 1-59493-032-5 $12.95

ABBY'S PASSION by Jackie Calhoun. 240 pp. Abby's bipolar sister helps turn her world upside down, so she must decide what's most important.   ISBN 1-59493-014-7 $12.95

PICTURE PERFECT by Jane Vollbrecht. 240 pp. Kate is reintroduced to Casey, the daughter of an old friend. Can they withstand Kate's career?   ISBN 1-59493-015-5 $12.95

PAPERBACK ROMANCE by Karin Kallmaker. 240 pp. Carolyn falls for tall, dark and . . . female . . . in this classic lesbian romance.   ISBN 1-59493-033-3 $12.95

DAWN OF CHANGE by Gerri Hill. 240 pp. Susan ran away to find peace in remote Kings Canyon—then she met Shawn . . .   ISBN 1-59493-011-2 $12.95

DOWN THE RABBIT HOLE by Lynne Jamneck. 240 pp. Is a killer holding a grudge against FBI Agent Samantha Skellar? ISBN 1-59493-012-0 $12.95

SEASONS OF THE HEART by Jackie Calhoun. 240 pp. Overwhelmed, Sara saw only one way out—leaving . . . ISBN 1-59493-030-9 $12.95

TURNING THE TABLES by Jessica Thomas. 240 pp. The 2nd Alex Peres Mystery. *From ghosties and ghoulies and long leggity beasties* . . . ISBN 1-59493-009-0 $12.95

FOR EVERY SEASON by Frankie Jones. 240 pp. Andi, who is investigating a 65-year-old murder, meets Janice, a charming district attorney . . . ISBN 1-59493-010-4 $12.95

LOVE ON THE LINE by Laura DeHart Young. 240 pp. Kay leaves a younger woman behind to go on a mission to Alaska . . . will she regret it? ISBN 1-59493-008-2 $12.95

UNDER THE SOUTHERN CROSS by Claire McNab. 200 pp. Lee, an American travel agent, goes down under and meets Australian Alex, and the sparks fly under the Southern Cross. ISBN 1-59493-029-5 $12.95

SUGAR by Karin Kallmaker. 240 pp. Three women want sugar from Sugar, who can't make up her mind. ISBN 1-59493-001-5 $12.95

FALL GUY by Claire McNab. 200 pp. 16th Detective Inspector Carol Ashton Mystery. ISBN 1-59493-000-7 $12.95

ONE SUMMER NIGHT by Gerri Hill. 232 pp. Johanna swore to never fall in love again—but then she met the charming Kelly . . . ISBN 1-59493-007-4 $12.95

TALK OF THE TOWN TOO by Saxon Bennett. 181 pp. Second in the series about wild and fun loving friends. ISBN 1-931513-77-5 $12.95

LOVE SPEAKS HER NAME by Laura DeHart Young. 170 pp. Love and friendship, desire and intrigue, spark this exciting sequel to *Forever and the Night*. ISBN 1-59493-002-3 $12.95

TO HAVE AND TO HOLD by Peggy J. Herring. 184 pp. By finally letting down her defenses, will Dorian be opening herself to a devastating betrayal? ISBN 1-59493-005-8 $12.95

WILD THINGS by Karin Kallmaker. 228 pp. Dutiful daughter Faith has met the perfect man. There's just one problem: she's in love with his sister. ISBN 1-931513-64-3 $12.95

SHARED WINDS by Kenna White. 216 pp. Can Emma rebuild more than just Lanny's marina? ISBN 1-59493-006-6 $12.95

THE UNKNOWN MILE by Jaime Clevenger. 253 pp. Kelly's world is getting more and more complicated every moment. ISBN 1-931513-57-0 $12.95

TREASURED PAST by Linda Hill. 189 pp. A shared passion for antiques leads to love. ISBN 1-59493-003-1 $12.95

SIERRA CITY by Gerri Hill. 284 pp. Chris and Jesse cannot deny their growing attraction . . . ISBN 1-931513-98-8 $12.95

ALL THE WRONG PLACES by Karin Kallmaker. 174 pp. Sex and the single girl—Brandy is looking for love and usually she finds it. Karin Kallmaker's first *After Dark* erotic novel. ISBN 1-931513-76-7 $12.95

WHEN THE CORPSE LIES A Motor City Thriller by Therese Szymanski. 328 pp. Butch bad-girl Brett Higgins is used to waking up next to beautiful women she hardly knows. Problem is, this one's dead. ISBN 1-931513-74-0 $12.95

GUARDED HEARTS by Hannah Rickard. 240 pp. Someone's reminding Alyssa about her secret past, and then she becomes the suspect in a series of burglaries.

ISBN 1-931513-99-6 $12.95

ONCE MORE WITH FEELING by Peggy J. Herring. 184 pp. Lighthearted, loving, romantic adventure.

ISBN 1-931513-60-0 $12.95

TANGLED AND DARK A Brenda Strange Mystery by Patty G. Henderson. 240 pp. When investigating a local death, Brenda finds two possible killers—one diagnosed with Multiple Personality Disorder.

ISBN 1-931513-75-9 $12.95

WHITE LACE AND PROMISES by Peggy J. Herring. 240 pp. Maxine and Betina realize sex may not be the most important thing in their lives.

ISBN 1-931513-73-2 $12.95

UNFORGETTABLE by Karin Kallmaker. 288 pp. Can Rett find love with the cheerleader who broke her heart so many years ago?

ISBN 1-931513-63-5 $12.95

HIGHER GROUND by Saxon Bennett. 280 pp. A delightfully complex reflection of the successful, high society lives of a small group of women.

ISBN 1-931513-69-4 $12.95

LAST CALL A Detective Franco Mystery by Baxter Clare. 240 pp. Frank overlooks all else to try to solve a cold case of two murdered children . . .

ISBN 1-931513-70-8 $12.95

ONCE UPON A DYKE: NEW EXPLOITS OF FAIRY-TALE LESBIANS by Karin Kallmaker, Julia Watts, Barbara Johnson & Therese Szymanski. 320 pp. You've never read fairy tales like these before! From Bella After Dark.

ISBN 1-931513-71-6 $14.95

FINEST KIND OF LOVE by Diana Tremain Braund. 224 pp. Can Molly and Carolyn stop clashing long enough to see beyond their differences?

ISBN 1-931513-68-6 $12.95

DREAM LOVER by Lyn Denison. 188 pp. A soft, sensuous, romantic fantasy.

ISBN 1-931513-96-1 $12.95

NEVER SAY NEVER by Linda Hill. 224 pp. A classic love story . . . where rules aren't the only things broken.

ISBN 1-931513-67-8 $12.95

PAINTED MOON by Karin Kallmaker. 214 pp. Stranded together in a snowbound cabin, Jackie and Leah's lives will never be the same.

ISBN 1-931513-53-8 $12.95

WIZARD OF ISIS by Jean Stewart. 240 pp. Fifth in the exciting Isis series.

ISBN 1-931513-71-4 $12.95

WOMAN IN THE MIRROR by Jackie Calhoun. 216 pp. Josey learns to love again, while her niece is learning to love women for the first time.

ISBN 1-931513-78-3 $12.95

SUBSTITUTE FOR LOVE by Karin Kallmaker. 200 pp. When Holly and Reyna meet the combination adds up to pure passion. But what about tomorrow?

ISBN 1-931513-62-7 $12.95

GULF BREEZE by Gerri Hill. 288 pp. Could Carly really be the woman Pat has always been searching for?

ISBN 1-931513-97-X $12.95

THE TOMSTOWN INCIDENT by Penny Hayes. 184 pp. Caught between two worlds, Eloise must make a decision that will change her life forever.

ISBN 1-931513-56-2 $12.95

MAKING UP FOR LOST TIME by Karin Kallmaker. 240 pp. Discover delicious recipes for romance by the undisputed mistress.

ISBN 1-931513-61-9 $12.95

THE WAY LIFE SHOULD BE by Diana Tremain Braund. 173 pp. With which woman will Jennifer find the true meaning of love?

ISBN 1-931513-66-X $12.95

BACK TO BASICS: A BUTCH/FEMME ANTHOLOGY edited by Therese Szymanski—from Bella After Dark. 324 pp.

ISBN 1-931513-35-X $14.95